CACOPHONY

THE REALM TRILOGY
BOOK TWO

L. MARIE WOOD

MOCHA MEMOIRS PRESS

COPYRIGHT NOTICE

PRAISE FOR L. MARIE WOOD

"There's a wicked atmosphere which grows page after page right until the end..." —Buried.com

"A chilling debut and a must-read for lovers of Horror and Mystery." —C. Highsmith-Hooks, author, *The Soul of a Black Woman*

"L. Marie Wood... might be rewriting existences and what we thought we understood reality and free will to be." – R. J. JOSEPH, AUTHOR OF MONSTROUS DOMESTICITIES

"Cacophony keeps the reader on the edge of her seat, guessing until the end, never quite sure who to root for as events unfold and secrets are revealed." – MELINDA CLAYTON, AUTHOR OF MAKING AMENDS

"L. Marie Wood crafts psychological horror you can't put down." – JOHN EDWARD LAWSON, HORROR WRITERS ASSO-CIATION PRESIDENT AND AUTHOR OF BIBLIOPHOBIA

f

For SAW, BKW, and MDW... again... always

Acknowledgments

Three people let me be who I need to be when I need to be. They know who they are. I thank them from the bottom of my heart.

CHAPTER I

Run.

Tara's legs and arms pumped as she ran away from the house where Mileeha lay dead, afraid of what waited for her in the darkness but knowing she couldn't stay where she was. Monsters inside; monsters outside. She could hear the Hunters in the distance, could imagine their hot breath on her neck, their sharp teeth grazing her vulnerable flesh. A shriek threatened to escape her lips when the thought of their hulking forms, the scaly skin over writhing muscle, massive claw-like hands, and bulbous, swiveling eyes pervaded her mind again and became too realistic and Tara pushed harder, running until her legs gave out. She didn't notice the blood on the grass, as black as tar in the moonlight... not at first.

It was the iridescent skin that caught her eye.

Lydjauk's flesh, smooth and unblemished and from another world, shone beautifully in the night, shimmering in a way that brought the blush from a lover's touch to mind. That only his severed arm was visible, torn roughly from his body such that the ragged edges of skin lay fanned against the grass, registered a second too late.

"Lydjauk," Tara started, before she realized that her friend could not hear her, and would never hear her again.

As Tara's hand reached towards Lydjauk's arm seemingly of its own volition, her eyes took in the carnage around her. Blood dotted the ground in splotches and droplets, pooling in some places, puddling, painting the landscape like a macabre Pollock rendering. It was then that the view widened, expanding to show her more of the carnage, more of the gore.

Body parts lay scattered in the clearing; fingers, hair, swatches of scalp littering the landscape: the debris of battle. There was nothing she could identify as specifically Sebastian, Kincaid, Aadi, or Qiao, yet she knew she was looking at what was left of them... her friends: The Watchers. All of the flesh strewn across the clearing, the heat emanating from it creating a hazy cloud that hovered above the marred grass, was non-descript, pulverized: ruined. Tara imagined her friends' bodies as they broke apart, reduced to scraps that dropped from The Hunter's mouths, discarded, base understanding hitting her at once.

Tara's head filled with the sound of her own fearful whimpers as the reality of being by herself in a world where she was prey descended upon her. As whimpers turned into cries, they became desperate and guttural. She cried for her friends and the brutal end they suffered. Never had she realized how much they meant to her – she hadn't wanted them to become her world the way they had. Tara had made them feel like she didn't care most of the time, with how distant she behaved, how aloof... never sharing details about her lives unless utterly unavoidable, never truly becoming one of them. But she *did* care, for each and every one of them and she would never have the chance to show them. Tara cried for herself and her fear of traversing The Realm utterly alone, and she cried for her love, Mileeha. Part of her didn't want to admit that she shed tears for the demon who had corrupted her very being in the first place, but she did. Mileeha was the love of her life. He was the one she had adored through space and time, the one she had been baptized in blood with, the one she had been crucified side by side with more times than she could count. And he was finally, unequivocally dead. He wasn't coming back. Not this time. Tara had looked into Mileeha's eyes for the last time, as his life was snuffed out. There was something in his eyes as he left her, something that she had never seen before. Was it recognition? Yes, indeed it was. Mileeha finally saw her, knew who she really was. Something about that made a chill run down her spine.

A pit settled uncomfortably in Tara's chest, wide and heavy enough to slow her steps. Her legs felt weak under the weight of what happened, and she couldn't shake it. Was Tara the reason her friends had been killed? She couldn't help but wonder. Did Mileeha command the Hunters to slaughter them because Tara would not take his hand? Mileeha wanted her to rule The Realm as second in command, collecting souls and creating monsters as she lived in the luxury of her choosing. But she couldn't do it. Tara didn't think it was in her to be evil even though she had done things in life that made her skin crawl upon reflection. She wanted to change, wanted to be someone different. But that wasn't what Mileeha wanted. When she turned him down, had she signed her friends' death warrants? Tara wanted to let all those inconsequential questions fill her mind, let them occupy enough space that she didn't have to think about the only one that mattered, but she couldn't. The question reverberated in her mind, repeating itself over and over again: would Mileeha have issued a Hunter to kill her too?

There was no way to know, not now. Not ever.

What Tara *did* know was that the ones she had come to love, her friends from all over the world and beyond, had died horribly, yet she still lived. She had to avenge their deaths. Standing there among what was left of those she had suffered through The Realm with, Tara realized that she could not curl up and cry; she couldn't give up. She was not ready to bare her neck to the Hunters and let them do what they would.

Tara willed herself to stand, not remembering when she had sunk to her knees, but knowing she had to get up, to get away while she still had a chance. The dark was impenetrable, but normal. Everything in The Realm looked so normal, so average, so basic. It looked like the places she had experienced during every life she lived on Earth. Now, in the woods, Tara could have been absolutely anywhere.

The Realm may have looked normal, but it was anything but. The wet sound of the Hunters' eager mouths salivating at the prospect of the hunt was proof of that. Tara wondered distantly what The Realm was like for Lydjauk, her friend from beyond the galaxy. Could he sense the Hunters better than humans could? Did Lydjauk actually see the Hunters stalking him, saliva dripping off their canine teeth - teeth that were elongated and thick like the beasts of prehistoric times - in anticipation of his flesh? Tara pushed those thoughts away quickly. Going down that path would do nothing but make her hesitate, make her cry bitter tears. Going down that path might get her killed.

Tara couldn't see her hand in front of her face, but that was ok. She had lived in The Realm, creeping along the fringes, long enough to find her way to shelter. Tara moved swiftly, keeping an eye out for the Hunters that she was sure were on her heels.

Mal must have known she was in the house with Mileeha,

she thought. If he figured out that Mileeha was plotting against him, there was no way he didn't know that Tara was there listening to the plan. Was Mal toying with her, then? Watching her like a movie projected onto a screen as she skulked around The Realm, her hair snagging in the thicket, twigs scratching her arms, her legs, her face, as she inched forward? She couldn't think about that. All Tara could do was get to shelter and hunker down. Only then would she allow her mind to do what it begged to do: think about what she would do next, mourn her friends, and cry for herself.

CHAPTER 2

Joanne's cracked lips split into what used to resemble a smile as a memory came back to her, vibrant and textured, manifesting before her very eyes.

"It was a stupid story," Dylan said, reclining in his seat, his hands making their way to his deliberately unkempt hair. "The one about the house was so much better."

Joanne smiled as she listened. She agreed with him and said as much, to his surprise, before separating the class into groups for the debate. Her students' reactions to her honesty always made her laugh. They always stared at her, eyes wide with shock when she lamented the inclusion of romance-laden classics in the Gothic horror canon or professed her undying love for George Romero because he gave the world Night of the Living Dead. *Joanne took those moments to remind them that they are in a Horror Cinema and Prose Comparative class and, because of that, all bets were summarily off. Even though the students loved the freedom of expression her curriculum provided, the formalities of academia still tripped them up from time to time.*

Joanne looked at Dylan's body language, all bluster and arrogance. She couldn't help but laugh because she knew what was coming.

"What do you know? You probably didn't even read it, Dylan," Chelsea, a student with a proclivity for quoting text (especially her go-to, Wuthering Heights), cut her eyes at Dylan as she spoke. "The stuff Gilman's talking about is too much for your little brain to comprehend." Chelsea smiled as she opened her book to look for a suitable quote, pleased with herself.

"What? Mental illness? I've been putting up with yours since 4th grade!" Snickers make their way around the 50-student class. Small towns mean students that traverse education together, even through college.

Laughing, Dylan continued, "What do you see in the wallpaper, Chels?" The snickers turned into full-on laughter as Jessica's cheeks flushed. Unable to stop himself, Dylan finished, "Those eyes are staring at you again."

"Ok, ok, let's get back on track," Joanne says, corralling the conversation through a smile of her own. "Consider the symbolism in Jackson's and Gilman's stories and form your best argument within the context of present-day impact. You only have 40 minutes to prepare, so let's get to work."

Joanne felt like she was still in the room with her students, enjoying the exchange of ideas and good-natured ribbing. She missed that version of herself, the quirky English professor whose curriculum explored the darker side of genre fiction; the aspiring novelist whose idealism spilled over onto her unedited pages of narrative. She was in her element then, in front of students interested in learning how to write by first doing the requisite research, paying homage. As Joanne sat in the dark room and the movie of her life turned off like a light switch, she lamented the loss with every fiber of her being. *That* was living.

That was life. That, she knew as well as she knew anything anymore, was over.

Joanne pawed at the wall to get her bearings. She stood on legs that felt asleep when she tried to take a step. An embittered laugh escaped her lips. That she should feel anything at all was ridiculous, after all. She was dead. Long dead. Dead was supposed to mean Heaven or Hell, angels or demons. It wasn't supposed to mean a locked room that smelled of dirty skin and torturous images plucked from her memory to be played before her over and over and over again like some cut-rate snuff film. Because that's what it was, wasn't it? A movie that showed her death and dying. It was revealed little by little instead of in one full grotesque blast, admittedly, but it was her death just the same. Every day something new from her memory showed itself, stirring a longing in her that could never be sated. Was this what she would have to live with for eternity?

Joanne had long since given up finding ways to die a second time.

Instead she willed her mind to go to sleep, to shut down, to separate itself from consciousness forever. Then she could be here, but not be, watching the memories that made up her life replayed before blank eyes. But it didn't happen. She hated herself because of it.

Joanne heard sounds coming from outside the four walls that she now called home. A woman screaming, perhaps? It didn't alarm her; the sounds of this new place had burned themselves so keenly into her psyche that they became soporific to her, as her mother's lullaby once was. She only half-heartedly raised her hand to beat against the wall in response. As she slid back down to the floor, the interest in moving to another place in the room disappearing as quickly as it came, she wasn't sure if she had banged in the hopes of being heard or to admonish the screaming woman to be silent.

CHAPTER 3

Patrick and Doug looked at each other during the silence that ensued after Mal left. The air was thick between them, as full of Mal's presence as if he was still in the room. Patrick wanted to ask Doug if he saw Mal's metamorphosis, his face changing right before their eyes. Or was that reserved only for his benefit? Somehow, Patrick didn't think Doug had. It was as if Mal was looking into Patrick's soul, staring, capturing his eyes and forcing him to watch as he killed Mileeha from afar. And Patrick saw. Oh, what things he saw in Mal's dark eyes. Strength, dominance, control. The heady combination made Patrick feel invigorated, though he would never admit that aloud. No, the glimpse of what Patrick could have for himself was a vision designed for his eyes alone.

Doug's eyes were unfocused and wet. He hadn't said a word since they were left alone, hadn't been able to. The whirlwind of events had left him off-kilter to the point where Doug wasn't sure he would ever be righted again.

Patrick knew the feeling.

"So, we run The Realm now," Patrick started, the overwhelming need to fill the silence with something - anything - boiling over.

"Yeah, I guess we do," Doug replied, his tone emotionless.

Patrick paced the sparse room, a blank slate for he and Doug to decorate in whatever way they chose. They could make it look like a room in their family home or one from a dream home that neither of them had ever been able to buy. But none of that mattered. They weren't there to live in the lap of luxury. The Realm, for all the delusions and allowances it could offer, was a far cry from hospitable. Patrick and Doug would never be safe, regardless of what Mal said. Hadn't Mal killed Mileeha, his right-hand man, right before their eyes? Patrick didn't think he would ever be able to forget the sickening keening that came from the back of Mileeha's throat when -

"So, what now?" Doug asked, jarring Patrick away from the memory. Hi voice was raw with emotion, painfully so. When Patrick looked at Doug again, he saw the toll the stress of the situation was taking on him. The sight almost broke him. Death was supposed to be manumission; it was supposed to be deliverance. Watching his son fall apart was almost more than Patrick could take.

"Now," Patrick said, his voice exuding more confidence than he actually felt, "we figure out how to save Gabby."

CHAPTER 4

Mal watched as Tara crept through the brush in an effort to mask her movements from the Hunters. He had called them off, but she had no way of knowing that. It would have been easy to let them devour her and some part of him admonished his momentary weakness for the woman, but there was something about her that appealed to him. Tara was formidable, even if she didn't believe as much herself. She also had a skeptical nature. Mal thought that might come in handy with Patrick and Doug at the helm. Putting Patrick and his son, Doug, in charge of The Realm was his way of keeping his enemies close. Patrick couldn't be allowed to ruin things. The wonders of the house had much to reveal to the inquisitive and Patrick was that, if he was nothing else. Mal wished he could make himself destroy Patrick, eliminating the threat and manifesting his own destiny at the same time, but that was not the way it was written. Patrick was a part of the puzzle whether Mal liked it or not, and if he touched a hair on the man's head, the repercussions would be felt for millennia.

Much like security system cameras projecting captured images onto monitors, Mal's mind switched to Patrick and Doug. They were holed up in that room, restless and unsure, anxious to act but not knowing how to. He wondered how long it would be before they took action - any kind of action. Doug looked broken already - the prospect of living in The Realm even another day was too much for him to handle. Patrick, on the other hand, was gaining his composure. He was starting to look more focused than he had before as he considered what had to be done next. Mal knew that Patrick wanted to save Gabby, but he also knew that Patrick had no idea the road that lay ahead as he strove to that end. Mal wanted to keep it that way. He had to make sure that Patrick never figured out the truth, never put two and two together. He needed Patrick to remain ignorant for his plan to work. Mal was so close, he could almost taste it.

Ah, taste. Mal stirred at the thought. He let his mind shift away from Patrick and Doug and over to Joanne who lay helplessly in her room. He still had a taste for her, even after all the years they had spent together. Admiring her from afar as he did so often, he remembered how salty her tears tasted, calling up a memory from a time long past when he had sampled them. Her tears were like a balm in the way they had soothed him, aroused him. Dare he partake now? Her sobs had slowed, and the tears had dried at the crest of her cheeks, pooling only at the corners of her lips. Mal had to fight himself not to kiss her there, not to lick out and capture those tears with his hot tongue.

Did she know?

Mal often wondered what Joanne felt when he visited her in that way, appearing disembodied, more imagination than reality, to pleasure her as an incubus would a sleeping beauty. He tried to penetrate her mind as he had Mileeha's to read her thoughts and know her intentions, but he couldn't, at least not as completely as he would have liked. Be it by love or by hate, she blocked Mal from her thoughts like no other had been able to. It frustrated him, not being able to read Joanne, control her, dominate her very being. But more than that, it frightened him.

She knew more than she should.

Mal blew a kiss to Joanne, his lovely prisoner, leaving her to suffer her misery alone.

CHAPTER 5

They could see her. Time passed so quickly in The Realm. It seemed as if they had only blinked and Gabby had changed from a child to an adult with children of her own. Patrick already knew what to expect having experienced it when watching Doug's life go by in a flash. Even knowing how it felt to see his son become an older man with infirmities that weren't even on the horizon the last time they had stood before each other, nothing prepared him for the anguished cry that emitted from Doug's lips.

Doug watched Gabby's gymnastics classes, singing lessons, temper tantrums, and birthday parties replete with cake and frosting piled high in abject horror, whispering her name over and over as though it were a chant. He cried over the volleyball games, the prom, college orientation, then college graduation, his voice elevating in the most alarming ways at what were happy times for his little girl. But that was the problem. Gabby wasn't his little girl, not anymore. She was a grown woman.

It was all happening too fast.

They hadn't even begun to figure out what to do next.

"We have to hurry up. We have to figure this out before -." Doug bit back the words as if saying them out loud would make them come true.

Patrick nodded, the urgency palpable inside the ramshackle house within which they stood.

CHAPTER 6

One on her hip and one wandering around the store laying sticky fingers on everything he sees. Gabby started to tell her son to stop touching everything for the seventh time, started to reach for him and guide him away from the chocolate-covered coffee beans and all-too enticing cake pops, but decided not to. Pick your battles and all that. At least he wasn't running up and down the aisles, screaming all the way.

"That'll be $5.99," the purple-haired barista told her. Baby Autumn wriggled in Gabby's arms. Christopher touched something else. Gabby nodded apologetically, handing the woman her credit card, trying to ignore the younger woman's eye rolling. The barista smirked as she put the card in the chip reader for the haggard mom. Gabby was rapidly starting to hate the facial expressions that young people made when they saw her, disheveled and stressed-out mess that she was. That judging, contemptuous smirk that people in their 20s give to anyone not as trendy as them; that look of disdain that people without children cast onto moms trying to juggle babies and groceries - it's disgusting, really. So what if she couldn't bother to match her son's socks or take a brush to her own hair before racing out to get that coffee fix, the one that always made her mouth water? So what if she had joined the legion of ladies that deemed leggings pants and wore them anytime and anywhere? She was allowed, right? She had two kids, after all.

Gabby looked over at her son. Her handsome little three-year-old boy turned holy terror was eyeing the mugs that lined the display in the middle of the room, contemplating whether or not to touch them. His hands were empty. They shouldn't have been.

"Christopher, where is your book?"

He turned to her, that little cherub, and said, "Book?"

Gabby couldn't hide the exasperation in her voice. He had begged her to bring that book on their trip to the store, wanting to carry it around even though she knew he was going to leave it somewhere. It wouldn't matter, would go forgotten entirely until it was time for his nap, and he wanted Mommy to read it to him. Then he would scream and cry and sob until he almost made himself sick. That's why she had been watching the book like a hawk, keeping it in sight all day, reminding him to keep his hands on it so he didn't lose it. Until they got in line to get coffee, of course - the coffee she desperately needed to get through the next few hours of finger painting, hide and seek, and Sesame Street.

"Yes, honey. Your dinosaur book. You had it when you came in. Please take a look around for it."

Gabby found the book with a quick scan of the room, the bright reds and yellows adorning the cover causing it to stand out amidst the muted black and brown tones of the coffee shop. The contemporary, stylish black and brown tones of the furniture and tables, sofas she used to sit on while reading a book and sipping coffee midday on a Saturday. Back when she didn't have any place in particular to be, didn't have something pressing that had to get done. She would sit there with her hair done up in a messy bun, chick-lit held in her manicured hands, strong coffee on her lips. Manicured hands. It had been so long since she'd had a manicure. She looked at her fingers and dry, cracked cuticles stared back at her. She couldn't stop the frown that crossed her lips as she brought one of her neglected fingers to her mouth and...

"Ma'am." The purple-haired girl's voice was insistent. Gabby turned toward her in surprise. The pitiful smile on good ole purple hair seemed to glow in the dark. "You can take your card out now."

It was then that she heard the incessant beeping of the card reader, shrill and high-pitched like a neglected alarm. She had been slow; she had spaced out. Gabby could only imagine how many eyes were boring holes into her back.

She fought back the urge to roll her neck and mock the silly girl, settling for a well-placed glare instead. Gabby let the machine beep a little longer before snatching the card out too, never saying a word. Gabby had bigger fish to fry. Her lovely son was looking for the book all right, but in all the wrong places. The book sat on the floor near the coffee bean display. Christopher was clear across the room, looking for his book near the candy. Strategic, yes. In proximity, no.

Gabby stepped out of the line and waited for her drink, letting Christopher search. Everything's a lesson, right? Finally, and before he could aggravate another 30-something person impatiently waiting for their cold brew, Christopher brought the book over to her and slammed it into her hands, giving Gabby that heart-melting smile that always wiped away her memories of "life before", that trademark megawatt beauty that made her grateful for the here and now, in one swipe.

"Here it is, Mommy."

That angelic voice. Oh, her little baby boy!

She picked up Christopher's book, stuffed it in her massive diaper bag, grabbed her coffee and her kid (Autumn had remained perched on her hip, enjoying a front row seat to the mayhem that was her life), and made her way to her sensible SUV with a backseat big enough to fit two car seats comfortably. As she strapped the baby in, she felt the all too familiar jiggle of the fat on her arms and sighed.

Tonight, damnit, she thought. *I'm gonna start tonight.*

CHAPTER 7

These baby monitors are shit.

The static emanating from the video monitor was enough to drive anyone crazy. Gabby knew that, even as she bought another one (she planned to use the second one as a back-up for the on-its-last-legs first one). Whether it was crap or not, she had to have it. The monitor gave her peace of mind. It let her look at her baby's face whenever she wanted to without barging into the room and potentially waking the little one up. And she always wanted to look, so it was always with her. The baby monitor was attached to her hip when she sat on the deck, when she went to the mailbox, when she went to the bathroom. Gabby had to have the volume turned up super loud so she could hear it when a movie was on, causing her husband and anyone else watching to suffer through that mind-numbing static she seemed oblivious to. But Gabby wasn't oblivious. She heard the incessant hissing just as much as everyone else did. The difference was she *needed* to hear it. The static, the absence of any other sound, let Gabby know everything was ok.

She knew it had to stop.

Gabby was trying to wean herself off of the monitor. It had become the crack she was afraid it would be. But as the saying from the 80s goes, the one that was spray-painted all over the sides of buildings and handball courts in New York, crack kills. Every time she said that, she laughed. The flair for the dramatic was strong in her.

That's why the monitor was with her in the makeshift gym she had set up in the basement. Among boxes labeled KITCHEN STUFF and GUEST BEDROOM, boxes that held the contents of her mother's life, Gabby had set up a workout area complete with free weights, a stationary bike, and an iron man she was pretty sure she'd never use. She sat in front of the television, previewing the workout she had planned to do that night.

Stretching, Gabby gave herself a pep talk. "I can do this," she said under her breath. She was finally ready to start losing weight. Baby weight isn't baby weight when the baby isn't a baby anymore. She had a realistic goal - she wanted to lose maybe 15 pounds and tone up. Not a whole lot. Not looking for a bikini body anymore. At 38 and with two little ones, Gabby didn't know if she wanted to show her belly off anyway. Even if it flattened out, there were battle scars there. Ones that she was happy to have, but they were not for everyone to see. No, a tankini would do just fine. She would do anything to avoid that skirt contraption. It reminded her of a bathing suit her grandmother used to wear on sunny days in New York at Orchard Beach.

Gabby stood in front of her old big box television set with its wide base and huge picture tube perched precariously on a cheap TV stand and stared at the screen. Jab, jab, jab to the left. Kick, punch, squat to the right. Now pulse, pulse, pulse. Repeat. Gabby watched for a while - longer than she should have if she was ever going to get up and join in. The perky little instructor made her tired. The background exercisers, with their perfect smiles and sweatless bodies, annoyed her for reasons she couldn't identify.

Maybe starting today had been a bad idea.

I mean, there's no rush, Gabby rationalized. *I could always start in the morning instead of trying to do it at night.* The logic was starting to sound good to her. Who works out at night anyway? The day was long and there was no way she could give it her all, not after a full day with the kids.

Sigh.

Gabby looked over at the darkened baby monitor screen. Crack, pop, everything's fine.

As she turned back to the TV, Gabby caught a glimpse of herself in the full-length mirror she'd propped up there one day while making room for more boxes, almost as an afterthought.

Damnit.

As much as she wanted to turn the TV off and go upstairs and eat everything she loved, she didn't let herself. The mirror held truths she had to deal with. Her face was bigger than she was comfortable with, so said that poorly timed glimpse. So were her stomach, her arms, and her thighs according to that hateful strip of glass. It was time. No more excuses.

Gabby started moving, following them move for move. It was awkward at first - years of inactivity reared its ugly head as she plodded through. Her feet felt heavy and uncoordinated. This was not the way she remembered herself being... not at all.

Gabby slowed to a stop, standing still at first then sitting on the floor to watch the DVD like it was a movie again. Except she wasn't watching this time, not really.

Gabby kept looking over at the boxes, reading each label and mentally flipping through the contents – the culmination of her

mother's life. She had packed the boxes haphazardly, roboti-
cally, quickly – not letting get bogged down with the task... not
letting herself think about what storing it all away meant.
Gabby knew she would have to put her mom in a home one day.
When the doctor said her mother had Alzheimer's, Gabby's
pessimistic nature took hold, even in the face of her mother's
optimism. She knew that her mother would start to forget
things and that once she started, she would never stop. It was
inevitable. Gabby would never hear her mother tell her children
stories about their Grandpa Doug and how he was when they
were young – what he liked to do, how he treated her when they
were dating - stories that even she didn't know about. Gabby
knew her mom would never be able to reminisce with her about
their trip to Paris and how they arrived at the Louvre only to
find out that it was closed. All Gabby could do was retell that
story to her mother during visits, showing her the pictures of
them together in front of the iconic glass pyramid. Gabby
reminded her mom about how they pulled up a picture of the
Mona Lisa on Gabby's cell phone, joking that they really *did* see
the Mona Lisa at The Louvre. To anyone looking at them, Gabby
might have appeared to be laughing so hard that she was
crying, but she knew the truth.

As teeny tiny little women in bright pink exercise bras
bopped around the screen (it wasn't quite Jane Fonda-esque,
with leg warmers and leotards, but it was close enough), Gabby
made her way over to the boxes.

KITCHEN.

LIVING ROOM.

GUEST ROOM.

Since getting her mother situated at the yellow-walled,
carefully planned elderly campus, Gabby hadn't done much
with her things. She couldn't make herself move them into the

storage room at her own house, let alone a storage facility because she claimed she wanted to sort through them. Her husband offered to do it with her, but to that she said no. She wanted to do it herself but going through her mother's things brought a finality with it that she was not ready to embrace, no matter how much her pessimistic side told her that she needed to prepare for it. Going through her things felt like the last time she would ever visit with her mom again.

Except that day was different.

DINING ROOM.

BEDROOM.

GUEST BATHROOM.

That day Gabby wanted to go through her things. Not every-thing - she didn't think she could handle seeing the pictures that were tucked away in those boxes or smelling the nearly empty bottles of perfume that her mother had left behind. Gabby was afraid that she might not be able to pull herself away. But she did want to find one thing. It wasn't even her mother's, not really. She had it by default, handed down twice over by death. It was her grandmother's unfinished manuscript that Gabby was after that day. The desire to find it was so profound that Gabby suddenly felt like she wouldn't stop digging around her mother's things until she had it in her hands – even if it took all night.

Gabby had started reading it back when her mother was healthy, eclectic and oddballish in the most endearing ways, but fine just the same. Gabby wishes she had finished reading it then - they could have talked about it. Maybe Gabby could have gotten more insight into what her grandmother, the elusive Joanne, was like. Gabby only knew bits and pieces – Joanne had been an English professor, a deep thinker, and an unabashed dreamer, but that was all she knew. Gabby always wanted to know personal details like what her favorite color was or her favorite food. Where was her favorite place to write? What was her favorite pastime? Who was her favorite author? Why? She wanted to know the little details that people pick up on just by being around each other. In Gabby's imagination, Joanne was larger than life - a free spirit ahead of her time. She didn't know why she painted her grandmother in that light, but she always had. Maybe it was the wistful way her father had looked when he spoke of his mother or the fact that she brought a passion to the classroom that was different from other professors (at least according to quotes from students memorialized in several of the yearbooks). Maybe it was the coy smile that seemed to tease the corners of her lips in most of the pictures Gabby had seen, as if she knew a secret that the world didn't. She had this Indiana Jones quality about her; she was the unattainable icon in Gabby's life. Although Gabby had always asked, craving more information about the woman who wore floral sneakers with ankle-length maxi skirts to class before that was a thing; who had died before she was born, no one ever told her much. Her father told Gabby that his mom gave the most amazing hugs, but that was about it. When he died, Gabby thought that the chance she had at understanding the woman that Joanne was had left with him.

Until she remembered the unfinished manuscript.

Gabby wished her grandmother had finished writing the manuscript, but then again maybe she shouldn't have. Maybe not finishing it was deliberate, some twist of fate that the universe made so, shifting responsibilities into view that demanded her attention while at the same time, stilling her pen. Maybe Gabby not reading all of it before was somehow right too. Maybe fate was a real thing and Gabby was supposed to read the manuscript now, the way it was - unfinished and unchecked. Having the manuscript in whatever form was better than having nothing at all.

REC ROOM.

BASEMENT.

OFFICE.

Gabby opened the box labeled OFFICE in search of the hard-copy of her grandmother's unfinished manuscript. Finding it was like finding a bar of gold.

"Goodbye," Gabby said to the perky instructor on the DVD as she turned off the TV, put on some music, and made a beeline to the old stationary bike tucked away in the corner - the one she hadn't touched in years.

Gabby turned the bike on and then looked at the cover of the manuscript, reading the title. *Sanguine Paradise* by Joanne Richardson. The yellowed pages on top curled toward the middle at the corners, as drawn to the words typed dead center on the page as Gabby's eyes were. The title page brought a flutter of excitement to her stomach.

Sanguine Paradise.

Intriguing, to say the least.

Pedaling slowly, she started to read.

CHAPTER 8

Gabby marveled at her grandmother's even tone right from the beginning. Her pacing seemed practiced, making Gabby wonder just how long Joanne had been interested in trying her hand at writing a novel. Tears prickled at the corners of her eyes as she read the words, lyrically composed, flowing like a river from sentence to sentence. The prose was hypnotic and Gabby couldn't wait to read the next sentence - every sentence. She was engaged, totally submitting to the ride without knowing where the car was going. There were no notes to give Gabby an idea of what her grandmother had planned for the story, no outline, no back-cover copy - nothing. And that was just fine. She found that diving into the story without any idea of where it would end up felt like those Sunday drives she and her mom used to take. They would just pick up and go, destination unknown. Sometimes they ended up at a coffee shop hours away from home, looking at the water and talking about their hopes and dreams. Sometimes they ended up at a roadside fair getting on rides like they had when Gabby was young and eating funnel cakes until their stomachs hurt. Times like those were the ones she missed most - when she and her mother just *were* and no one and nothing else matters. If reading her grandmother's manuscript could bring that feeling back to Gabby, even if only for a minute, she would grab onto it for dear life.

They never ceased to amaze me, the deep waters. Darkened to a midnight blue with the tiniest bit of aqua flashing bright against the stark white foam, the waves broke along the surface, moving the water to and fro, hither and yon. It seems so long ago that I traveled the seas, passing lands and people that were as oblivious of me as I was of them. I have the same thoughts when I fly, her grandmother started. *Joanne* started. Gabby decided she would read the manuscript written by *Joanne*, the woman, the author, separate from the larger-than-life grandmother she had created in her mind. Gabby thought it might give her more of a view into Joanne's thoughts, her struggles, and interests. It might be interesting to see her grandmother the way that other people saw her: as an adult with mature needs and problems. At least that's how she started. Gabby wasn't sure she could handle reading a sex scene, but she'd cross that bridge when she got to it.

Gabby felt her cheeks warm up at the thought and couldn't suppress a smile. This was going to be fun.

Water, flying, being oblivious, she thought, shaking her head and getting back to the story. Her feet were slowing to a stop on the stationary bike, but she didn't notice... not really.

CHAPTER 9

When I fly, I think of all the people below me sitting in their houses and watching television, living their lives unaware of me coasting above them, sharing their space for a moment in time. I've always thought the concept of travel was amazing, covering ground in hours rather than days, weeks, or months. I used to relax into the trip, used to, "enjoy the ride" but now I find the time spent getting from one place to another unbearable rather than cathartic. Could it be the hunger that rumbles in my stomach and constricts my chest during the journey? Maybe. Is it the night sky, inky and black, unyielding as it showed the flickering lights below – these views my only showcase now and forevermore? Perhaps. But there is something more, something I have not allowed myself to think about since before.

I can't help but remember my last cruise. It brings so many emotions to the forefront, emotions that I don't want to think about, don't want to feel. But no matter how I try to divert my attention to something else, the feelings still rise to the surface. Maybe it's because the rest of my shipmates are sleeping, boredom taking over to force uncharacteristic lethargy; maybe it's because I am to be punished for what I allowed to happen. I don't know. The only thing I know is that in a world where few things can harm me, my memories pose a heavy threat.

The others don't seem to suffer the same way I do. I am not the youngest by far, but I seem to be the most sensitive, the most unable to let go of the past. Letting go has always felt like forgetting to me and I don't want to do that. If I forget the way my mother's hair smelled or how soft my first kiss was, I will lose a part of me. I can't afford that considering how much I have already lost.

My last cruise was to a place very much like where we're going now, with rolling mountains and beautiful views. I was with my girl-friend of two years. I was serious about her, that much I can recall, but I can't remember her face anymore. I've tried before, alarmed that the features of someone so important to me could disappear from my mind. I struggled but nothing came except that she had long brown hair and held me tightly when she hugged. And her name. I remember that much at least. Gillian.

But that time with Gillian was long ago. She had surely moved on to bigger and better, fulfilling her dreams of marriage and chil-dren with someone who could give her that life. I hope she's well, if for nothing more than the sentimental notion of karma. I hope she made it through this dark time that doles punishment on the world as though reprimanding a wayward child. I hope she is safe, though I know she can't be. If the uprising that ruined England, France, and Egypt is happening where she laid roots, she is as dead as I am.

Dead.

It's something I don't allow myself to think of, let alone label myself as. But it's the truth. I am dead, and have been for more years than I care-

"'It's the truth. I am dead and have been for more -'" Thomas' mocking voice sullied the tranquil sound of waves splashing against the hull. I rolled my eyes in disgust.

"A little privacy?" I feel like I've said this a million times in the past few hours. Thomas could be as annoying as a bored child and twice as snarky.

"Why? So you can write more of that sensitive nonsense? Really Aaron, you are becoming quite the lightweight." Thomas laughs as he always does; poking fun at me seems to be his only pastime besides the hunt.

"Not all of us are hardened to it, Thomas," I said, my response sounding whiny even to my own ears.

"That's the problem, Aaron! You've had how long to get used to it? Sixty-five years?"

CHAPTER 10

Gabby, now sitting on the stationary bike without even the pretense of working out any longer, chuckled out loud. What are they, vampires? It didn't really surprise her. Her grandmother was into horror fiction - that much her father had been able to tell her. She read it and taught it, and apparently wrote it too. Gabby couldn't help but smile as she read her grandmother's work. Joanne definitely had a way with words.

Getting off the bike without even a backwards glance, Gabby walked out of the exercise area and upstairs to the living room sofa. She let her body drop onto the cushions, eyeing the cookies calling to her from the kitchen counter (chocolate chunk - the best batch she'd ever made, if Gabby was being honest) all the while. She tried not to give in, if only for a second. Cookies and a good book... who could resist?

Not Gabby. Not at all.

With cookies in hand and a blanket covering her legs, Gabby settled into the vampire tale.

CHAPTER II

Answering Thomas won't make him lay off. In all the conversations we've had about this, I haven't figured out what will.

"What you need," Thomas states as usual, "is a good lay."

I look at him incredulously. With hunger roiling in my stomach, I can hardly think about anything other than sating it. Carnal pleasure is the last thing on my mind.

"Why not?" Thomas continues, "You're a good-looking guy and the island has to be full of women ready to... enjoy themselves with men speaking with strange accents." Thomas spoke with exaggerated British flare.

"I don't think American accents would be considered exotic. This island sees thousands of American tourists in one season, I'm sure."

Thomas smiled mischievously. "I'm sure you'll find some other attribute to accentuate." He licked his lips, a gesture meant to be lascivious but doing nothing more than making my stomach growl more.

"We don't even know if anyone is there," I said, turning back to my journal.

"Don't we?" Thomas turned his attention to the ocean, its cerulean water rolling and churning as our ship cut into it, surging forward to the island due north.

For better or worse, it wouldn't be long now.

"Why do you doubt what you've been told?" Thomas asked, his back still turned to me.

"Why are *you* so anxious to believe everything you hear?" I retort, unable to bite it back.

Thomas turned to me then, his blond hair blowing in the wind. He was striking a pose that was lost on me; his enigmatic disposition, his allure, has yet to affect me like it had most of the others. He knew it. He made a game out of trying to tempt me... Every. Single. Day.

"Why, you ask? Because others have been here, have seen it with their own eyes. How do you think we found out about this place? Did you think Raymond thought it up on his own?"

Raymond. The designated leader of our band of thieves, as I like to think of him. There was no ceremony about his position, nothing formally documented for posterity; there was little need for such measures anymore. Raymond had just emerged as the leader when food started getting scarce. He was one of the few who kept his head. He made and kept contact with others who roamed for food, be they sects with several members or vagabonds who lay in wait for the first person to walk by. He heard things that way — things the rest of us didn't. Because he kept his ear to the ground, Raymond seemed to have all the answers, so we went where he said we should go. I am still not sure

Raymond is right, but it's not like I had anywhere else to be either.

"Raymond heard from Jacob, who found out from Cecelia," Thomas continued, "She's been all over the world looking for the best place for us to start over."

"Hmph," I snickered, "a regular world traveler."

Thomas turned toward me now, giving me his full attention. The effect that the sea spray dancing around his frame gave off would have pleased Thomas greatly if he had seen it.

"Must you be so disagreeable? We are on our way to salvation, Aaron! It's all there, ready and waiting for us. We can almost pluck it from the trees, it's so plentiful." Thomas' theatrical arm sweep was almost comical.

"Because Cecelia said so," I can't resist goading Thomas when he gets this way.

"Yes, because Cecelia said so. She is one of us. She understands our need. She wouldn't falsely lead us here if there were no bounty, as it were, to claim."

Theatrical lilt. Head turned just so. Thomas can't help but turn on the charm. It's exhausting to watch.

"If there is so much 'bounty' here, why didn't Cecelia keep it for herself?"

For the first time, Thomas didn't have a quick comeback. I pressed, "With the shortage going on right now, I don't understand why she wouldn't hoard it. If what Raymond says is true, there is enough here to sustain us for decades. Why not harvest it and keep it close to the vest? Does it make sense that she would share this secret with an old flame who is attached to ten ravenous men? I understand the need for companionship, but are you telling me she couldn't find it here?"

Thomas' sigh was audible, but it didn't do much to hide the hesitation – the confusion - flickering in his eyes. No one could answer the questions I had asked. Cecelia hadn't been heard from after her second message to Raymond. She said she found an island where the problem of diminished food supply crippling Europe, China, the Middle East, and North and South America had not manifested itself. She said she was alone there and was willing to share the place with Raymond if he would come. That she extended refuge to him made sense. Raymond and Cecelia had been lovers a long time ago; their love affair was as romantic as it was tumultuous. The invitation itself isn't what bothered me, that was just something to tack onto my argument for good measure. That we haven't heard from Cecelia since is what worries me.

Thomas leaned in conspiratorially, lowering his voice to a whisper, as if that could stop Raymond from hearing if he really wanted to. "Between us blokes, Cecelia was always a bit of a flake."

Thomas' dramatic pause made me turn to him, readying myself. Thomas was about to go too far as he always does where Cecelia is concerned. He always manages to say something about her that makes me question his intelligence, his understanding of the world in which he now lived... the one he always claims I need to embrace. The disdain I feel for his past utterances must be showing on my face because a question has taken residence in Thomas' eyes. It is only there for a second if it was ever there at all. It gives me pause, that look.

"She may have already found a companion," Thomas continues, "She might have even found one as soon as she sent for Raymond. This could all be an elaborate game to her, something designed to tease Raymond, to make jealous so he'll fight for her... whatever, I don't care," Thomas dismisses. I cast my eyes around us cautiously before leveling a look of admonition upon Thomas to rival a parent. It was one thing to disagree with

Cecelia's decisions - what leader didn't have their share of dissidents, after all - but to speak of her in such a way as to make her appear less than capable, foolish even? I wouldn't have been surprised if a spear appeared out of nowhere to bleed the silly fool on the spot.

I snickered, realizing that I would have been even less taken aback if the hand holding the blade was his own. Thomas, however, was unperturbed. Waving off my warning, indeed missing the sentiment of it entirely, Thomas continues, "All that matters is that there's food here, Aaron. Sustenance. She wouldn't lie about that, not to Raymond. He'd have her head for it - queen or no."

Thomas turned back to the water, finding it more appealing than my furrowed brow. I looked past him at the island slowly coming into view, my hand resting on the ornate rail that would soon tarnish for want of attention. There it is - the island we have hung our hopes on; hung our very lives on. I can't help but feel optimism stirring in my belly. Maybe Thomas is right and we can start over here. I want to believe that could be real and push away my skepticism, but it doesn't feel right. Something about Cecelia's silence is wrong.

We're almost there.

"St. Martin," I say under my breath, pulling the name of the island from a distant corner of my memory. "Bonjour ."

CHAPTER 12

"What are we going to do?" Doug's voice was nearly frantic. Gabby sat serenely reading in her living room, cookie in hand and coffee steaming on the end table, oblivious to the fact that her father and grandfather were pacing the floor in a nondescript room in a dilapidated house in The Realm at that very moment, trying to figure out a way to save her soul.

"I wish I knew," Patrick replied, lost.

"You *wish*? *You wish*?"

Doug's eyes were wild. For a fleeting moment, Patrick thought his son might strike him.

"Doug, I-"

"How can you *not* know, Dad? How can you stand there and tell me you don't know what to do now, after everything?"

"Doug -" Patrick started but the words died in his throat. He felt so helpless. Doug was right - he was right about everything. He *should* know something. It didn't make sense that he couldn't remember what heinous thing he did to land himself and his whole family in such a place, but the truth remained elusive to him.

"I mean, what the fuck?" Doug continued, "We're here because of…"

"I know, I know. This is all because of me." He didn't mean to make it seem like he was looking for pity, the kind that wanted to reflect in Doug's face but didn't quite hit the mark, really, he didn't. Patrick just didn't know how to get the self-loathing out of his voice. "I know and I'm sorry."

"Sorry?" Doug sounded as though he couldn't believe the words coming out of his father's mouth. He sounded as if he were hearing the world's worst news delivered with the most sickeningly sweet cadence ever imagined. His own words were laced with disgust.

Patrick hated the look on Doug's face.

"Doug, I-"

"We just saw a man die right in front of our eyes. Nothing even touched him - he just… seemed to draw into himself like someone was wringing him out like a dirty sponge from the inside." Recounting Mileeha's death felt necessary; it grounded Doug. They were really in the godforsaken place. They were really about to watch Gabby succumb to the same fate.

"Son -"

"What could do that? What could make a man's face contort like that?"

"He was evil -"

"That's supposed to be enough of a reason? He's a sick bastard so it's ok for him to die like that?"

"Doug…"

"What about me? What did I do to have to see it, huh? What did I do to make anything about that ok? Tell me that, dad!"

"I… I -"

"Just -" Doug held his hand up to his father, quieting his speech. Had he caused him to flinch too? To pull away in an effort to dodge his frenzied, gesturing hands? He hoped not. God, he hoped that wasn't true. But he did want to shut him up. More than anything, Doug wanted to leave his father standing there, mouth agape in that irritatingly confused way he always adopted when at a loss, mind grasping at straws, tears threatening to spill out onto his hot cheeks... unequivocally alone, but all he could do was turn his back to him. Because that was his dad. Because Doug loved him.

Patrick gave Doug a minute, considering it a win that he hadn't left the room. When he thought Doug was in a better position to listen than before, he continued, his voice thick with humiliation, "I wish I had answers. I just don't. We will figure this out together. You and me."

Gabby's voice was low in the background. She wasn't reading aloud, but Patrick and Doug could hear her thoughts as clearly as if she were. The words were familiar to Patrick - he had read them himself so many years ago. It was Joanne's book. Inspiration for the tome came from out of nowhere, it seemed, and like a light switch turning on, Joanne hit the ground running, researching writing, editing, outlining - doing something related to the book every single day. She poured so much energy into it, was so possessed of it that it made Patrick nervous at one point. For a span of four months, all she did was wake up, write, go to work, teach, come home, and write until after midnight. Then get up and do it all over again.

Then she just stopped.

Joanne put the book down as quickly as she had picked it up and never touched it again. Patrick hadn't had the heart to throw out the unfinished manuscript after she died, nor could he bring himself to read any further than she had let him before.

It was as if her blood, sweat, and tears had been spilled on those pages and it still wasn't enough. Joanne hadn't been able to finish the story. There was a vulnerability around it for the rest of her life - a deliberate avoidance. It seemed to Patrick that if Joanne could have wished those days and weeks of working on the manuscript away, wiped it clean of everyone's memory and gone on like it had never happened, she would have. That's why he never bothered her about reading it, even though he wanted to know what monsters had been bouncing around her mind and found themselves on the page. That's why he felt like he was trespassing every time he eyed the cover, even after she was gone. Still, he couldn't part with it. Doug had, apparently, felt the same way. He wondered what Doug remembered about those few months - his mother had been so distant from them then, so caught up in the story that it was almost as if she didn't see them in the room with her... when she was there at all. More often than not, Joanne stayed away, writing in solitude. Patrick used to joke that it was them, not her characters sitting at the table with her at dinner. The thin smile she gave in reply used to raise goosebumps on his skin.

Patrick raised a hand in the air to quiet his son, who had started raging again, but Doug never saw it. He still had his back turned to his father, trying to shut him out. Patrick tuned Doug out and listened to Gabby as she recited her grandmother's words. Patrick felt a strange pull toward Gabby's voice. He forced himself to listen closely to the timbre and cadence, allowing himself to truly appreciate every word Gabby was saying.

Doug was beside himself. Rarely had he ever been that angry. His heart beat wildly in his chest; his breathing was erratic. But was it? As he placed a hand on his chest, and watched it rise and fall with each exhalation, reality came crashing down on him again. He willed his chest to stop heaving; told himself that it was all his imagination. He was dead. Dead and gone. All the heavy breathing was a façade that his mind was throwing up to distract him. Doug no longer needed his lungs; he didn't need to breathe at all, and all that gesticulation was like playing pretend.

Doug wanted to look at Gabby to reassure himself that she was still alive, still able to be saved, but he was afraid of what he might see. Would she be like she was before, a woman in her late thirties reading her grandmother's unfinished manuscript instead of exercising, or would she have aged to a gray-haired, cane-toting woman in her seventies? Time was transitory in The Realm and he hadn't been paying attention. Doug couldn't shake the thought that if he looked now, he would see death reflected back at him.

He looked at his father instead, noting the faraway expression he held on his face. He assessed the man before him, let the love he felt creep in and break away the disdain that threatened to take over. Doug loved his father, he truly did. Patrick had been a wonderful man in life and was trying, with everything he had, to make things right in death.

They would figure it out together.

If it took everything he had left, Doug was going to find out what his father did to get them in this predicament so that he could save his daughter. He only hoped it didn't mean he would have to lose his father to do it.

CHAPTER 13

Vernese saw the ship, still majestic looking as it glided effortlessly on the water, coming toward the island and knew what it brought with it. She shivered in the warm wind as it drew nearer to the dock, a dock that had been renovated and prettied in preparation for a busy tourist season that would never happen. The empty shops along Front Street and the rotting food in the refrigerators of the boardwalk restaurants confirmed that. Tears stung her eyes as she thought of the plans she had made for the future before the world, as she knew it, ended. Vernese had just completed a management program at the hotel and had received a promotion that lasted all of three days before the news of what was happening in the US came. It was like watching a movie, exactly like that, she thought not for the first time, only instead of zombies taking over the world, eating people's brains and slogging around in mindless marching repetition, it was vampires. Vampires drinking the blood of the living until they fell dead where they stood. When they said it on the news, she thought that was the most ridiculous thing she had ever heard. Everyone thought it was some elaborate hoax, maybe a promo for a blockbuster movie. But as reports kept coming and coming, and as flights started being canceled and never rescheduled, the people on the island started to wonder. Stranded guests called home and got no answer. The airport lost contact with the towers first in the US, then in Europe.

Vernese had started to believe what was being reported, as crazy as it sounded. And she started to get scared.

The wind blew her hair gently, as if caressing her with an unseen hand. She smiled ruefully as she watched the ship draw nearer and nearer. Vernese remembered a guest from Europe, where exactly in Europe wouldn't come to mind. The woman had been in the lounge with the rest of the guests, watching the news and contacting the airport to find out the status of her flight. The din in the room was loud but not alarmingly so; just a bunch of people wondering out loud about what could be happening back home. Wondering if their dog was ok, or if their parents were worried. That's all it was in the early days: wondering. Vernese remembered the woman hanging up the phone and whooping in triumph. People turned to look at her and were met with a beaming smile and nothing else. She left the lounge and went up to her room as though floating on air. Vernese never saw her leave but assumed that was exactly what she had done. By the next day, flights to Europe were being canceled, but surely the woman had made it home. Knowing what came after, Vernese wondered what the woman found when she opened her front door. Vernese wondered if she even got that far.

Vernese, new manager that she was, tried to take care of the guests that remained at the hotel as best she could. The week the trouble started was a busy one for the hotel - they were full, as were many of the hotels on the island. Her General Manager had gone on vacation to California the week before, so Vernese held down the fort alone. She hadn't reached out to the other two shift managers for help, not even when flights started getting canceled. She was determined to handle it on her own, to prove she deserved her new position. She was sure the general manager would be impressed by her dedication when all was said and done. *It won't be long*, she assured herself in the early days. *This will all blow over soon.*

The memory of how naive she had been made her stomach turn.

Vernese parted her lips involuntarily, a small, tortured gasp escaping her lips at the thought of her General Manager. Boyd had been a friend to her, had been her mentor. He sponsored her through management training, and had actually hired her on at the hotel two years before. He had shared his family with her, included her in their celebrations and gatherings. Boyd cared about her genuinely, the way her father might have had he not moved to Grenada and cut ties with her mother before Vernese had even turned four years old. Boyd was even there for her when her mother died the year before. He gave her the moral and emotional support she needed. Vernese was afraid that the same fate might have befallen Boyd that the news talked about. Melancholy newscasters, faces crestfallen, clothes disheveled, and hair loose in a way that said they had stayed up all night, that nothing was ok and would never be again. The newscasters, those that hadn't left the station for a home that may or may not exist anymore, made it seem like everyone had succumbed to the plague or virus or whatever it was being called. They made it seem like most people had gotten it and it was just a matter of time before the others did too.

The newscast she watched was out of California.

Boyd and his family were vacationing in California.

Vernese wanted him to be safe for his wife and two children. She wanted him to be safe for her. Part of the appeal of accepting the manager position was that she would be able to learn more from Boyd, and not just about hospitality, but also about life. She thought she'd have more time with her mentor; her friend. Thinking of Boyd made her sad deep down in her soul.

Vernese knew what happened to Boyd, just like she knew what happened to that woman and anyone else who had left the island – she wasn't stupid. Vernese called Boyd. He didn't answer. She knew.

They were dead.

They had been bled.

And if she wasn't careful, she would be too.

The ship seemed to coast slowly, peacefully, as if a ship full of weary seamen was coming in, just tired souls looking for a place to rest. But she knew who sat aboard the ship waiting to drop anchor and wreak havoc on a place that would otherwise have been considered paradise... and there was nothing she could do to stop them.

CHAPTER 14

The sudden appearance of light frightened Gabby to her core. She jumped, snapping out of her reverie harshly, casting a glance around the room to get her bearings. It was just the baby monitor, the crappy thing that it was. Any movement her little one made in her crib caused the thing to erupt into cracks and pops and bright white light that seared into Gabby's eyes. Only this wasn't a little movement. Autumn was rolling around in the crib, arms reaching, legs twitching. Gabby looked over at the clock: 12:18 a.m. She shook her head. How could that be right? She felt like she had only been reading for 30 minutes, not 2 hours.

Autumn whimpered.

So did Gabby.

It was time for the nightly cuddle, the one she couldn't seem to break her daughter of... the one she herself didn't want to give up. Except tonight. Settling Autumn wouldn't take long, Gabby knew - they both just needed a simple touch, a nose nuzzle, and a kiss, really - but this time Gabby didn't want to do it. She didn't want to move from her seat. She was engrossed in the book her grandmother had written all those years ago. Gabby wanted to keep reading, to push through, go the whole night if she could. There was something about Aaron and his forlorn demeanor that spoke to her. Something about Vernese's unexpected rise to leadership that compelled her to turn the pages. Would the two of them meet? Would Aaron drink from her? Would Vernese try to kill him? Gabby really wanted to know.

Autumn's whimpers were more insistent this time. If Gabby didn't do something, whimpers would turn to whining, which would quickly degrade to shrieking.

As Gabby stood, preparing to make her way up the stairs and to her little girl's bedside, she knew that one day she would have to let Autumn cry if she was ever going to get a full night's sleep again. It was a fact and she knew it, but what bothered Gabby, what made her turn back and look at the open pages of the manuscript on her sofa as she climbed the stairs to her daughter's room, was that the voice saying it wasn't her own.

CHAPTER 15

Mileeha hadn't seemed right.

In those last moments, Tara thought something was off, something different. He had seemed cold to her, vengeful even. Very unlike himself - at least the part of himself that Mileeha had let Tara see. Mileeha had always shown her his sensitive side, if you could call it that. He loved her and she knew it, right from the very start when they shared their first life together. Reincarnation after reincarnation brought them together and he always managed to find her, woo her, and love her all over again. They were inextricably connected, for better or worse. Soulmates. Even when their connection landed her in The Realm at the mercy of the Hunters as he sat second in command, they were each other's heart and soul, even if she hadn't wanted to admit it. Tara wondered if, in the face of the true death, - because he was gone, completely gone - the connection was still as strong.

Still, something had been different about Mileeha in his last moments. Tara lay on the makeshift bed that had belonged to

Sebastian, instinctively going there instead of to her own out of a need to be close to him in some abstract way. Mileeha had spat insults at her, calling her on the table in a manner that he never had before. *"I don't believe in the idea that someone can make you do something. You would have been killing on your own if I hadn't come along. If you didn't want to kill, you wouldn't have,"* he had said, venom lacing his tongue. She felt weak replying that she would have lost him if she hadn't. She hadn't wanted to admit that to him even after everything they had been through, but she had to. It was what she had always believed, after all. Life after life, she simply had no choice.

It was over so fast.

One minute he alternated between asking her to join him and insulting her entire being, and the next, he was dead. Truly, forever dead. A sob breached her lips and echoed in the too empty ramshackle lean-to she and her friends used to call home. Mileeha was gone.

When she had just gotten to The Realm she stumbled upon the body of a leathery-faced man. He had drawn a crucifix in blood on a nearby stone and seemed to have been gazing at it in the moment of his death if his upturned chin and fixed eyes were any indication. He was fresh, newly dead. In her curiosity she had touched his skin to see if he was warm. He was and that threw her for a loop. It took time to realize that he was warm only because her mind *thought* he should be warm. In all actuality, his body temperature was likely room temperature - the feeling of nothing at all. It was her mind that insisted otherwise because that is what she was used to when she was alive.

An hour later he was gone.

Someone could argue that the Hunters consumed the flesh of the ones who died in The Realm, but she knew they didn't. The flesh ripping and bone chewing was mostly for show. They wanted the victim to suffer, hearing his bones crack between the teeth of the beasts. They wanted the other prey to hear the person's demise to strike fear in them. Fear smelled good to the Hunters and it tasted even better. Once the victim died, they left the bodies, in whatever state, where they were to disappear when it was time.

That's what had happened to Mileeha – he had disappeared.

When a body was gone - completely gone: no bones, no clothes: nothing - it was because they had been wiped away. It was the true death - as far as she knew, there was nothing else afterward. She didn't know what infraction the true death punished – condemnation to The Realm forever seemed enough to keep them in line to Tara's weary mind. But no, apparently it wasn't. All Tara knew was that the true death was the end of everything, for once and for all.

Tara sniffled in despair. Maybe if she had gotten to Mileeha sooner, tried to make him see that there was another way, this wouldn't have happened. Tara struggled to remember how many romances they had enjoyed together before ending up in The Realm for good. New York in the 1950s. California in the 1980s. Paris, France in the early 2000s. Different names, different cities, different skins, but still them to the core. Seven romances; seven lives. It was all a blur now. Mileeha had explained over and over again that the only reason they were in The Realm was because they had kept failing; they had never gotten it right. Mileeha told her that most people didn't know they were reincarnated, that they had something to fix. Mileeha said they were lucky because they knew what was going on but knowing hadn't changed anything in the end; they squandered every chance they got and ended up in The Realm after all. Tara knew he was right. Hell, she hadn't even tried to do the right thing after the third or fourth go 'round. What was the point?

Mileeha was never going to change - he enjoyed the blood too much. With every life his bloodlust grew stronger until he was ingesting it for emotional sustenance towards the end. She had never gone that far; Mileeha was elixir enough for her tastes. Tara had never gone as far as drinking blood, but she hadn't stopped him from doing so. She never interfered. And yes, she spilled more than her share of blood for him to savor. It was exhilarating, holding someone's life in her hands. She couldn't help but to indulge from time to time. God gave them seven tries to get it right - seven reincarnated lives to do something different with, to make amends with and buy their way out of eternal condemnation, but Mileeha and Tara had chewed up that promise and spit it out with zeal.

Tara figured she'd go to Hell when she died the last time considering the crimes she had committed, and some part of her soul had relished the idea of atoning for her sins. She felt so unclean, so damaged. She needed to wash the blood off of her and if paying in the afterlife meant she could do that, she'd readily acquiesce. But atonement wasn't what she found, not in any way that might be restorative. Once Tara and Mileeha closed their mortal eyes for the seventh and final time, they awoke in the only home they would ever know again: The Realm, dark and dank, unforgiving, and preternatural. Their names had been etched in Mal's Book of the Condemned - she envisioned them scrawled in beautiful calligraphy that contradicted reality. Tara hadn't been surprised she ended up being chased by monstrous beasts after she awoke; she found it rather appropriate considering the beast she had been in life. She deserved the fear of impending death, knowing that if she died in The Realm she was truly gone. Some part of her liked that idea more than she was willing to admit. Tara knew that Heaven and even Hell were out of reach for her now and she had made her peace with that. But the idea that she could be finished, annihilated; no more – that she could cease to exist... The thought was intoxicating, if she was being honest. With every life she lived she lost more and more of who she thought she really was. By the time they had been condemned to The Realm, Tara didn't even recognize herself. How she could kill so many people all the while claiming she didn't want to was a mystery to her. Maybe she was just bad. Bad to the core. If that was the case, then disappearing was probably the right thing to do for everyone's sake. But just as she was in life, every single time she had been faced with a choice to kill or not kill, Tara was afraid. She was scared to be honest. She was scared to go against Mileeha.

When Mileeha opened his eyes in The Realm and found a way to make a better life for himself than he ever had when he was alive. Tara knew the true death would be their fate. Mileeha would never be satisfied. He used the Hunters to kill even when it was not warranted, sometimes watching as the blood splattered in torrents from the victim's body with a smile on his face. His bloodlust hadn't disappeared, even with condemnation. He was every bit the monster he used to be.

Tara shook herself from her reverie. She wanted to stop herself, save herself from all those thoughts of the past. Reminiscing was not a luxury she could afford, not with the Hunters out there. But still Tara couldn't shake the thought that she hadn't stuck around to see what happened to Mileeha. She knew he had died the true death - there was no way around that. She went back to make sure, to see with her own eyes even as she knew the truth. But maybe she should have stayed with him, watched him disappear or disintegrate - whatever it was that happened when someone died in The Realm. Leaving him alone felt cold, callous: wrong. Hadn't they shared lives together? Hadn't they shared their hearts and their beds? Didn't he deserve to die with someone who loved him by his side? Tara knew she was that person for Mileeha, for better or worse. She always had been, yet she ran when he needed her most.

Tara stared at the floor forlornly, her emotions rising to a head. Mileeha was dead and it broke her heart.

The anger welling inside her was like an old friend.

"I'll make them pay, my love," Tara said to the empty room louder than she should have, but not caring. The fact that she could summon the murderous side of her and call it into action so easily disturbed her, but she would deal with that later. Patrick and Doug would die for what happened to Mileeha; Tara would see to that. She'd make sure they hurt. She'd make sure they bled. Tara would fight until her dying breath to make sure they got what they deserved.

CHAPTER 16

Patrick heard Doug when he left the room, but he acted like he was oblivious to it. He couldn't blame Doug for leaving - he was mad. More than mad: he was afraid, helpless, frustrated, livid. All of those emotions were turned toward Patrick and he knew it. Doug wasn't wrong. Whatever happened to land them all in The Realm was his fault.

But what had he done? Patrick had no idea - didn't even know where to start to figure out what happened. But he *had* to figure it out. If he didn't, they would all be stuck there in that nothingness of a place. And that's only if the Hunters didn't tear them apart first.

Patrick needed time to think.

Doug needed to *do* something.

It was good that they were getting time apart.

Gabby's melodic voice bounced off the walls, the sound reverberating beautifully around the room and into his ears. It made him want to cry. This child, this beautiful woman with babies of her own, a life of her own, was going to die and end up standing where he was if Patrick didn't figure out what was going on. It was a paralyzing thought that he couldn't shake. Then his mind did something shifty that he wasn't entirely sure was a good thing. In big white letters against the black backdrop what was his mind was spelled one word:

Joanne.

She was here. He knew it. With all the activity he had been through since entering the house, he had forgotten about finding his wife. Patrick saw her walking by a window when he was hiding outside, cowering in the shrubs and tall grass as he cased the house in those early days. Now the realization broke its way through the frenzy of emotions crowding Patrick's mind.

Joanne was there!

Patrick jolted as if he had been shocked and turned toward the door that Doug had just exited. He had to find Joanne.

Patrick started to walk, started to leave the room he had been anchored in since Mileeha's death, in search of his wife. Thoughts about where he was going or how Joanne could have been there and not have uttered a peep didn't enter his mind. He only knew that he needed to find her. Being with Joanne again would make everything all right. She would know what to do next. She would know how to get them out of The Realm.

Joanne always knew what to do.

Joanne had always been there for Patrick, even before they were married. He would see her at the park reading a book on a bench while he jogged along the trail. One day he got a charley horse near where she sat and collapsed to the ground, writhing in pain, much to his chagrin. Joanne hopped off the bench and applied pressure until the damned thing let up. Another time a mama duck got a little aggressive toward him when he ran too close to the water's edge. Patrick weaved out of the animal's way but bumped into another runner and dropped his water and there she was, sitting on her favorite bench holding out a fresh bottle of water. She was his editor when he had a big presentation, his stylist when he couldn't figure out what to wear, his nutritionist when he wanted to change his diet and eat right. So, where had she been when he woke up in The Realm? Why had she not been there for him when he was running for his life, the breath from the Hunter's open, salivating mouths hot on the back of his neck? Patrick desperately wanted to save himself, to stop the diatribe playing inside his head and pull himself out of the rabbit hole, but it was too late. It didn't matter that his rational mind knew Joanne hadn't been there to greet him in death because she was locked away in that house. The irrational part of himself was steadily trying to convince the former that she hadn't been there because she was too busy painting her toenails in her new, fancy bedroom.

The two voices warring with each other in Patrick's head created a devastating cacophony that drove him to his knees.

Then he heard Gabby laugh.

It was a bitter laugh, rueful in a way that normally would have made Patrick sad for her, but that jarred him back to reality instead. It also did something else for him, something he had desperately needed more than anything else at that moment. Gabby's laugh made Patrick focus.

Gabby was muttering to herself about climbing the corporate ladder, snickering disdainfully about something Vernese was talking about in the book. He wasn't sure what the emotion represented for her - did she miss working but was home with the kids, or was she tired of trying to make her mark in corporate America? Patrick didn't know, but that detail didn't really matter to him at that moment. Gabby's sardonic muttering was hypnotic. Patrick was compelled to repeat her words over and over again, both in his mind and out loud even though Gabby herself had moved on to something else.

Trying to go up, ha! Want to climb up?

Up?

Patrick stared at the walls as if he could see the words manifesting there, the type done in huge, neon block letters.

What was he supposed to get from that?

Patrick looked up at the ceiling. Was there an upstairs to the house? He remembered it as a rambler, a one-story, sprawling beast of a thing that seemed to have endless corridors covering acres of land, but was it? Mal told them they could make the house look like whatever they wanted it to. Did that mean that there could be an upstairs if he wanted there to be? Would Joanne be in a room up there just because he wanted her to be?

Was it that simple?

Patrick didn't allow the thought that he might have just witnessed his own mental break to take root. Instead, he replayed Gabby's words in his head. *Trying to go up.*

Something broke inside him; some tenuous hold he had over his emotions just snapped like a rubber band stretched too far. Patrick called out; he couldn't stop himself.

"Joanne?" Patrick said, his head turned toward the ceiling. His voice was weak and noncommittal, the words more a plea than anything else, but he did it just the same. He wasn't sure if he really wanted a response.

CHAPTER 17

Gabby was hooked.

At a time when she thought it impossible to add anything else to her plate, she found a way to squeeze in reading her grandmother's manuscript. Every chance she got, Gabby's nose was stuffed in the pages kept together in a loose-leaf binder. She cooked dinner with it propped up next to the stove, carried it while vacuuming, read before bed and then again, first thing in the morning, before the kids started their day. She couldn't put it down. The story was captivating. She felt as if the characters were speaking directly to her.

Gabby wondered why her grandmother never finished the manuscript, why she never tried to get it published. Her dad hadn't known. When Gabby asked him about it, he said she had just put it down and never went back to it. That sounded like the memory a child might have - she had become keenly aware of how little we understood about adult behavior when we were kids after having her own. No, there was something more to it, Gabby was sure. She just didn't know what.

The house was quiet except for the sound of her husband snoring from their bedroom. The kids were asleep too, worn out after a busy day of playing in the park, reciting the alphabet (the lot of them singing it, saying it, screaming it over and over again), and meeting up with friends to play some more at dinner. Gabby knew she should be tired too, but she wasn't. Instead, she was anxious. She wanted to get back to the book, to see what was going on with Aaron and Vernese and the others. She had been frustrated earlier at the park when, thinking she could grab a few minutes to read, she turned to where she left off only to be interrupted by chatty moms and bratty kids whining and crying and being so loud that she couldn't hear herself think. Then later, when the kids were napping, she got a phone call that lasted longer than expected, eating away her reading time. And then, of course, there was dinner with some of her mom friends and their little cherubs. The conversation cycled over and over between the kids' eating habits *("Mine will only eat chicken nuggets. How about yours?")*, to missing adult conversation (even though now that they were having it, it revolved around the children anyway), and back again. There was no opportunity to take out the manuscript and get some quiet time. The thing had been burning a hole in her diaper bag all day long.

But with everyone asleep and the house quiet, Gabby could read for as long as her eyes would let her.

Gabby settled down on the sofa and pulled the soft, fuzzy blanket that adorned the armrest over her legs. With a contented sigh, she found the page where she left off and rejoined the adventure.

CHAPTER 18

SANGUINE PARADISE

She had really been there. Aaron was sure of it. There was a woman standing on the deserted pier looking out at the boat as it made its way to Saint Martin's shores. He couldn't see her well, but he saw all that he needed to.

She was there only for an instant it seemed, though he knew it must have been longer. No human could move in the blink of an eye the way some of his kind could, yet he saw her for the fastest of seconds, and then she was gone. As he stared at the place she had occupied moments before, he wondered why he cared. She was just a girl that would, more than likely, end up as their evening meal, knowing how ravenous his shipmates were. She wouldn't live past next week, of that he was sure. So, why did he care to see her face, to see how her hair, dark and curly like corkscrews, blew in the wind? Why did he feel himself respond to her - to life? He couldn't deny the tension that roiled in his stomach when he looked at her, but it was more than a sexual reaction. In that instant, that moment in time when he saw her standing alone on the dock, he felt a pull, a longing. Her hair was unkempt and blowing wildly around her head as the tropical winds sent word of an impending storm. Her face was solemn, her almond-shaped eyes looking dull, as if lifeless. Her lips, full and pouty, were downturned, tugging at the corners. There was no happiness there, no contentment. Only sadness and, Aaron thought for a fleeting moment, bitter recognition.

The others rumbled below deck, moving boisterously in their sleep as they prepared to wake. They were excited about docking, thinking the islanders were unsuspecting, but Aaron knew better. The girl knew who was in their solemn vessel, and if she did, he thought others might as well. The hunt may not be as easy as the others thought it would be. Aaron knew this would do nothing but heighten the anticipation. If there was anything his ilk enjoyed it was the smell of fear that exuded from human's pores when they tried to escape. Thomas' excitement was already bursting at the seams. The thrill of having to catch their prey rather than just plucking it from the streets would be scintillating on several levels. He too was ready to disembark and set foot on Saint Martin, but for another reason.

He wanted to know her.

CHAPTER 19

Dr. LaFleur had said they would come and she believed him because he, of all people, would have no reason to lie. Some of the guests thought he was crazy, raving after days alone on the open seas. But Vernese didn't. She believed every word the doctor said, not because he was a scientist and a man of unwavering logic, but in spite of it. Dr. LaFleur was trying to help them because doing so meant helping himself.

He came to the island the day the news stopped broadcasting - the day the world went silent. Vernese and the guests that remained were sitting in one of the penthouse units watching television and trying, as they had for eight days by then, to figure out what to do next. The guests still had their assigned rooms but had designated the penthouse as their new lounge. There were usually several of them in there at any given time commiserating, strategizing, or just looking out over the ocean in utter hopelessness. Vernese was guilty of the same. She left the hotel a couple days after the report of rampant vampirism on the news (she found humor in that term, even then, with the creatures breathing down their necks), wanting to check on the apartment she shared with Constance, a friend from school. She found it empty, entirely so, like no one had ever lived there. Vernese found a hastily scribbled note on a tattered piece of paper pinned to the refrigerator by a magnet that said, 'I love the beach!'. It said what she had already guessed - Constance had gone to stay with her boyfriend. She thought if they were going to die, they wanted to be together... and that was it. No 'Goodbye, old friend', no well wishes or hopes for safety. Just an empty space after the words ended that did more to express the way Vernese felt right then than anything else could have. A profound sadness engulfed Vernese then, as she stood in the kitchen with the note in her hand. Constance leaving wasn't what was bothering her - Vernese hadn't really expected her to be there anyway, at least not alone. It was that she herself didn't have anywhere to go or anyone to be with. No parents, no boyfriend anymore - he had moved to Antigua behind some tramp he met at the casino school - no one she would consider friend enough to spend what could be her last days with. She was utterly alone. Vernese realized that the people at the hotel were the only people left in her life. They needed her and she needed them. They were all she had.

After standing in the sparsely furnished living room, and looking over things that meant nothing to her, after trying not to let feelings of loneliness and despair root her, Vernese packed some clothes and left the apartment too. She went back to the apartment once more, the day she visited Phillipsburg to find a cruise ship approaching the island's abandoned dock, only to find that it had been trashed.

The penthouse was relatively empty the morning that Dr. LaFleur's boat was spotted in Simpson Bay. Vernese had taken a seat on one of the penthouse's four balconies to get some air. One of the guests - residents were more like the truth by then - had engaged her in conversation about what was happening in Iowa, where his daughter lived. He had given up hope. He had no faith that his daughter was alive and was hiding out like they were. Even when Vernese suggested the possibility, he rejected it. He told her there was no point in living if she was dead and that he couldn't go on knowing his daughter hadn't made it. Vernese felt sorry for him, but there was nothing she could do. She'd heard many people say the same thing, some threatening to jump off the roof if this went on much longer. She and Spencer, the one security guard who had stayed at the resort, took turns guarding him, but he never made any attempts to take his life. But someone would, she knew. It was only a matter of time. The prospect made her tired.

And scared.

Vernese couldn't help but wonder when she would crack. Would it be when people started jumping off the roof in line, going over back to back like that cult lining up to drink the Kool-Aid in Jonestown? Or maybe she wouldn't lose it until the last of the food they could scavenge ran out and they started hunting the strays that roamed the streets yowling and barking, suffering from their own starvation? And what then? Would she abandon these people, and leave them to fend for themselves? Would she run into the streets raving? Or would she follow them off the balcony, without so much as a backwards glance at the next doomed soul?

Vernese shivered involuntarily, the thought making goose-bumps stand out on her skin.

CHAPTER 20

SANGUINE PARADISE

Vernese sat on the balcony in one of the chairs lined up to face Kimsha Beach thinking about what comes next. The air felt good against her face and the smell of saltwater caressed her nostrils, pulling her back to the beauty of her little island and away from the dark thoughts that threatened to take over. Vernese had always liked the smell of the ocean, even when she was a little girl. She remembered walking past the beach where the locals went, going all the way down the hill to feel the sand beneath her feet and hear the water unencumbered by Soca music and idle chatter, even though Friar's Bay was ten minutes out of the way between school and home. Times like that morning brought back memories of normalcy, when people weren't brandishing fangs and biting their neighbor's necks any other time than Halloween.

Memories like that coupled with the smell of the ocean

could almost lull her into believing the rumors were nothing more than the last vestiges of a dream; what lingered from a crazy nightmare.

Vernese heard them shouting but thought it was someone breaking down. It made her feel tired to hear the elevated voices filled with emotion yet again. Vernese knew they couldn't help it, but that didn't make it any easier to hear. She kept looking at the water instead of going inside to help, hoping that someone else would play savior this time. But then the sound of the waves rolling onto the surf was disturbed by screams - it was the would-be jumper again, Vernese knew. Maybe he had finally decided to do it and was standing on the top rail of the balcony off the bedroom, his favorite spot to contemplate ending it all. She was afraid of herself suddenly, goosebumps rising on her skin not because his life might be hanging in the balance, but because it didn't matter to her if it did.

It was better for Vernese to stay where she was.

She didn't know if she had the strength to deal with his grief, not when her own loneliness was starting to engulf her like a shroud. She might make things worse, her apathetic face driving his hesitating form over the edge, finally. Vernese didn't know if she could live with that.

Vernese shut her eyes to the ocean and tried to close her ears to the screams. She was just about to give up and leave the penthouse, to sneak out, hiding her footsteps in the din if she could, when she realized the screams were not of grief and loss but of excitement.

"Look! Over there!" the would-be jumper yelled, his voice excited.

"Is that a boat?" Someone else chimed in.

Vernese opened her eyes and saw what they were shouting about. Off in the distance a little boat - nothing more than a modest fisherman's vessel - made its way to the shore. It was slow going, even in the calm waters. It was as if the person in it was spent, just riding along, hoping to hit the shore before he passed out. Vernese came to know later that her assessment wasn't far from the truth; Dr. LaFleur was so fatigued, he could hardly hold his head up.

Vernese and the others raced down the stairs (they didn't dare use the elevator anymore - if it stalled, they would never get a crew to the hotel to fix it) and out to the beach in silence, afraid to say anything for fear of being heard, and apprehensive about who - or what - might be in the boat. Morbid curiosity trumping all, they waited, half expecting to meet a beast with fangs that dripped with blood.

What they saw shocked them just the same.

CHAPTER 21

Doug had started investigating the house. It beat standing in the same spot ineptly listening to Gabby reading his mother's unfinished manuscript. His father was so drawn to it. Patrick wouldn't leave the room no matter what Doug had tried. But this wasn't the time for nostalgia; his daughter's life was at stake. He had to do *something*, unlike his dad who had done nothing to stop this runaway train to Hell. So, Doug snuck out.

But that wasn't really fair. Patrick had been trying. From the moment he found himself in The Realm, Patrick had been doing everything he could to change things for Doug and Gabby. Doug knew that was true, but it didn't matter. None of this would have happened if it wasn't for Patrick. He was at the core of the whole shitball of a scenario and Doug couldn't get past that point. He was dead and stuck there because of some great wrong his father had committed. Sins of the father and all that. So would his daughter be if he couldn't figure out how to reverse the curse.

As Doug left the room, he caught a glimpse of his father's profile. Worried, haggard, pensive, and something else. Something wholly unto its own, intense in a way that the other emotions were not. Doug couldn't decipher it and decided he didn't want to. He couldn't stand the idea that something else could be preoccupying his father's thoughts at a time like this. This was no time for self-deprecation, wistfulness, or (good God, could that really be what he sees?) longing for times past (for the *woman* from those times, perhaps?). If Doug put too fine a point on it, he was afraid of what he might do.

His father had put them there. His father had condemned them.

Doug allowed his mind to be filled with that sentiment, sounding like a mantra in his head for as much as he repeated it over and over as he turned down endless corridors and opened innumerable identical-looking doors. It still didn't make sense to him that this was reality but as he cast his eyes around the unfamiliar walls, he couldn't help but accept it. The mild-mannered man Doug knew growing up didn't seem capable of doing something so heinous that he could damn his whole family for all eternity. What did that even mean, anyway? Religion and the Bible had never been his strengths. He enjoyed a level of ignorance about Heaven and Hell, God and the devil that only a casual churchgoer could claim and that had been more than fine to him. Talking about eternal retribution and condemnation in some nether region in any real sense was as foreign a concept to him as the impromptu appearance of stigmata on the innocent. He would have dismissed it out of hand had he heard about it while standing upright in the only life he thought possible. But now, as he stood on feet that should be immobile, in a place that only loosely resembled his habitat, he knew that all of the allusions he held to be true before were bullshit. Utterly and completely so.

So, what the fuck had his father done?

Doug placed his hand on the fourth (or was it the fifth?) door and pushed it open. The room was empty except for a chair covered with chipped black paint. It sat at the perfect right angle, as if it were tucked under an imaginary dining room table with its three accompanying imaginary chairs surrounding said table just so. There was nothing on the walls, the same as in all of the other rooms, and there were no windows. He closed the door and moved to the next one. This one had an empty coat rack sitting on the far side of the room and nothing else. The next one had three throw pillows on the floor, lined up as if they were ready to accent a sofa as soon as one materialized beneath them. Doug sighed deeply. He knew there was more to it than this, knew there was some kind of riddle that he was supposed to solve. The thought made him tired.

As he shut the door to the next room, the one that had board games stacked one on top of the other almost up to the ceiling - titles like Life, Jenga, Monopoly and Scrabble mixed with older boxes with muted colors carrying names like Stop Thief and Feeley Meeley - Doug dragged his mind back to his father and what he had done to land them in The Realm. Was it murder? Sex? Pedophilia, though Doug could hardly allow himself to finish that thought. His father had always been on the straight and narrow. He helped with Doug's Little League team, tutored kids, shuttled him and his friends back and forth. But isn't that the way it always goes? It's always the one you least suspect, right?

No! His dad was not a pervert, Doug screamed inside, drowning out all the crazy thoughts coming at him from every angle. The thought of his father being that way made him sick to his stomach. He would kill him with his bare hands if it was true.

But it's too late for that now, isn't it?

Doug was starting to hate that little voice inside him, the one that kept planting the seeds of doubt at every turn.

So, what was it, then? Going back to the original problem made the most sense, at least that's what his anxious mind told him as he walked through what seemed like endless corridors. He could hear sounds from outside, low, guttural, wet ones that sparked a slow churn of fear in his gut, but he reminded himself that there was nothing to be afraid of in The Realm anymore. He ran the place now - he and his father. They controlled the beasts that hunt in the night. They controlled who lived and died. A smile played at the corners of Doug's lips at that. For a guy who never ascended past individual contributor status at work, never managed anyone, never had the chance to choose his projects: never controlled a goddamned thing other than what side of the desk he would keep his sticky notes and pens, the power was unexpectedly heady. He considered going back and reminding Patrick of that. In the end, if Gabby ended up in The Realm it wouldn't be that bad after all. They would make sure that she had safe passage, would even make the damned things that were the Hunters carry her around in a chariot if that would make her happy. She would be safe. They would all be safe, and they would all rule. They would be like a royal family from medieval times with dragons protecting the kingdom. They could do whatever they wanted because they would be in control.

Easy. So easy to get lost in the fantasy.

Doug shook his head, willing his rational mind to wake up and take control before things got out of hand. Sure, they would be rulers, but for how long? Mileeha died right before their eyes

- couldn't the same thing happen to them? And how long could they control the beasts? Were he and Patrick strong enough to dissuade them from fresh meat? Doug stopped walking, a thought assaulting his mind. Where was his mother? Where would his wife go? If this curse was only on his paternal bloodline, would he never see the love of his life again? Never kiss his mother's cheek? If there was one thing that religion extolled the most, it was being with your loved ones after death. If they choose to stay in The Realm, wouldn't they be forsaking that eternal promise? That he hadn't thought about that first bothered Doug to his core.

Doug walked down the corridor, thinking, looking. What was upstairs? *Was* there an upstairs? Was there a cellar? Doug traced his hand along the wall as if the space was dim and he needed to touch to confirm where he was, but the corridor's lighting was as good there as it had been in his own home. Doug wondered if the corridor was lit that well because that's what he willed it to be. After all, he controlled things in The Realm now, didn't he? He opened the next door, keeping puppies in his mind. He didn't know what he would do if he opened the door and found a bunch of puppies bouncing, tumbling, writhing en masse on the ground, but he didn't have to waste energy on it. He opened the door and found an empty easel set up in the middle of the room and nothing else. Doug didn't know how to feel about that.

He turned to look back the way he came, envisioning his father sitting on the floor listening to Gabby's voice intently. A sound not unlike a sob emitted from the back of his throat. How he had judged his father for the emotion he was displaying, for the weakness. Doug had let his anger cloud his mind and remove rational thought. He didn't see what his father knew, didn't feel the impending loss that threatened to breach reality and make itself known. Doug hadn't understood any of it. But now he thought he did, clarity lifting the darkness around him the way a groom does a bridal veil. Ruling in The Realm would mean saying goodbye to his wife and mother forever.

Doug braced himself against the wall, the revelation nearly knocking him off his feet. He took in a few breaths, steadying himself for the search ahead, now more focused than ever. He had to understand the place, know all the nooks and crannies, if he was going to be able to manipulate it. Doug cast his eyes around the hallway he was standing in. It looked just like the one he had left a moment before, which looked just like the one leading to the room where he had left his father. The place was a rambling maze with all its twists and turns, but Doug couldn't let it get the better of him. He had to search for clues about Mal, where he was or if he only existed in spiritual form. And, most importantly, he had to find out what his father did, not to castigate him with it, but to figure out what could be done to make it right so they could all be freed from The Realm so that they could all be reunited.

CHAPTER 22

Mal was as enthralled by Gabby's voice as Patrick was. It was melodic, captivating, really, but that wasn't the reason he couldn't stop listening. It was the words she spoke, her mind caressing them as she read to send them through the ether to their waiting ears. She spoke truths she could never imagine; sang lyrics to a song she had never heard. Those words were a symphony to long-deafened martyrs. Gabby couldn't know what she was awakening by simply reading the words on the forgotten pages.

But Mal knew.

Mal knew every syllable of what was being read, could feel each word regaining its fervor, filling in like mercury in a maze, fleshing out dead skin to make it plump and malleable once again. He was powerless to stop the poison from flowing.

Mal ran a finger along the ornate door, the pattern etched deeply in the jarrah wood. How he longed to see her. It pained him that he still felt the same way about her. That the thought of her could derail him; that the prospect of seeing her sent tingles up his spine frustrated him. Feelings like these – any feelings at all - did not serve him well in The Realm. Feelings could get you killed, as Mileeha found out for himself.

Things would be so much easier if he didn't care. She was part of his past, after all - a connection that had served him well but was of no real use anymore. Now she was a detriment to him. If only he could convince himself that he would be better off without her around.

Mal fancied he could hear her breathing on the other side of the door.

Mal cast his eyes down to the floor, the rotting mass of over-grown vegetation, mud, and waste that he masked with images of a rustic tiled floor and smirked. Ah, Joanne. The bane of his existence, most unexpectedly so. The love of his life. The two sides of her were inextricably linked and while he wanted to keep them separate, to only reveal himself to one side - the one he could control - he knew it would never work. The book was being read. It had begun. There was nothing he nor Joanne could do to avoid the inevitable now.

CHAPTER 23

Dr. LaFleur, after falling out of his boat and standing unsteadily on the shore with his feet buried in the wet sand, brandished what could only be described as a sword and shouted as loud as his hoarse voice would allow,

"Éloigne-toi de moi! Me partir seul! Me partir seul!" *Stay away from me!! Leave me alone! Leave me alone!*

He looked scared, terrified in fact. His face was ghostly white despite the raw sunburn that dotted his forehead and cheeks. His fingers twitched along the base of the weapon he held in a vice grip. Vernese believed the man standing in front of them in tattered clothes even if she couldn't understand him. Her gut feeling was enough to show Vernese that he was human and not one of those vampires trying to lure them in, not that she had ever seen one to know what to look for.

Vernese took a step toward the man but was stopped by a

stiff arm in front of her. One of the guests, a man who had, by and large, kept himself together, said in a hushed tone,

"Wait. We don't know if we can trust him."

From behind him, the jumper said, an almost shrieking quality in his voice, "What did he say? What the hell did he say?"

The guests looked at Vernese and she met their eyes with a blank stare of her own. Even hough the island was split between the French and the Dutch, she was a Dutch resident and had never learned enough of the French language to do anything more than say hello, goodbye, and ask where the library is.

Vernese hadn't realized Spencer had joined them on the beach until he spoke to the man, his voice rich and clear over the excited chirping coming from the bewildered guests who alternated between asking what the man in the boat said and suggesting they kill him to be safe (Vernese couldn't allow herself to think about the fact that the guests had degraded to murder to protect their safety pretty much right away. It was another one of those things that might push her over the edge).

"Nous sommes normaux ici," Spencer said, his French impeccable. He would tell Vernese later that he told the man that they were normal and that he would be safe if he was also, knowing neither one of those statements was entirely true. "Si vous êtes aussi, vous êtes sûr."

The man, whom they would later know as Dr. LaFleur, blinked once, twice, three times before exhaling a pent-up breath. His shoulders slumped as his guard came down. He laughed, the sound raspy and humorless.

"Sûr? Il y a aucune les chose telle que sûre. Pas plus." The man dropped his sword in the sand and sat down hard, pivoting as he dropped to look out at the water.

"What did he say?" Vernese asked Spencer. It was as if he

hadn't heard her. Spencer stared at the weary traveler with a look of such sadness in his eyes it could have brought tears from a lesser man.

The guests that remained, the people Vernese had been relegated to spend this new existence with, leaned in to listen. The effect was chilling. Even with only eight of them left, they affected the appearance of an angry mob.

"Spencer, what did he say?" Vernese tried again.

After a deep breath, Spencer responded, "He's no threat to us. I told him that we were normal and that if he was too, he was safe. He said there is no such thing as safe."

Vernese looked away from Spencer, back at the ocean. She was afraid to hear any more, but Spencer moved closer to her, to the guests who were still asking questions about where the man came from and what was going on there, raising their excited chatter to a near deafening level yet again.

"Vernese, this man didn't speak Creole. He spoke formal French like they speak in Paris, and Nice, and Versailles. Proper, like in school. Do you know what that could mean?"

Vernese sat in stunned silence, unwilling to let the possibility seep into her consciousness, though it had festered in her subconscious for longer than she cared to admit. Where had this man set sail? What had he seen, what had scared him so badly that he took to the water to run?

Vernese couldn't bring herself to look at Spencer while he spoke, couldn't acknowledge the train of thought he had embarked on. She knew all too well what it meant. It meant the end of the world.

The guests were firing questions at the man from the boat now that he had dropped his sword. They inched toward him, pressing.

"Who are you?

Where did you come from?

What's going on out there?

Have you seen any of them?"

The barrage was relentless. The man had started to back away, dragging himself backward in the sand toward the water. His face registered fear once again.

"Me partir seul! Me partir seul! Je ne sais pas ce que tu veux de moi!"

"Leave him alone," Spencer boomed. "He doesn't understand – can't you see that? Have pity! My god, this man has been through enough!"

Hearing Spencer speak so loudly after having not said more than a hundred words since they had been holed up together shocked the guests into silence and stilled their advancing steps. The man from the boat stood on tired legs and whispered, "Merci."

"You are welcome to stay with us," Vernese said, speaking up. "We don't have much food, but we are willing to share it with you."

While Spencer translated, Vernese ignored the angry looks from the guests. This was still her hotel and she would make decisions accordingly. One of the guests, a woman from the U.S. who had been practically invisible, dealing with her fear alone in the confines of her room and rarely commiserating when she did come out of her room, spoke up,

"We don't have much left. How can we bring someone else in?"

"We can't leave a man to die," Vernese said, fatigue lacing her words. "Who knows how long he's been in that boat. He needs food and medical attention and while we can't provide much, we should give him what we have. It's the right thing to do."

The woman didn't say anything more, but Vernese could see she didn't agree. She was going to have to be stern with them moving forward, Vernese knew. With sad recognition, Vernese knew they were only steps away from every man fending for himself... at any cost.

This is what Vernese was thinking as she stood on the pristine shores watching that ship, a ghost ship if ever there was one, come in. She remembered her last moments of ignorance, her last moments of freedom. With bittersweet clarity, she shed a tear. It wasn't only for herself that she cried, though the mourning of a life spectated rather than lived sat like a stone in her chest. She cried for the people that would die when the ship docked and the jackals descended. She cried for the people whose blood would run in the streets only to be lapped up by those living a new horror. She cried because she didn't know if any of them would see the break of dawn.

CHAPTER 24

SANGUINE PARADISE

"Sanguine... sanguine..."

The man mumbled in his sleep but Vernese had expected as much. He had been in the boat for God knows how long without food or fresh water. He was sick, she could see that. She knew the others were right when they protested bringing him in, but she couldn't leave him out there alone to die.

"Sanguine..." he croaked.

"Sanguine?" Vernese ventured, coaxing him back to reality. "Do you mean blood?"

His eyes opened, lids squinting as he searched her face for understanding. Vernese leaned closer and gave him a drink while he was awake enough to swallow.

"Are you talking about blood?" she repeated, trying to keep him talking, raising her voice a little in the hopes that Spencer would hear and come to translate.

"Yes. They drink blood." The man's voice was no more than a whisper, but he wanted to speak. His eyes, ever clearing, were urgent.

"I heard that on the news... when we could get a signal." Vernese fanned herself. The heat was becoming unbearable during the day.

"Not them. The sanguinarians," he croaked, his voice trying to recover from disuse. "They drink blood. They say it - it heals them."

English.

Vernese was surprised to hear the man speaking English after the confusion on the beach. She didn't say anything though, choosing instead to let it go. That he had taken refuge in his mother tongue in the face of unbearable fear need not be called out into the light now.

Vernese listened intently. If Spencer came, he did not make himself known and that was good. There was much to be learned from this man who had actually been out among the vampires, as they assumed he had. Why else would he have fled in a rickety little boat and risked his life on the open sea? Better to let him continue without an audience.

"It... heals them?" Vernese asked and he simply nodded in response. She didn't understand what he was talking about and desperately wanted to. She had never heard anyone speak of sanguinarians. Blood suckers and vampires were the labels of choice, at least around here, but even that was short-lived. Everything happened so fast. Before she knew it, no one was talking about anything anymore.

Vernese busied her hands, smoothing the wrinkles in her pants just to have something to do. Her eyes implored him to continue, but she didn't want to say anything. She was afraid he would stop talking, keeping the secrets he knew about what was going on in the world to himself. If he did that, Vernese thought she might just go crazy.

Vernese had to keep him talking. This was the most he had spoken since they found him.

"I met one in the bathroom," he said after a long pause within which Vernese felt she might pass out, soul drained in desperation. "We weren't supposed to see our subjects - our interactions were supposed to be carefully orchestrated to keep us apart, but somehow, this man and I were in the bathroom at the same time. He looked pale, like he was about to be sick."

The man paused to catch his breath. He took another sip of water, looking stronger by the minute. Vernese offered him a piece of the bread she had set out for him, which he took gratefully.

"I asked him if he was ok," he continued, chewing while he spoke. "He said he needed to drink. But the way he looked at me, I knew he didn't mean alcohol... or even water."

Vernese sat up, understanding tickling her senses as if for the first time. "You don't mean he-? He didn't-?" Her eyes searched the man's body for a bite mark frantically, her eyes crawling over the exposed skin and peering at the rips in his clothing to see if the material was dyed in blood. Vernese's mind screamed at her for having been so stupid, for trusting him blindly, as if she hadn't heard of all the horrors, hadn't seen the destruction in the world playing out on the TV screen. She could hardly feel her extremities; her hands and feet had gone cold as if all the blood had fled them in an instant. Vernese had to fight the urge to run from the room.

"No, no, I wasn't bitten," the man said, reading the sudden panic on her face. "I left the bathroom right away. Miraculously, I haven't come close to that." Vernese visibly calmed, shoulders unbunching, eyebrows unfurling, legs giving way to the seat beneath her in utter relief. "I was too unsettled by the way he stared to stay. But that's when I got my idea, and I just knew it would work"

He shook his head incredulously, looking around the hotel room with a mixture of disdain and chagrin painted on his face. Reality had never seemed so absurd. He sighed heavily, running a weathered hand across his sunburned face purposefully, as if he could wipe his folly away. After some time, he spoke again. "I was going to cure cancer, AIDS, every disease known to man if my results were positive. I thought I would change the world."

"What are you talking about?" The man's introspection unsettled Vernese. She wasn't sure if he was delirious or not.

"I'm talking about terminal diseases. If my research had worked, there would be no such thing as dying from leukemia anymore. What I was doing was the natural progression of modern science. It was revolutionary."

"You're a doctor...?"

"I'm a scientist," he snapped. "I was going to change the world as we know it, but then," he propped himself up on a bent elbow. "Then he died."

Vernese felt a chill even as the heat bore into her skin. She needed to hear what he was saying but was glad that she was the one in the room. The others might have thought he was raving, might have overreacted because of it. They were so on edge that they might have tried to kill him when he started talking about the blood, making themselves believe they were in danger. And really, she couldn't blame them. First he raved on the beach, brandishing a sword and speaking in a language they didn't hold in common, then he slept like the dead before waking to mumble about blood, and now this talk of death? Part of her, the part that didn't care for the fact that everything that had happened the past few days seemed like a scene in a movie, the part that couldn't shake the thought that she was sitting with the mad scientist, his entry into the film precisely on cue – that part of her knew that what she was hearing was important but was terrified to her very core.

"*Who* died?" she asked, forcing herself to keep engaging no matter how outlandish the story got, no matter how the hairs on the back of her neck stood up. With a voice laced with trepidation, she prodded as gently as she could, "Who?"

"The first of them. Patient Zero, I guess you could call him. He wasn't alone for long. He made more just like him right away."

"How? What happened, Dr.-"

"My name is Dr. LaFleur," he said tiredly. "I was running a test group to see how sanguinarians' bodies reacted to drinking human blood versus animal blood. No one knew which type of blood they received. The ones that got the animal blood thrived, claiming to feel more energetic and clear-headed than their counterparts, who received the human blood they were accustomed to. That was a breakthrough, to say the least."

Vernese listened though her stomach turned. The idea of drinking blood - anything's blood - made her feel nauseous.

"I was preparing to conduct my third round of testing when one of the patients from the first test group barged into the office, dispensing with the guard that sat outside our door as if he was a gnat flying around his head."

Vernese squirmed in her seat, the story seeming to take a turn down a road she was unsure she wanted to travel.

"We couldn't see the guard. We didn't know what happened to him at that time. I'm not entirely sure that I know what happened to him, even now," the doctor said under his breath, the memory distracting him. "But I knew at once that something was wrong with the man standing in our lab."

"How?"

Dr. LaFleur considered the question, measuring his words carefully before responding. "There was something in the way that he was standing that gave me pause. The stance was too wide; his arms hung unnaturally at his sides, muscles tensed as though ready to strike. He seemed primed for battle." The doctor paused at that, finding himself back in the room with his frightened colleagues at the mercy of Patient Zero. The sound of his own breathing flooded his ears as it did then, sharp intakes and dry huffs mingling with the incessant hum characteristic of HVAC units and the intermittent whines, moans, and sobs that his colleagues let slip through their clenched jaws. The cacophony was so all-encompassing, he didn't think it would ever abate. Vernese's voice pierced the din sounding in his mind, bringing the doctor back from the laboratory of his nightmares and into a fresh sort of hell.

"What happened, Doctor?"

Dr. LaFleur's eyes were wild, but he fought to keep his voice under control.

"This, my dear girl, *this* happened. All of this, the blood, the death, the veritable feast they make of us... *this* is what happened."

The doctor kept talking, kept explaining how Patient Zero had barreled through the scientists in the room, ripping necks open and splashing the walls with blood. He spoke of three people who escaped the carnage, one of which didn't get five steps outside of the building before falling prey to the feral sanguinarians. That's what he called them - feral - because that's what they were, wasn't it? Reverted. Wild. Ferocious.

They were beasts, now, truthfully.

"Which blood did he drink?" Vernese asked tentatively,

afraid of the questions as much as of the answer. "Patient Zero. What blood did he have?"

Vernese would ask again but the question would remain unanswered, giving way instead to details of carnage and suffering that Vernese wished she had never heard.

Dr. LaFleur considered the meaning of the words he spoke, working through them with more verbiage, more chatter, more noise, but Vernese didn't care about any of that. What she knew now, after the doctor talked of mistakes and outbreaks and dystopia of such fantastical quality as to have been born of the mind of an author, was that there was no getting out of this. The proverbial game was over, and she hadn't even begun to play.

CHAPTER 25

It was there as it had been so many times before and she rose to greet it swiftly, her actions masking the hesitance she felt in her soul. Even as she tried to keep her emotions at bay, hidden within her, and silent, she was sure they sat on her skin, shimmering like rhinestones in the sun. Joanne swallowed, willed herself to be strong, but she was sure it knew. She was as enamored of it then as she always was.

The realization frightened her.

"Who are you?" Joanne asked the entity in the room. She could sense it; feel its presence caressing her skin like a silk blouse. Her mind willed her to sink into the feeling, to let the sensation distract her, please her the way nothing had since she had awoken in that barren, desolate place, but she couldn't. Not yet.

"Answer me," she pleaded, eyes suddenly wet. "Please."

"I am me." The voice was silky and deep, the pitch a breathy baritone that licked at her soul.

He, then.

"Me?"

"Yes."

Joanne had to shake her head to stay grounded. "What does that-? Am I supposed to know who-" She was stammering and couldn't stop. She wanted to feel embarrassed, but it wasn't a reaction she could summon then.

"You *do* know."

They stood in silence; his countenance as yet unseen.

As usual.

"Let me see you," she begged. She just wanted to know if his face looked as regal as his voice promised it would, if the lips that formed the words he spoke were as plush as she imagined. She just wanted to -

"And what good would that do?"

The voice was so sure, so strong.

So familiar. Perhaps because his reaction was always the same.

Defeated, Joanne changed tack. "Tell me," she implored. "I beg you, tell me what you want from me. Tell me who you are and what you want."

Joanne waited. The silence was deafening.

"Can you hear her, Joanne?" the disembodied voice asked kindly, as though making conversation on a warm spring day. "Her voice echoes through the halls."

Joanne was thrown off guard. She listened but heard nothing more than her heart beating in her chest, no doubt a figment of her imagination, but ringing in her ears, nonetheless. But then there was the tiniest of sounds...

"I don't hear anyone but you," she lied, wanting to keep that little voice at the edge of her perception to herself.

Joanne let that sit, hoping that she had been alluring enough to entice him to speak. She laughed self-deprecatingly after more silence followed. It was futile. Joanne knew she could never make him do anything he didn't want to do.

"Please..." she tried again, letting her words trail off unspoken.

"You know me, Joanne. You know me as well as you know yourself. You always have."

His voice sounded in her ear like the whisper of a lover. She jerked her head toward the place where she thought he was standing but saw nothing. Joanne searched the room, eyes peering into the darkness hoping to find a silhouette. But there was none. There never was.

"I could never hide from you," he continued. "No matter how much I want to."

Joanne opened and closed her mouth, voiceless in the face of this confession. One word rose in her mind blaring like a neon sign with a definitive quality she had not known since she was among the living: Liar.

"What do you mean you couldn't hide from me?" Try as she might, Joanne couldn't wait for a response. It was all pouring out now - the frustration she felt about being strung along, the anger she harbored for ending up in that lonely place, the dull ache of desire she tried to tamp down even now, as it roiled in her stomach. "I have no idea who you are or what you are talking about." Joanne's voice began to rise, becoming shrill despite her effort to control it. She wanted answers. She deserved them. "Why are you keeping me here?"

Disregarding her outburst, Mal spoke calmly again, "I knew this day would come."

Joanne was beside herself. She knew he was involved with why she was there instead of in Paradise, knew he might even be the one pulling the strings in that godforsaken place, but none of that mattered. Now that she had found her voice,

Joanne didn't want to be silent anymore, no matter what it cost her.

"My god, why can't you leave me to suffer death in peace?"

The room was still, so much so that Joanne thought he might have gone. But then, from the shadows, he spoke once more, "It was always you, Joanne. In the end, I knew that too."

The incredulity died on her lips before she gave voice to the question she had repeated in her head like a mantra from the beginning, because as she listened to the cadence of the sensuous baritone as it lilted and swirled, closing the space between them to caress her ears, she knew. With stark clarity, Joanne realized she had known all along.

CHAPTER 26

Patrick saw it.

A sudden arching of the eyebrow; an almost indiscernible reaction, but it was something tangible - something real. He was almost giddy with excitement.

He made Gabby jump.

He wasn't entirely sure how he had done it - his mind had been on Joanne and whether or not he should go looking for her when he, rather impulsively, reached out - but he knew it worked. Gabby was reacting to it, this pulsation, vibration, little mental tap on the shoulder - he had no idea what to call it, but none of that mattered. Patrick had reached out to Gabby and she felt it. It took a herculean effort to do it once he has committed to try, but judging by her reaction, it felt like nothing more than one of those vein kinks that form from inactivity straightening out – Gabby reacted with the slightest of shivers like the ones brought on by a finger cascading along one's back.

Patrick had willed the action, telling his mind to reach out his invisible limbs to swipe at her through space and time and, by God, he did it. The strain was enough to drive him to his knees. It felt like he had run a marathon for nothing more than a blip on the screen in Gabby's world, but it was worth it. Patrick could almost feel the sweat beading on his forehead while his panting echoed off the walls; he mused at how his mind still worked overtime to send him images of himself in human form with human reactions. But this time Patrick didn't experience that frustration that usually followed the bubble-bursting reality that he no longer needed the air he was so desperately gasping for. All he felt this time was unmitigated joy.

Patrick could affect things in the real world.

He turned quickly, eager to celebrate this amazing feat with Doug, but found that he was in the room by himself.

"Doug?" He called his son's name cautiously, unsure if he really should - the Hunters were listening, after all - but still louder than he had called for Joanne. That he was the ruler of The Realm under Mal, the silent partner who was never there, wasn't real to him yet. That he could yell, scream, dance naked in the halls under a disco ball if he wanted to just didn't resonate. He hoped it never would. This wasn't what he wanted, not in the long run. All Patrick wanted out of the deal was the power to reverse the curse that put them there. Then Mal and whoever else wanted the helm could do with it what they would, including destroy him.

Patrick recoiled, taken aback by his own thoughts. That was it, wasn't it? He wanted to die. Thought he *should* die for damning everyone the way he had. He had no intentions of making it out of The Realm, did he? Patrick marveled at how he had hidden that truth from himself until just then, but he knew it was fact without even a moment's hesitation. When all was said and done, Patrick expected to die. His rational mind forced the thought away but didn't lock the door against it, even as his emotions begged him to.

Patrick looked back at Gabby who was curled up on the sofa with the pages of Joanne's manuscript held gingerly in her hands. He thought of how proud Joanne would have been to witness this moment. Patrick always thought she should have finished the book, but Joanne waved him off. Every time he would talk about the story and her descriptions of the island, she would shy away from it, feigning disinterest. She had lost interest in it, she told him. Said she didn't have anything else to write. Patrick used to make a joke about it, saying that her abandoning the book was like leaving those characters stranded on an island. He never knew how close to home that really was.

He tried reaching out to Gabby again needing to be sure he could do it. He focused, channeling his thoughts into one concentrated effort, and ended up producing the most under-whelming sound: a beep of sorts carried along the wind.

Gabby looked around her in surprise as something roused her from the words on the page. Was it a leaf fluttering in the wind? A branch tapping an upstairs window? Music coming from a car driving by? Gabby couldn't put her finger on what had made her look up from the manuscript. She couldn't tell if it was near or far, sound or scene. Patrick smiled. It was him.

Him.

It had been clumsy - he was shooting for caressing her cheek, something that would have been as light as a breeze. He had been trying for something that would make her react, swat at the air maybe like she would a fly - garner some kind of reaction, but he was happy with what he got. That weird, baseless sound that did nothing more than disturb Gabby's train of thought for an instant was proof enough that he had done it.

Patrick had really made something happen in the living world.

After another swivel of her head to peer into the four corners of the room, Gabby stopped looking, never rising from her perch on the sofa. And why would she? Whatever she heard, saw, or felt, was insignificant and fleeting - nothing to pay attention to. But to Patrick, it was everything.

As Gabby started reading again, finding Vernese and Dr. LaFleur on that doomed island paradise, her voice caressing the words rhythmically as though they were lyrics to her favorite song, Patrick smiled. This was big. He wanted to stop his mind from thinking it, but he couldn't - he was too late. If only he'd had this skill when Doug was alive. Then his son wouldn't have ever had to come to The Realm. Maybe he wouldn't have died yet, though there was no reason to think that was true. Still, Patrick wondered. If he had been able to interfere with Doug's death, maybe the next time they saw each other would have been in Paradise. Maybe Doug's eyes would hold such contempt in them when he looked at his father.

Patrick squeezed his eyes shut in an effort to stop the tears that welled there threatening to spill onto his cheeks. He let himself get lost in the sound of Gabby's inner voice reading his wife's words, words he had also read so many years ago.

Oh, Joanne, if only you were here to help me. Where are you now?

Patrick felt antsy. He needed to do something, whether that was find Joanne, find Mal and wrestle answers out of him, or fight his way down to earth and save Gabby. *Something.* Patrick looked back at the door silently willing it to open and for Doug to step in, but it didn't happen. He gave one more look at Gabby, his shoulders sagging into the turn of his head, as realization set in. He couldn't leave the room, not without someone to take watch. Leaving Gabby alone felt like knowingly leaving her to face a Hunter by herself, with its mouth agape and fangs bared. He couldn't do it. That was his granddaughter down there - the only reason he hadn't gone stark raving mad yet. He had to stay with her until Doug got back to take up watch. Joanne would understand, he knew with complete clarity. She would have done the very same thing.

As he watched Gabby sitting there, manuscript in hand, reading over the words in silence but her voice sounding like music to starved ears in Patrick's world, a new determination filled his mind, setting him to purpose. If he could make things happen in the land of the living maybe he could interfere with whatever might befall Gabby. Maybe that would buy him time to figure out the reason for the curse. All Patrick had to do was keep Gabby alive.

CHAPTER 27

Aaron inhaled deeply, the salty air still unusual enough to him that it made him smile when he let himself languish in it, even after two weeks on the island. Night covered the island like a blanket, thick and warm, suffocating in its humidity. Thomas and the others found it oppressive as most do, but Aaron relished in the feeling. The air stuck to him, cloying at his skin like a desperate lover. It made him feel needed, necessary. It made him feel alive.

He walked the lonely street aimlessly, though he was supposed to be on a mission. He had to feed, of course, but that wasn't the only thing he was tasked with that evening. Satisfying his thirst was the least of his worries. Finding sustenance that would last him and his merry band of vampires for an extended period of time was of most importance that night as it has been all of the nights of their stay. The island appeared deserted save for a few unlucky animals out near Loterie Farm, monkeys and goats that wandered away from their homes to find themselves in a vampire's grip. But that wasn't enough. Not nearly enough to satisfy a boat load of hungry vampires. A land wiped clean of food wasn't what they expected when they made the trip to that little French/Dutch island. It isn't what they sensed either. Indeed, they felt like there was something else going on, like the people were hiding or being hidden from them. Aaron could smell them even now, as he walked along one of Sint Maarten's quiet streets, empty as though the people had vanished into thin air. The Dutch side, where his search had brought him that day, was as much of a maze as the French side was, the city center packed with zig-zagging streets that interlaced and overtook each other, eventually giving way to a hilly countryside and sandy shores. There were many places to hide.

And hide they did.

Yes, Aaron could smell them; their blood was pungent and laced with fear. It was one of the most tantalizing scents he had ever enjoyed and would know it anywhere. No, the island wasn't empty, unlike he had feared. The people were smart, crafty. They were hiding from them. That meant they had known the vampires were coming, had been preparing for it. Maybe they had gathered supplies: food to sustain them for a long time, fresh water, and clothes. Maybe they had fashioned weapons to use against them, stakes and crosses like the tales of old instructed. Maybe they were readying themselves for a fight. That simply wouldn't do.

Aaron wondered who told them, who tipped them off. Could it have been Cecelia? That old distrust sprang up at the mere thought of her name, making the hairs on his neck stand on end. Would she have done such a thing? Sure, she would, Aaron thought. If it ensured the survival of herself and her flock, of course she would. If it separated Aaron from his group, all the better. Cecelia had never been known for her loyalty and vampires were a hinky lot to begin with. Aaron knew that Cecelia was capable of it, of luring them to the island, causing a war then marooning the survivors, but he didn't think that was what happened. Yes, Cecelia had called them to the island out of the blue, but somehow, he believed her when she said there was food. She would have no reason to want to kill them and she had loved Raymond at one time - truly loved him. To murder him unprovoked seemed unconscionable. Contrary to popular belief, there is honor among thieves.

Still, something was wrong. The streets were too quiet. There weren't many bodies lying around as one might expect if vampires had come through and snatched up the low hanging fruit. There were no broken windows from looting, no open front doors from burglars. Cars were parked neatly in spaces. Order had been maintained. None of this reflected a mad dash or any desperate effort to leave the island before it was overrun. The place still felt inhabited, just closed as the stores that lined Front Street might be at 3:00 a.m. It was as if the people were still there, wearing invisible cloaks and dancing before his very eyes.

Now he was waxing poetic. Aaron needed to feed.

He found the man crammed into a dark corner, pressing into the wall like discarded waste. He stank of piss and sweat; his skin marred by the dirt he wallowed in. Aaron was repulsed; his senses were so acutely offended that he had to force himself not to turn away. But the hunger was too great to be picky.

Aaron knelt before the man, seeming to appear in front of him from out of nowhere. The man, weakened by hunger, fatigue, and fear, could only shrink away, pulling himself closer to the wall. The small cry that slipped from his lips was barely audible, but it was enough to make Aaron's heart ache.

"Please no," the man uttered, his voice like sandpaper as it wrenched itself from his throat. "Have mercy on me."

Aaron cocked his head to the side as he peered at the shell of a man in front of him. He had been different, just a week before. Aaron could see it in his face, the way his eyes shone with hatred as his voice betrayed him. His shoulders had been straight, posture impeccable. His strong hands had been used to lifting things, rocks perhaps, or branches - Aaron didn't know. But the strength he was capable of was evident only in the curve of his muscles beneath the shirt that now appeared to be too big for him. Something broke him. Was it seeing his daughter ripped from his arms, her neck devoured by a waiting vampire while another nearly salivated at the sight? Yes, that is what it was, Aaron suddenly knew. The man's heart told the tale for anyone willing to listen.

Aaron stared at him, a mixture of intrigue and sympathy filling his own soul. This man whose voice used to be a rich tenor that caressed English words with a hint of his native Papiamento thanks to his time living abroad, seemed to sink into himself before Aaron, losing stature the longer that the vampire stared. It wasn't that he was afraid, Aaron discovered as he watched the man shifting on feet with soles so cracked, they looked as if they might bleed. He should be; Aaron's kind was not the winged mercy of death talked about in ecumenical fantasy. He was, without a doubt, there to kill the man in a most undignified way: Aaron would take his life's blood for his own purposes, leaving his body cold, lifeless, and drained. The dogs in the street might sniff at him minutes after he was dead, but in the end not even they would want to use his body for sustenance. The blood that might have preserved the tender flesh inside, at least for a little while, will be gone. The hounds would smell the rot on it and leave it lest they make themselves sick.

But the man didn't hold fear in his heart when he looked at Aaron, when he begged him to spare his life. At least, he didn't hold fear for himself and the fate that stared back at him. Instead, Aaron sensed a different terror in this man's eyes, one that was so all-encompassing that he was blind to anything else. His wife and son were still out there, still hiding, trying to survive. They had been separated and his daughter slain. He begged for his life - for Aaron's mercy - so that he could continue the search for the rest of his family.

How curious, Aaron thought.

Aaron could smell the woman and child in the distance. He could pick up their scent from the man himself, their distinct essence preserved on his tattered clothing from their last embrace. They were dead. Drained. Mere carcasses left discarded on that which had been the main road serving the island, the potholed mess that it was. They were less than a mile away. The man would have surely stumbled upon his wife and son by sunrise.

Perhaps this is how Aaron can show kindness to those that remain. Killing them before they find out the truth. The thought sparked a warmth in Aaron that permeated his otherwise cold body.

Aaron's smile didn't make the man return one in kind. Instead, his screams could be heard from blocks away.

CHAPTER 28

Still he hungered.

Aaron sated himself with the blood of that poor man and one other that night, quenching the thirst that threatened to tie his stomach into knots if unabated, but it did nothing for the thirst that dominated his senses. No, this was hunger of a different sort. It was a longing in his soul, and desire that he couldn't satisfy with drink or play. He had tried that as well, sampling the island pleasure from a woman he found near the beach. She had given up and splayed herself on the sand, waiting and available for anyone in need that happened by. Despair had ruined everything beautiful and joyous about her, leaving her delirious. She was lucky it had been him. Aaron told her as much, purring into her ear to arouse at least a modicum of pleasure in the doomed woman – the better for both of them. And it was true. Some of his shipmates might have torn her limb from limb, causing her more pain that she could imagine before her light winked out. Others might have kept her and bled her, affecting their own fountain of drink that could be visited every few days for as long as her body would allow. Aaron didn't think that was a bad idea, but not with her. She was tainted. The fight had been frightened out of her. She was nothing more than a mindless zombie when Aaron found her lying prone on the beach. Blood from a thing like that, one who willingly allowed herself to be milked over and over without putting up any fight at all, couldn't be restorative to a vampire like himself.

He almost felt sorry for her.

Aaron took her body first, trying to get at the itch that had been bothering him since he first laid eyes on the shore of this once vibrant island. But when that didn't change anything, not even the physical desire his body had thought so important five minutes before, he put the poor dear out of her misery, drinking only a taste of her to see if he was right about her damage and then leaving her to bleed out when he confirmed that he indeed was. A sigh escaped his lips as he sat some miles away on a rock overlooking the calm Caribbean Sea. It wasn't just the love of anyone, he surmised. It was the love of one. The woman standing alone on the beach, her face a mask of resignation with just the hint of pleasure as the sounds of the surf made their way to her ears. The woman he glimpsed from the ship all those days ago.

They had been on the island for two weeks and Aaron hadn't found her anywhere. He didn't know whether to be relieved that he hadn't found her in those early days, or not – he had been so hungry, he was afraid of what he might have done. But then he became worried. After quenching that initial thirst which nearly drove him mad with need, Aaron began looking for her. He scoured the beach where she had stood looking out at the horizon that day, searching for places where people might take shelter. There were closed shops with their gates drawn, touristy locations where cruise ship patrons shopped almost exclusively. Those places were buttoned up tight. Could people be in there? Perhaps, but he didn't think so. He can normally smell human blood, even from behind metal. There was no life there on Great Bay Beach save for the stray dogs and cats that wandered the island, thriving and taking over areas that were once off limits to them if they wanted to avoid the thwack of the broom.

Where was she?

He went up the coast, finding himself muddling through the strange vegetation covering the sand and shore at Guana Bay and marveling at the swells at Baie Lucas. He walked between the parasailing equipment littering the beach further up the coast, docked boats, and moored jet skis bobbing in the water, tethered to a brace below the surface. It was a veritable grave-yard, Orient Beach. For all of its activities - restaurants dotting the shore, ocean equipment meant to facilitate fun in the sun, and waterfront hotels, the place felt more like a ghost town than a tropical paradise. Gone were the sun worshipers and their glistening skin. Gone was the laughter carried on the air to vacationing ears. Everything - everyone - was gone. And where? Where had they gone? Aaron turned himself in a circle looking around futilely. How could a whole island population disappear into thin air?

Aaron returned to Phillipsburg, moving between the French and Dutch borders without notice. He had to be careful. If someone noticed that he was doing more than searching for food – that he was looking for someone specific - they might become curious. Thomas, harmless though he might be, even with all his huff and puff, might find it interesting that Aaron was looking around so intensely. It might make him remember that day on the boat when Aaron was writing in his journal about love lost. It might make him remember how sensitive Aaron was to all of this.

Aaron couldn't afford for Thomas – or anyone – to get curious.

As Aaron walked along the deserted street smelling for blood and listening to the surf, he lamented. If there was one thing that was certain, it was that Thomas knew him. Through and through. He knew about Aaron and his proclivity towards compassion. He always had. Thomas had been Aaron's companion for decades - he was well-versed in the things that piqued his interest – almost as keenly as was Aaron himself. Normally Thomas could be trusted to keep it to himself. Sure, he gave Aaron a good ribbing, but it never went further than that. But this? This was something more, something entirely differ-ent. While Aaron would consider it to be about companionship of another sort, shared interests, and, dare he even utter it - love -, Thomas would see it differently. It would be about the blood, nothing more and nothing less. The *hiding* of the blood. The proprietorship. The utter secrecy of it all.

Disembarking on this little island nestled in the Caribbean Sea had been anticlimactic, to say the least. They had been expecting hordes of people stranded on the island with nowhere to hide. The vampires could almost feel the blood coursing through the veins of the damned as their ship cut through the water to gain its shores. Cecelia had made the place sound so bountiful, ripe with life-sustaining blood, when she invited Raymond, though he wondered now how much of that was truth and what was desperate will. They needed the island to be plentiful, after all. So many places weren't anymore. They had tried some coastal communities, thinking that people might have run there to set their backs to the sea, in doing so, facing the demons head on. That's what the news suggested, anyway. Frazzled newscasters signed off their final transmissions urging people to get to the water because the vampires wouldn't come that way, couldn't come that way based on some rule a 19th century author put down on paper intending to for fiction, but ultimately laying the foundation for vampire canon.

How wrong they were.

But when he and his shipmates got to the North Carolina coast, it had been gutted. Vampires unknown to them had already been there, leaving bodies everywhere in their wake. Florida fared no better. Some of the towns were home to newly created vampires left to fend for themselves. They didn't survive for long, these fledglings. Having been abandoned by their makers, who likely created them by mistake during a fit of lusty blood swapping at the moment of death, these unfortunates were more apt to burn themselves up in the sun than to enjoy all the benefits that being a vampire afforded them. But that didn't stop them from being dangerous. So violent were they, so territorial, that Raymond had gathered the lot of his coven up and taken to the sea again to escape.

That's when Raymond got the message from Cecelia and he pointed the massive liner toward the little island upon which Aaron stood. The anticipation had been so thick on the voyage over, many stayed on deck until the sun drove them away until they reached the island's dock.

And then this... Decrepit. Sparse. Most of the island's inhabitants hidden away.

Gone.

The woman that Aaron sought wouldn't be special anymore, not to anyone but him. Instead, she would be food. She might potentially lead them to more food by revealing where everyone else was hiding, but food she would be in the end. Aaron couldn't let that happen.

Aaron considered walking up the other side of the coast to search along the many caves that lined Cupecoy Beach but thought better of it. Sunrise would soon come, and he didn't want to be forced to find shelter somewhere new. Just because he couldn't find many people didn't mean that everyone was dead or gone. The people were there somewhere, they all knew that much to be true. Aaron didn't want to run the risk of them finding him first.

As Aaron made his way back to the ship that had brought them to this desperate harbor, he cast a glimpse around for the woman once again. He had to find her before the others did and spirit her away, keep her safe. He didn't know how he intended to do that nor why he wanted to do it so desperately. All Aaron knew was that he was going to protect his mystery woman with everything he had.

CHAPTER 29

The newscaster spoke gravely about a murder in a small town whose name Gabby thought she had heard before. Gabby only noticed that someone was speaking at all because the name of the town had stuck in her ear, echoing there, teasing her with the glimmer of a memory. Shaddock. Shaddock? Saying it aloud didn't help her place it, but she was sure she knew the town, had been in the town, had done something in the town to make it seem so familiar.

"... Neighbors say the woman had lived in the home for more than six years and frequently used the walking trails in the community.

"'She always stopped to comment on my garden,' Ella Smith remembers Griffin's morning routine..."

Gabby looked up at the TV in time to see an elderly woman with watery eyes looking forlornly at someone off camera, her profile reflecting how saddened she was by the death of her neighbor. That, or showcasing her masterful acting skills as she basked in her 15 minutes of fame, Gabby couldn't be sure. It bothered her that she even thought the woman might be anything other than sincere.

She snickered to herself. Cynical much?

"'... don't understand why something like that would happen to such a young woman. Full of life, she was. Full of life.' Police are still investigating what occurred Thursday night and urge anyone who might have information related to this case to contact...'"

Gabby watched as the newscaster, an African American woman with sparkling eyes and a welcoming smile, moved on to another story, one equally as disconcerting as the last. She kept turning the name of the town over in her head having no real reference to keep it playing there, but it rooted itself in place like the lyrics of an old song.

Shaddock.

The newscast showed pictures of the woman's house. It looked like many of the houses in the planned communities that sprung up in the early 2000s: siding facades with brick wainscoting; solar lighting bordering the walkways; gold house numbers on painted metal doors. The woman had looked like so many of the people who populated suburban areas like those - fresh-faced professionals who like to jog or do yoga or some kind of crunchy activity in their off time. They shopped at farmer's markets because that's what you did when you lived in trendy areas (not because they were really interested in supporting the people who grew their food without the middleman taking their cut). They read self-help books and political tomes; they recycled diligently; they knew at least one person that drove a Prius if they themselves didn't. The woman was unremarkable, that much was true. But one thing kept bothering Gabby about it all.

The woman was dead.

Gabby didn't catch how she had died or if there was a suspect in question. By the time she realized the news story was on, it was almost over (enter the watery-eyed attention seeker).

A woman in Shaddock was dead.

Gabby felt like she should have some kind of reaction to that.

She stood and looked up the stairs, a premonition guiding her steps. *The baby is about to cry. The baby is about to cry. The baby is about to cry. The baby -*

The baby was crying.

She laughed to herself as she set the manuscript down on the counter. She hadn't realized it was still in her hands. She might have carried it all the way up the stairs and been forced to set it down on Autumn's dresser if she hadn't needed to free her hands to turn off the TV. Her husband always teased her about her habit of getting up to turn the TV off using the button on the set instead of using the remote. He had created all these macros (whatever *they* were) to allow her to turn the TV set, the cable box, and the receiver off at the same time, but she didn't care. She always used the button on the TV set to turn it off. She used the button on the receiver to turn it off too. Only the cable box posed a problem with no buttons to be found. She *had* to use the remote for that one. Every time she did, she had to fool with the universal remote her husband cherished so much to find the cable input and turn off the right thing. It took her longer than it did him, she knew, and that was because she just didn't care about all of that stuff. Why he couldn't just listen to the TV through the built-in speakers was beyond her. Gabby hadn't realized she had resisted learning how to work the whole contraption so much that she could no more decode that remote now than she could a physics textbook. Well, maybe she did know that. But knowing and caring are two different things.

Gabby got up to turn off the TV, setting the manuscript down in the process. As she reached for the button, she wondered when she had turned the TV on in the first place. She had been reading about Aaron and how he kept his need for blood at bay while he searched for the woman he saw on the shore. She didn't usually enjoy background noise when reading, and anyway, the insistent hum of the baby monitor provided more than enough in that regard. But there it was. Strange, but no stranger than her behavior had been since she found the manuscript. Gabby hadn't taken her nose out of the book in days. Interactions with her husband and kids had gone by in a blur intermingled with thoughts of fangs and blood and desolate island streets. It was disconcerting how completely her mind had been taken over by her grandmother's work. She'd really had a flair for storytelling. Gabby dreaded the day when she finished reading the book, knowing it would leave her hanging in its unfinished state; knowing she would never find out what happened to Aaron and Vernese and Dr. LaFleur because her grandmother's pen had been forever silenced.

Ha, she was even starting to think the melodramatic way Joanne wrote.

It was weird and knocked her off-balance, this whole experience, but in a way, it was comforting and endearing. Gabby was getting the chance to know her grandmother in a way that most people didn't. She had the chance to glimpse her creativity, her awareness of the world around her, and her concept of herself. All that was coming through in her writing and it made Gabby feel close to her, perhaps in ways that she hadn't been able to experience with her own mother.

Gabby couldn't put the book down.

She didn't want to.

But when had she turned the TV off?

As her hand cut through the air toward the power button on the side of her husband's newest favorite techie thing, she realized it was already off. She stood erect, straightening her back from the natural lean it had taken as she bent over to turn the set off.

A black screen stared back at her.

Gabby could see her reflection in it, could see the sofa further behind her and the glow of the lamp on the side table that she had been using to read the manuscript. The remote was on the ottoman, as it always was. But it was askew. It was only a little off, but Gabby could tell it wasn't the way she left it. Just like there was a macro for turning off the television, there was a place for the remotes. They sat in a nice little holder on the ottoman, a flat little thing with barely elevated sides - just enough to keep the remotes from sliding around. Easy to reach, easy to keep track of as her husband was so fond of saying. Except the universal remote that she would have used to turn things off was sitting on the ottoman, outside of the little holder.

It was also upside down.

Gabby stared at the remote reflected in the darkened TV screen, unable to tear her eyes away. There was just something about it, something that was disturbing about the state of the remote itself, but she couldn't put her finger on it, even as she admonished herself for the insignificance. She took a step closer to the TV, leaning in again, trying to decipher something – anything...

She gasped. The hand that had gripped the manuscript so tightly fluttered to her mouth.

Was that - could that have been...?

Did the remote just *move*?

Gabby willed herself to turn around, to look at the remote

with her bare eyes and not through some reflected image that was, no doubt, distorted by the curve of the screen or some such feature that her husband had drooled over, but she couldn't. Suddenly she didn't feel like she could ever turn around again. An icy chill had crept up her neck and sat, playing with the tiny hairs there. She was afraid of what she might have just seen in the reflection, sure, but she was terrified of finding that the reflected image might actually be true if she turned around.

Gabby wanted to clamp her eyes shut, to just wipe away the image of her world for just a second and start fresh. But she was afraid to move a muscle.

Autumn's cries rang out suddenly; the baby monitor, crackled, distorted, and unbelievably loud, almost made her jump out of her skin. Gabby was so thoroughly startled that she jumped and spun, immediately facing the sofa dead on. For a second, she didn't know where to rest her eyes. She hadn't intended to look at the sofa just then, ever again if it came to that, but now here she was, staring right at it.

Gabby averted her eyes from the ottoman.

Gooseflesh sat pert on her skin.

Her palms were sweating.

Thebabyiscryingthebabyiscryingthebabyiscrying.

Gabby sucked in a deep breath and let it out through her clenched teeth. 'This is my house, damnit,' she reminded anyone - or anything - that might be listening and looked at the ottoman before she talked herself out of it. The remote was in the holder, right where it was supposed to be.

Hmm.

Gabby looked back at the TV just to see what she would find. More of the same - the remote was in the holder on the ottoman - where it should be.

Gabby turned back to the sofa and snickered incredulously.

That's just great, she thought. *Now I'm turning into a chicken shit.* She giggled out loud, vowing she would keep this embarrassing little moment to herself. No sense in giving her husband another thing to tease her about alongside her need to turn on every light in the house when she's home alone and her lowkey fear of darkened hallways. No, this little episode will be between her and the lamppost, as her dad used to say. Or in this case, between her and the TV remote.

As Gabby left the room, she couldn't stop herself from glancing back at the ottoman just one more time to make sure the remote was there, in its holder, where it was supposed to be. The need to do it pulled at her like cold fingers on her neck that threatened to dig in for purchase and force her gaze if she didn't acquiesce. And it was there, as she had expected (no, she didn't really expect anything, if she was being honest. It could have been walking behind her on tip toe and she wouldn't have been surprised. Not really.). Where else could it have been? Gabby chastised herself for being so silly, so jumpy all of a sudden. Maybe it was because she was reading a story about vampires; maybe it was because she had lost time so completely that it felt sort of eerie - Gabby didn't know, but something was making her skittish. It was so unlike her; she didn't know how to process it. The self-deprecating laugh Gabby let out on her way to Autumn's room was as genuine as they come.

Gabby hated to admit it, in fact, she pushed the thought out of her mind almost as soon as it had formed, but the truth was the truth. That the remote was still sitting in the holder on the ottoman was the creepiest thing of all.

CHAPTER 30

Mal knew he should stay away from her. Joanne was dangerous to him, for him - whatever way he thought about it, she was bad for him. For everything.

She would never remember, he told himself. And so far, that had been true. She had been there for years and never gotten past the feelings that stirred low in her belly when he came near. He couldn't help but recognize that look in her eye when she was in that headspace, feeling him the way she had when they were alive together. Joanne still had her tells. Her increased breathing, lowered eyelids, the way she nipped at her bottom lip - these were the things she had always done when she was starting to feel amorous and she was doing them now, even in this desolate place. Mal would be lying if he said he hadn't tried to induce that reaction from her. In all honesty, he needed to. Their connection had always been something he could count on. Not showing himself to her, removing anything that might make her recognize him had meant that he wouldn't have that closeness anymore.

Except that she could sense him.

At first Mal thought it was a mistake. He thought he had misread her, had imagined the hitch in her breathing, the whimper that played in the back of her throat. It was slight, nearly inaudible, but it was there and he heard it. No matter how much Mal tried to talk himself out of it, he had to admit it. Joanne had reacted to him. And he liked it.

Mal found himself trying to draw more of a reaction from her. He wanted to see how far she would go - how far she *could* go in their new reality. Would she perspire when she felt her temperature rise? Would she moan sensually, the sound emanating from between her parted lips like a whisper? He needed to know. Mal would deepen his voice, hum in response to her words. The effect sent shivers down her spine the same way it did when they were alive in so many forms, and he reveled in it. He would stand just close enough that she could sense his presence, but not be able to find him with her eyes. It was driving her mad and Mal knew it - that was part of the tease. It was exquisite, really, playing with her in that way. The color rose to her cheeks and her breathing increased causing her chest to heave just the slightest bit. Joanne had always been so easy to rile up. That it hadn't changed now that they were in that godforsaken place filled Mal with a longing he was sure he would never recover from.

But he always recovered and then went back for more.

But now things had changed.

Now he had to be careful.

She had always danced around the prospect of knowing him, of remembering. And in truth, remember him wasn't the real problem. It was always when she felt herself falling deeper into the trap he laid, when she was nearly panting with a desire that had, only moments before, been nonexistent, that she noticed something familiar. Was it in the way his breath caressed her ear - there but not there? Was it the rasp he allowed her to hear in his voice - the one that showed her that he, whomever he was, was just as affected as she? Perhaps, but Mal thought it was more than that. Her recognition had a little to do with the sensations her mind conjured up when he was near. It also had something to do with her sense of utter aloneness in a confusing existence. Those reasons by themselves would have been enough to drive her to crave connection from someone, anyone. But there was more. There was true remembrance, Mal was sure of it. But of whom and how much, he was not. And that is what troubled him most.

Her lips trembled as she stood there in the semi-darkness. He saw her in his mind as clearly as if he were standing in the room before her, his fingers close enough to touch. He knew what Joanne would do next and as much as he knew shouldn't, he settled his eyes on her pulsating form, unable to tear his eyes away. But this time, even though his vision was gifted a most perfect sight, one to rival memories from times past in another lifetime, he wasn't seeing her, not really. He was preoccupied with the fact that *she* was starting to see, even more so than before. The knowledge made her nervous, edgy, even angry. Mal would be a fool to think things were the same as they had been before or could ever be again.

He was no longer safe.

Joanne was remembering and he was no longer safe.

That child was reading, Joanne was remembering, and he was no longer safe.

And now, amidst some of the most sinful sounds of pleasure he had ever heard in all his lifetimes, he felt impossible tears stinging the corners of his eyes.

CHAPTER 31

They moved. After what happened, they kind of had to. Vernese almost cried when they walked away from the high-rise for the last time. Even though they had the run of the place, they had chosen to hole up together in the penthouse that had been their meeting room when it all began. It had seemed smart to stick together instead of being spread out around the hotel. There was more than enough space for the few of them who remained and the room afforded them the chance to enjoy luxury for what could very well be the last time. They had worked out the logic of it. Claiming the two-story unit would be easy to defend, even with its wrap-around balconies and rooftop eatery access. They rationalized that no one would scale the building to gain entry – at 10 stories, it was too high up. A fall like that, with no doctor available and all the medical facilities pilfered, would most assuredly mean death. The rooftop access door was reinforced metal, near industrial strength in quality. Someone would have trouble busting it in with a battering ram, let alone their hands and feet. No, they decided that people who might want to gain access to their unit would try to come in through the front door. That door was flimsy, at least in the face of what they were up against now. Solid core, ornate, but could be knocked down, kicked down if enough people went at it. But so were all the doors in the hotel. They figured that people might give up after a while since climbing the stairs was the only smart way to get around anymore and the heat of the Caribbean was oppressive, sometimes even at night. Maybe people would decide that no one was staying at the resort on the upper floors because of it, that they were locked and not worth checking. If they didn't, if someone made it all the way to the top and still had some fight in them, well, they would be ready.

At least, that's what they thought before the knocking started.

As they left the penthouse just at the break of day, slinking out as soon as they thought they might be safe from both the vampires that wanted their blood and the humans that wanted everything else, they all knew they would never return, even if no one would say as much out loud. The knocking had been too insistent, too deliberate. Someone knew they were there even though they stood stock still, barely breathing, hidden in the darkness. Vernese and her people sensed a presence beyond the door. Somehow the person on the other side knew... they knew and they just toyed with them.

They simply couldn't stay at the hotel anymore; their sanctuary had been compromised. Whatever they had done to expose themselves had been noticed. It was likely something irrelevant, miniscule, so insignificant in the general scheme of things. But the world was different now. There were eyes everywhere, Vernese knew. She could feel them crawling on her skin when she ventured into the remnants of what used to be the marketplace she'd shopped in her entire life. She missed that life, the one where she could go to the market or to Rick's Ribs, or to the beach to sink her feet into the sand whenever she wanted. Vernese had never considered how carefree her life had been before all of this. She had thought the struggle of climbing the ladder at the hotel was difficult, time consuming, unrewarding. She used to gripe about all the hours she had to work and the scripts she had to perfect - the "Welcome to the island!" one, or of the "Are you having fun yet?" one that always worked on the older set. She remembered how tedious it had all seemed then, how disingenuous. *How fake, Vernese,* she chastised herself. *No sense using a $100 word when a $5 one works just as well - not anymore.*

She hadn't realized how good she had it, but who ever did? The grass is always greener elsewhere, right? What she wouldn't give to chat up one of those loudly dressed tourists clamoring for a drink on the beach right now.

Maybe someone saw her coming back to the hotel after she walked through the open market. She had been doing that a lot, needing to stretch her legs, to get away from the people she was holed up with for a little while: to think. Maybe someone had been spying on her as she moved among the rotting food, stray dogs, and tattered awnings. It was possible though she had taken great pains to mask her route. Patterns could be picked up, routines remembered. Someone intent on tracking Vernese might have noticed how she lingered in front of Tessie's johnny-cake stand a little too long, savoring the memory of their buttery taste. Maybe someone saw how she looked longingly at the rack that used to hold sarongs in vibrant colors, the tasseled ends blowing in the wind. It was empty now, that rack of sarongs that used to mesmerize her. She had always wanted one of those sarongs even though it wasn't what an island girl like her really wore to the beach. Those things were for the tourists - people who came to sunbathe, squint behind sunglasses, and dip their toes in the turquoise blue water. Those were for the people who wanted to take pictures on the beach wearing their beautiful sarongs so that friends and family would know they had been somewhere. No one she knew wore such a thing. Going to the beach was like going to the park when you lived on an island - it was just something that you did - nothing special, not a once a year respite the way that vacationers tended to view it. Islanders would no more dress up to go to the beach, putting on fancy cover ups, toe rings, and body glitter, than they would to go shopping at the market.

Ah, the open market again. Her mind flooded with the memory of the sounds, of the smells...

She wanted a sarong. Still.

Vernese had gone back to the rack the first day she felt confident enough to venture more than a block away from the hotel. She didn't know why she went - she was sure there would be nothing left: when looters loot, they take everything, even if they don't need or want it, just for the thrill of doing so. But still she went, piecing her way through the side streets carefully, trying to stay out of sight – evermore skittish in those early days. The rack was empty, like she thought it would be. Still she lingered, imagining the tasseled ends of vibrant sarongs floating in the air.

Such a small chink in the armor, that desire. But it was there and Vernese knew it.

Maybe someone else knew it too, knew that she would return there over and over again, becoming more lax in her approaches and retreats as time went by. If they did, they also knew they just needed to follow her back to find out where she laid her head; the path would be all but highlighted in yellow. And that was the problem.

It wasn't all bad.

Vernese had packed their meager belongings while Dr. LaFleur prattled on and on about the potential of the new space. He fancied there would be room for a lab, thought he would be close enough to the island's only college to pilfer materials that could be used in his experiments since they were moving inland. At first, he wanted to relocate to the college campus itself. It made sense considering the types of plans he had in mind to battle the things that had taken over the island, but in the end, they couldn't. The campus was too open and they would be exposed. The college was on flat land and only had one three-story building. The top floor of that building had been closed off years ago -Vernese recalled there had been a plan to revitalize the whole thing after asbestos was found on the top floor years ago, but it had never happened. They had all decided it made the most sense to seek higher ground - as high as they could - though the reason for this was unclear. Logically, they knew the height wouldn't make a difference, not to the type of predator that hunted them. They weren't dealing with rabid dogs that couldn't climb trees after all. The vampires that had taken over their little island were craftier than that.

Vampires.

That was the name that Vernese and the rest of her vagabond group had settled on calling those detestable blood-suckers even though the idea still made many of them laugh, albeit wryly. Vampires. What a ridiculous thought. Who would ever have thought that vampires, and Vernese meant the full-fledged, supernatural, blood-drinking creatures, not the energy-sucking new age cosplaying geeks from the continent...

who would have thought that vampires were real? That was the stuff of movies and books, Halloween costumes and campfire stories. Vampires of the Bela Lugosi variety were all that came to mind when she thought of the word, strange little men with heavy accents dressed up in penguin suits. But that's not what they were dealing with, by any stretch of the imagination.

The vampires they were dealing with were unlike anything they could have ever conceived of. Verense often wondered if it would have been easier to deal with a vampire that was like the old-time ones. Nosferatu skulking around in the shadows, emerging from his casket, face ashen and abhorrent. She thought she might have been able to process that one. It would be an unnatural beast, drinking blood for sustenance, leaving bodies in its wake. It would have made more sense. When something can be categorized as "other" it is easy to put it in its place and process around it. But these - these were detestable, grotesque beings in their beauty. They didn't inspire fear from a glance at their deformed countenances. Quite the contrary. These vampires were positively stunning to behold. They possessed none of the paleness that movies would have people believe is indicative of the undead, none of the marble-esque, unnatural quality to the skin either. These people - these vampires - looked quite healthy, as though they had died in peak form. Their eyes did not seem unfocused and far away; their canine teeth were not grotesquely proportioned, though Vernese wondered if they always looked that way or if they grew when about to strike, as the movies were fond of showing. Their faces were most pleasant and inviting. They could pull you into their gaze without even trying. And that was the problem, wasn't it? The alluring nature of these beasts. They were so all-encompassingly beautiful that it was hard to look away. But if you looked too long, you would never see anything else ever again.

That's what happened to Andrew.

Andrew, the one who said he had come to the island to figure out his next step, had done so, and felt good about heading home and facing real life again, come what may; Andrew, the one who never seemed to panic, not even when food was getting scarce. Andrew went out to scavenge what was left in the French bakery around the corner from the hotel on the off chance there might be flour and sugar. Vernese had gone with him just to get out of the penthouse that had become her prison - a place where she was both warden and inmate. It was dusk when they ventured out, still unaware of the best times to do such things. But even then, it should have been too early, Vernese thought again for the hundredth time. It had been barely dark when she and Andrew entered the bakery's jimmied back door to find the place looted of everything of value. They tiptoed inside, hoping that no one had started squatting there, bodies tensed in anticipation of a battle. That was their reality now, the prospect of having to fight for their lives ever-present. Though it was never said, Vernese and the others had gotten used to it faster than they would have liked.

There was nothing left to take. Sugar had been spilled carelessly on the counters and unceremoniously licked up by a passing animal, leaving only a sticky residue behind to show it was ever there. Tins were turned over, bread ripped into, the jagged remnants now moldy, refrigeration unit left open. The cash register had been stolen, carted off to be pried opened at a later date. There was a lone can of ginger ale on its side at the back of the now hot refrigeration unit and Andrew grabbed for it. Vernese remembered the smile that spread across her face when they looked at each other. They were going to share that drink between them and not take it back to the hotel to ration out, unsaid but true. It was *their* find - they were the ones who stuck their necks out to look for food and damnit, they were going to savor this. It's amazing how special one hot ginger ale can be to people who had lost hope for anything else.

Andrew opened the can and the contents fizzed up and out, coating his hands in white foam. They laughed at this - actually laughed. It was like they were real people again, not the hunters and gatherers of old, nameless and faceless as they used the shadows to navigate the island that was their world. Andrew's laugh was deep and genuine. It was a sound she hadn't heard before and she relished the idea of hearing more.

Vernese wondered what Andrew would sound like moaning under her too, coming undone as she rode him urgently, desperately, chasing her release...

Andrew tilted the can of ginger ale toward Vernese, pulling her away from the thought that had invaded her mind out of nowhere. She wasn't even attracted to the man, hadn't even given him a second thought since they met. Nor he her, at least as far as Vernese could tell. She was almost positive Andrew's time on the island had been spent deciding whether or not to come out. Whatever the decision had been had made him happy enough to go home and face what waited for him. But now, as he stood there in the empty bakery backlit by the fading light outside, none of that mattered anymore. She noticed how sharp his jawline was, how trim his waist. He had good legs - strong, muscular thighs, just the way she liked. With the right amount of stamina, they could make each other forget about the hell they were living in and just *feel* again.

"You want it?" Andrew's voice caressed the words as he looked at her with a question in his eyes. For a second, Vernese thought he had peeked into her mind and taken stock of what was going on in there. She almost believed it - his stare was very intense all of a sudden, eyes staring into her own, the hint of seduction playing at the corners of his lips. It took everything she had not to utter a breathy 'yes' in response.

Instead, she looked at him, grunting a sound that means 'excuse me?' in the universal language that humans share. Andrew tilted his head toward his outstretched hand holding the leaking ginger ale. He was offering her the first sip. That's all it was. But Vernese couldn't help but let her mind wander to less civilized things as the foam billowed over his hand.

Finding her voice, Vernese declined graciously, saying something profound like, 'It's your find. You take the first sip." Details like that didn't seem to stick anymore. She could no longer remember those simple exchanges with any reliability, her mind was so consumed with finding a way to secure their hiding place, finding more food, finding a way off the island. There was no room for particulars, such as what color shirt a guest was wearing or even what day it was anymore next to that mantra. But Vernese did remember what she and Andrew saw that day. It was clear as a bell, rich and vivid in a way that many memories weren't anymore. Vernese wished she could purge it out of her mind, wipe it clear, remove it in some way. But, and she had no doubt about this, not after everything she had seen and heard since then, she would never be able to. The indelible image would be with her until the day she died.

CHAPTER 32

Doug found Patrick positively giddy when he came back to the room where their lives, if you could call them that, changed, and he had been ever since. Patrick had discovered something amazing - something that neither of them thought could happen, not in any real sense. Sure, they knew they needed something to work for them - need a win in the biggest way - but neither of them really believed they could pull it off. In the end, Doug realized he and Patrick had fully expected to lose this battle. They were coming in late and at a massive disadvantage. The stakes were too personal; too high. They had only just woken up in The Realm themselves. To now be in control of it seemed nonsensical at best. To also need to manipulate it as well as the natural world to save his family? Pure fantasy. As much as he hadn't wanted to, Doug expected that he and his father would welcome Gabby to The Realm and, together, they would usher in the rest of their lineage.

But Patrick had done something remarkable. He had manipulated things in the real world.

He made things happen - that was really the only way to
describe what was going on. Doug came back from his self-
indulgent pity party to find his father nearly bouncing up and
down in excitement. He could hear Gabby's voice reverberating
off the walls, the sound of her reading filling the room. Doug
wanted to tell his father to be quiet, wanted to tell him that he
needed to hear his daughter's voice to ground himself, but
something in Patrick's eyes made him bite it back. It was in that
moment that Doug understood everything. What Patrick had
experienced was still mired in what could only be described as
horror. He still blamed himself. He was still *to blame*. He needed
this win – more than anything, he needed to be able to help fix
things.

Doug believed him when he said he didn't know what was
going on or why they were in a place that had never been
defined in theology, kept hidden from view as an afterthought...
or an abomination. Doug had tricked himself into thinking he
believed otherwise - that he thought this father was lying about
something. He thought he believed the stories his mind
conjured up, images of his father being like John Wayne Gacy
the most prominent. Half-baked notions at best, but there just
the same. As he watched his father move about the room
animatedly, alternately listening to Gabby speak then chattering
about channeling his energy to interact with the only world they
ever knew, Doug was certain he had been wrong. Better, he
knew that he - the real Doug, the one that was still mourning his
own death even in the face of the calamity he found himself in -
that Doug never believed his father was a monster. The man
who had laughed with him when match after match showed

itself in a spirited game of War, forcing them to duke it out until they ran out of cards and neither could declare war on the other; the man who blinked back tears as he clapped Doug on the back at his college graduation; the man who brought flowers to his wife's grave every holiday and anniversary, the pain of losing her as visible in his eyes years later as it had been the day she died - that man had not deceived his family. He had not damned them all to a place worse than Hell. He wasn't capable of it; he had far too much of a capacity to love. It simply could not be.

Doug knew, without a shadow of a doubt, that Patrick was just as much a victim as he was. In that capacity, indeed in all capacities, they needed each other. They had to lean on each other for support if they were ever going to save anyone else from The Realm. They would need each other more to endure eternity there.

Doug took a deep breath as his eyes kept pace with his father. His mind was a blur of thought. *So, who then? Another family member? Someone who came before?* Doug dismissed that thought - Patrick had already gone down that road and found that he was the source. *Reincarnation?* Doug had never given much stock to the notion when he was a living, breathing person, but it seemed like the only option now. And anyway, was it such an unbelievable idea? Doug glanced at his daughter while she read, taking note of the shape of her mouth and the way that it formed words. Was it not like that of his mother's mouth? Didn't he himself share his father's eye color and even some of his mannerisms? Heredity and reincarnation have such close ties – who's to say that the link doesn't go deeper than biology? He'd read the stories about people having similarities to others that were biologically unconnected to them. He had witnessed it himself when a cousin started saying the very same phrase that a friend of his used to say, using the same inflection and same gestures. This cousin was younger than Doug and his friend by a decade, if a day. The problem was this friend had died about 12 years before Doug had heard his words echoed out of his little cousin's mouth. Isn't that what it was – that uncanny, hard to put your finger on thing you just shrug off as coincidence rather than give credence to?

Maybe living past lives was a real thing, but then how could someone not know it was happening to them? His cousin hadn't known he was repeating words Doug had heard his friend utter time and time again verbatim, as if he had heard him say it himself. Indeed, it freaked him out the way Doug talked about it once he found the courage to say something. But then didn't he know something wasn't kosher when he started gesturing with his hands in ways that didn't even feel natural to him...?

If you didn't know, maybe that was a good thing. To live day in and day out in a body that you know isn't yours... to know that you weren't you – or at least, not *only* you. The thought made Doug shiver.

Maybe something gets left from those past lives that impacts the new one, like some kind of cosmic residue.

What if his father is a -

Something pulled Doug's attention to the far corner of Gabby's room. Movement? A flash of light? As soon as Doug reacted, he forgot why he was doing it. But something pulled him out of his head and into the room within which Gabby sat, happily reading her grandmother's manuscript. Her voice was tranquil. She caressed the words in her mind, pronouncing each one in such a lyrical fashion that Doug felt like he was listening to a singer or a poet. It lulled him, soothed him; he wanted to keep listening. All he wanted to do was listen to it -

There.

Again.

Something.

Just outside his view, something was moving. Was it swaying? Undulating?

Was it *laughing*?

Doug looked closer, trying to see what was just beyond his reach.

Then Gabby looked at him.

Or did she? Doug couldn't tell. It seemed like she had pulled her eyes away from the manuscript with visible effort to stare right at him. Could she see him? Doug wasn't sure if what he saw in her eyes was recognition or empathy. Wouldn't she be surprised if she saw him – actually recognized him? Wouldn't he be an apparition - some wispy, translucent thing wearing her father's face? Wouldn't that scare her?

Doug thought about that for a moment, caught up in the idea. What does he look like now? Maybe she wasn't afraid because he was otherworldly in the most appealing of ways, appealing in a way that humans aren't – beautiful, for lack of a better word. He had a hard time wrapping his mind around that. Beauty, the glowing angelic-type visage of those who would meet you in the afterlife, is for angels, isn't it? Not those who have been condemned to a netherworld with a name unknown to human sensibilities. Nor did Doug think he took on an evil form like something straight out of Hell. Heaven was Heaven; Hell was Hell; The Realm was The Realm. Distinctly different places, all three, with their own play actors dotting the stage. No, Doug didn't think he looked like the archangel Gabriel any more than he looked like the devil's demon, Apollyon. But what, then? What did Gabby see staring back at her, if anything at all?

Whatever it was, Gabby noticed *something*. Her face softened a little, eyes opening wider from the squint the lids had settled into as her eyes grew more and more fatigued. Her lips took on a softness too, almost as if she wanted to smile but wasn't sure if she should. Her body had that quality of one receiving an unexpected shoulder massage, face slightly upturned, eyes hooded now, lips slightly parted.

Did she see him?

Gabby stared in his direction, eyes growing more and more unfocused, while at the same time more insistent. Doug stared back incredulously, never realizing that the thing in the corner at the far side of Gabby's room was staring at him too.

CHAPTER 33

Things were changing.

Just little things, here and there, but Gabby noticed. Things felt different. Everywhere she went, people seemed more guarded, less friendly. Before, getting into a conversation about crafting while shopping for supplies was a common thing. The people who frequented stores that peddled those types of goods were not a quiet lot, despite what people might think. Give a scrapbooker the chance to talk about her latest project and she would regale you with page layout designs, stenciling, and gluing techniques, all the while proclaiming undying love of her trusted Cricut. Gabby could spend hours in stores like that, alternating between window shopping, trying out tools, and filling her cart. She could easily have talked with at least five people during that time, having real, meaningful conversations about new trends, swapping ideas, and just enjoying each other's company. But now people shopped with their heads down, ducking in to pick up what they needed and nothing more - rushing in and rushing out.

Gone was the milling. Gone was the carefree banter. Gone was the feeling of being safe.

Someone was terrorizing her town.

Coverage was all over the news. Women were being targeted, but that was all they knew. The killer was indiscriminate otherwise - old, young, active, lethargic, fit, or plump - women in her neck of the woods were being slaughtered. It didn't matter where they were either. This killer would attack whether the woman was home alone or in a public place. The effect was crippling. Businesses closed early. At places like nail and hair salons, this was to be expected since their clientele was mostly women, but restaurants changed their hours as well. Not because they wanted to but because they *had* to. Slowly but surely, female workers stopped coming in for their shifts. Female guests stopped going to restaurants to eat. Women, by and large, started to stay inside, working from home more if they could, going out in groups whenever possible, limiting the amount of time they spent outdoors. The fear was debilitating, even for the holdouts who tried to live life as usual for as long as possible.

Gabby was one of those holdouts. She refused to let someone change the way she lived her life. It felt like 2002 all over again, when the Beltway Sniper attacks hit the DMV. Muhammad and Malvo frightened people with their unpredictability. Even the most mundane tasks, just pumping gas in the car, sparked such fear in people that they were paralyzed. People forgot about happy hours, forgot about going to the movies: forgot about living life. Gabby had been one of those people ducking at the pump, feeling eyes on the back of her head as she walked into a store. Even though she lived some twenty miles away from where most of the attacks happened, that wasn't far enough - not for her nor the people that lived near her. They hunkered down until the pair were captured. It took months for them to recover from the trained behavior they had put themselves through. Sometimes she looked toward the tree line for the smoking muzzle of a gun after a surprisingly loud sound, even now.

Gabby didn't want to go through that again, but it didn't seem like she had a choice.

This new killer was crafty. No one had seen him or *her*, Gabby supposed, not even when the women had been killed in popular places. And yes, there had been a fair share of murders outside. On a trail in a park, near a lake, in a convenience store parking lot, on a basketball court. Even in the back of a supermarket near the bakery, which was closed at the time. Gabby thought the cameras sprinkled all over the place should pick something up. Isn't that what people were always complaining about? Big Brother in the sky watching every move? But there was nothing. Either the cameras were malfunctioning, the images were full of static, or the equipment was improperly connected, if connected at all. Where was Big Brother now, when they needed him most?

Gabby sighed as she pushed her shopping cart through the aisles. The supermarket was pretty much empty, a veritable graveyard. She thought herself morbid for that thought, but it was accurate. There were only a few other people in the store with her and all of them were male. Where that wouldn't have bothered her before, now it made her hyper-aware of herself and where she was in relation to them. The little hairs on her neck stood on end as she navigated her way through the store at an admittedly faster pace than she would have assumed before the murders started. All the while, her mind was conflicted. She couldn't decide if it was better to be closer to the men in the store or far. Solidarity in numbers is a real thing. And Gabby couldn't deny the aspect of the safety that their maleness would provide even though she hated that such a chauvinistic thought could take root in her mind. If the killer was looking for women, they might be better at handling one that wasn't surrounded by potential adversaries. But chivalry being what it was, she wasn't entirely sure if the men would come to help her if called or run away as fast as they could. She couldn't avoid them all together and that reality ignited a bit of panic in her stomach. Could one of them be the killer? Could he be hunting her, following her around the store to track her habits and use that information at some later date? Gabby didn't know. She just didn't know, and it was driving her crazy to vacillate between possibilities so much.

Taking a deep breath, Gabby set her mind back to shopping, checking off items on the list in her head. As she pulled a 12-pack of toilet paper off the shelf and into her cart, her eye caught movement.

There was a man at the end of the aisle... staring at her.

Gabby stopped moving involuntarily. She wanted to put the toilet paper in the shopping cart naturally, deliberately placing it in there instead of letting it fall the way she did, but her mind shut off for a second and, not knowing what else to do, her body shut off too. The man at the end of the aisle hadn't moved. He wasn't looking at the shelves, deliberating over paper towel brands. He wasn't looking at his cellphone or staring at a list scrawled on a stickie note to see what was left. He was simply standing there staring at her. Gabby swallowed. Gulped really, though she had wondered, distractedly, if that's what gulping really was. If gulping was the forced swallowing of air and spit that felt so thick, a person thought they might choke on it before it made it down their throat, that's what she did. She stared back at the man, trying to decide what she would do if he took a step toward her.

Maybe he's not looking at me, she thought to herself.

Yeah, right.

Gabby knew he was, no matter what she tried to trick herself into believing. It's like when a person knows not to walk down a particular alley or to look again before crossing the street. There was a sixth sense about things like that, some knowledge that a person knows without question, as if it has been whispered into their ear. He was looking at her, that much was true. Why he was doing so wasn't.

Do killers need a reason? Hissed the voice inside her head that always told her to run when running was right.

Gabby pulled her hand back to herself as though rescuing it from the open air. The man at the end of the aisle stood stock still. He wasn't particularly tall, wasn't wearing anything overly flashy, Gabby noticed. She figured she better take a good look at him just in case she needed to give the police a description. Part of herself swore she was blowing this out of proportion. It told her that she was likely reading too much into this, that the man was just another customer who happened to be at the other end of the aisle from her. She wanted to believe that side - it sounded a heck of a lot more rational that the paranoid, every-body-is-after-me side that currently had hold of her - but she didn't want to be naïve. If something was about to go down, was going down right now, she needed to be ready. Deluding herself wouldn't help, as much as she wanted to stick her head in the sand.

The man at the end of the aisle turned a bit, giving her his profile. The effect was like the noonday sun on asphalt. The man's form slimmed, fuzzed, and elongated. Backlit by the windows that lined the front of the store and the headlights of oncoming cars parking in the lot, his form seemed to shimmer, moving like asphalt does when it smokes in the heat. Gabby blinked, trying to clear her vision. When she looked back, his form was smaller, more proportioned, more normal. She took a tentative step forward, pushing the cart with her hip as she rubbed at her eyes. The man kept changing. Smaller, smaller still, disappearing before her eyes. With one last blink, he was gone.

Gabby let go of the breath she hadn't realized she was holding and looked again. The aisle was empty. Gabby turned her head to look behind her instinctively, but no one was there either. Instrumental background music played over the speakers. The clank of shopping carts rolling on the tiled floors sounded in the distance. The normal din of the supermarket was back. Gabby hadn't realized it had been gone in the first place.

Gabby knew she should have felt relieved, but she didn't.

Maybe the man had just been picking up something at the other end of the aisle and left the way he came. That was the better reason for him not being anywhere to be found - it sure was the more rational one. It was better than believing he had disappeared out of thin air. Even she didn't believe that, not really. Gabby didn't know what was going on , but she wasn't *that* far gone.

Maybe the man had been playing a trick on her. Maybe he watched her in silence and made a sneaky escape when she looked like she was out of sorts. Gabby could only imagine what she must have looked like rubbing her eyes like that. Maybe he was some asshole that got off on teasing women. A copycat without the balls to go all the way. A fire rose in Gabby at the thought. She thought about reporting the incident to the store manager, just so he didn't get away with it. But what would she say? That someone looked at her from the other end of the aisle and then disappeared? Gabby couldn't describe the man - not his hair or build, what the man was wearing, his nationality. She had been too far away to see any of those details clearly. And he never did anything to her, besides. He didn't approach her, say anything menacing, touch her in any way. Now, after her eyes had cleared and she was alone in the aisle again, Gabby couldn't be sure if the man was even looking at her in the first place. Maybe he was looking in her direction, but past her. Maybe he was lost in thought and didn't see her at all.

Maybe, but did she believe that?

Gabby took a deep breath and told herself to shake it off. She was letting the media spook her. She had never been one to be jumpy and she shouldn't start now. That's what she told herself and she meant it. Gabby pushed her cart forward defiantly. She was going to exit the aisle the same way the man had. She wasn't going to allow herself to be afraid to walk in that direction, as the hair standing on end on her neck wanted her to believe. The hell if she was going to let someone change the way she lived her life.

But it wasn't just "someone", was it? It was a killer. A killer with no M.O. It was a killer who might very well be hunting in her town.

As Gabby turned the aisle to enter the main corridor, self-checkout bound because being tough was all well and good, but so was removing herself from a possibly bad situation, he cocked his head, letting her perfume fill his nostrils in the most all-encompassing of ways.

CHAPTER 34

SANGUINE PARADISE

He stands over there, a picture of beauty. Vernese struggled to find a word for it other than such a common one, but nothing else could come close to defining what he was. He was the personification of the word itself; beauty seemed to emanate from his pores. And it wasn't the standard beauty one might think of; it wasn't the definition of the word as it pertained to women or shiny things. It was more than that somehow. The man in front of her was perfect in ways that no man or woman had ever appeared to her before, lovely in ways that both warmed her core and made her feel disconnected from it. He was a vision in the purest sense of the word.

Tall, tanned skin, of Asian descent but sporting the high cheekbones of long-lost Indian tribes, and the full lips of those sharing her African heritage. Oval eyes of gray hue and black wavy hair - opposing characteristics juxtaposed in the most impossible ways, creating the scintillating work of art before her that demanded attention. And attention he got, from both Andrew and Vernese. They stood transfixed.

He was more than gorgeous or exquisite. More than resplendent or breathtaking. To say that he was androgynous wasn't enough, nor was it entirely correct. Though he had a delicate round to his face brought on by the apples in his cheeks, his sharp jawline and prominent Adam's apple were undeniably masculine. The sensual quality of his features came together to present a visage that was at once sensual and ethereal. He looked otherworldly, almost as if he had been created, like CGI characters in live action movies

That beautiful creature was almost the last thing Vernese ever saw.

The man walked toward Andrew effortlessly. Vernese didn't see him lift his leg to get over the downed tree trunk or sidestep the puddles that pooled outside the door of the bakery, even though he would have had to do that to get inside. She was too busy looking at the way his broad shoulders moved, one first and then the other, with the swing of his arms, almost undulating. He wore a black polo that hugged his biceps and sat unbuttoned at the hollow of his long neck, giving a sneak peek at the pecs below. The v-taper of his back was mouth-watering as it met the top of his khaki shorts. Vernese saw his teeth, long and pointed, but she didn't care.

The man stood before Andrew and smiled. It was an alluring smile, mostly lips and eyes. He beckoned Andrew to come to him without ever saying a word and Vernese couldn't help but feel jealous that she hadn't been the one he chose. Andrew took a sure step toward the man, who had opened his arms to embrace him, without ever looking back at Vernese. *Son of a bitch*, Vernese thought, hating how smug his posture was. Vernese hated Andrew just then, even as the image of the two males together, bodies pressed close, muscles rippling sparked something hot in her stomach. She didn't try to conceal the salacious exhale that hissed out of her mouth.

With his next step Andrew faltered, because by then the man had latched on to his neck and had begun to suck his blood. It happened so fast that Vernese couldn't register what was happening right in front of her eyes. Andrew was in the arms of the most beautiful man she had ever laid eyes on. His head was tilted at an unnatural angle, exposing his neck. The man was holding Andrew in place while he sank his teeth into his neck to let blood. The man was drinking Andrew's blood.

He was drinking Andrew's blood.

Vernese looked at the man, his face still so beautiful even as it sucked the life out of one of the people she had shared a home with. His eyes seemed to dance even as blood coated his lips.

Man? This was no man. It was a vampire, like the ones Dr. LaFleur talked about.

A vampire.

Andrew flailed, swinging his arms wildly. He tried to rip the vampire's face away from his neck, tried to beat at his arms and chest, but to no avail. Vernese snapped herself out of the trance she was in a took a tentative step toward Andrew. She didn't know what she intended to do - if a strong man like Andrew couldn't stop the assault, she would never be able to, but she tried anyway. Call it human nature, fight or flight. Maybe her first inclination was to fight after all.

Andrew had been facing the vampire when he latched onto him and was still stuck in that position, however his head had been manipulated so that the vampire had easy access to the blood he so craved. This meant that Andrew was able to plead silently with Vernese to run. When he saw her rooting around, looking for something to use against the bloodsucker at his neck, he widened his eyes and darted them toward the door, signaling for Vernese to move, to leave, to get out while she still could. With tears of concession in her eyes, Vernese complied - what else could she do? She was no match for the vampire, who had nearly bitten all the way through Andrew's neck in his zeal. She would have only succeeded in getting herself killed too.

She eyed the door over the vampire's shoulder but thought better of it. She would never get by him, she surmised. She would find herself in his clutches before she could blink if she tried. *The back door!* Her mind sent her the message as loud as an air horn on a quiet night and she jolted at the revelation. It was the only way out. Her last look at Andrew was filled with sorrow and solace combined; he met her gaze in kind before squeezing his eyes shut against the pain. Vernese slipped out the back door amidst the lewd sounds of moaning and slurping.

She was almost out of the bakery when she felt a hand caress the side of her neck from behind. Her heart jumped into her throat as her legs stopped dead in their tracks. She turned to look, to see who was touching her so intimately, knowing she didn't want to see at all, and found no one there. The vampire who would haunt her quiet moments forever remained in the center of the room with his teeth pressed against Andrew's ruined neck smiling coyly, blood staining his teeth.

The vampire's laugh was deep and melodic; tenor, baritone, and bass all rolled into one. The effect was hypnotic; she could feel the reverberations deep down in her soul.

Vernese never told the others what happened, just like she didn't speak up when they wondered who was on the other side of the door banging and banging and banging. She knew who it was. She knew because she had seen him standing outside their hotel staring up at the building that night and every night since. He just stood there, looking. He never tried to come in, never tried to frighten them. He just stood there, watching. Smelling the air.

Smelling her.

Vernese never told them but she was the first to suggest they leave the place they had called home since the event happened. She argued that higher ground was better, though she didn't really know if that was true. She said that looters would be making their rounds and were bound to find them. She reminded them that if they were trapped, they would have no way to escape given they were on the 9th floor. They would have to fight and who among them, in their weakened states, really wanted to do that, she asked. People agreed easily enough. Just like when she came home without Andrew - she told them that he lost his head and ran off and they believed it. She didn't know why she concocted the story instead of just telling the truth, but she did. Trauma can make people do some crazy things, running off and leaving the safety that they had experienced thus far in favor of the unknown among them. It can also make liars out of good people. Vernese was willing to accept that.

Bang, bang, bang.

That sound would surely make its way into her dreams.

As they trekked into the thick brush that would lead them to their new home, Vernese thought about all that banging again. It had been incessant, desperate. There was something needy about it. The realization straightened Vernese's back even as chills ran down her spine. Were the knocks and bangs coming from people desperate to claim their space or was it coming from the vampires? They wouldn't need to bang on the door, would they? Vernese would have thought they would be strong enough to rip the door off its hinges if they chose to. But they didn't. Were the vampires toying with them? Or was the gang human with something other than fun and games on their minds? She didn't know. It didn't matter. They had to leave. They had no choice. Whether human or not, *something* was on to them.

The walk was hard. It didn't help that Vernese was exhausted. She hadn't slept much since that day at the bakery. Every time she shut her eyes she saw the vampire sucking at Andrew's neck, his bloody lips curled into a smile reserved just for her, as the ginger ale spilled onto the floor from the over-turned can on the counter.

CHAPTER 35

"We have to send them," Patrick said, but he wasn't happy about it. His concern was reflected on Doug's face.

"Isn't there some other way?"

"Like what?" Patrick didn't mean to be sharp, but he was. He didn't want to do it anymore than Doug did. He knew firsthand how dangerous the Hunters were with their bulbous eyes and massive jaws. What if something went wrong? What if they hurt her?

He shook his head. Patrick couldn't allow himself to think like that. Doing so would paralyze him.

"Honestly, Doug, what other option do we have?"

Doug was silent at that because there was no other option. Sure, Patrick had made things happen in the real world, but it was a small display. With time, he could get better and do bigger things that had more of an impact, but they didn't know what kind of time they really had. They could have 40 years or 4 days, and both would pass in the blink of an eye in The Realm.

They couldn't just wait and see, not with Gabby's eternity on the line. Something had to be done and this was the only thing they could come up with. Doug sighed audibly, the weight of the world on his shoulders.

"Anyway, we control them now. They work for us." Patrick stated this as if it was a matter of course. Sure, they controlled the Hunters now - they ruled The Realm, after all. But suddenly he didn't feel so confident in that anymore. Mal had been strangely silent since he killed Mileeha. He turned over the keys to the kingdom so easily, it was as if the whole thing was just a matter of going through the motions for him.

Why was that?

As he stepped out of the dilapidated house where he and Doug had spent their entire reign thus far, Patrick started to feel uneasy about the exchange of power, and not for the first time. Why had it seemed so simple? Why had Mal chosen them as the new rulers? Where had Mal disappeared to?

Patrick stood outside, feeling every bit the sacrificial lamb in the open clearing, a final thought plaguing his mind: *How do we know they'll listen?*

Patrick stood still silent. Doug took a tentative step out of the house and onto the packed dirt as well. Everything inside Patrick wanted to tell Doug to go back inside, to shut the door, wait for him to call out his name and tell him everything was ok; to do what his father says. But Patrick couldn't say any of that. The corners of his eyes prickled with fresh tears as he looked at his full-grown son stepping into the clearing to stand by his side. His full-grown, dead little boy.

CHAPTER 36

Tara saw them emerge from the house from which she had so recently fled and felt the absence of a weapon in her hand. She had gravitated there after mourning her friends so keenly, she could feel their presence in the space they shared. It frightened her. They called to her from wherever they had gone, wanting her to come to them. That's not what bothered her. What made Tara leave their camp was how much she wanted to figure out a way to do exactly that.

So, Tara found herself in front of the house again. What she saw there stopped her dead in her tracks.

Patrick and Doug stood among the Hunters.

A chill ran down her spine at their brazenness. How could they stand there without a care in the world? Didn't they fear the Hunters as she did? Tara could barely control her breathing from fear that one of those monstrous beasts would sense her presence and set its jaws upon her. Tara blinked back tears at the thought, but it wasn't for herself that she was crying, not entirely. She was thinking of her friends, limbs strewn grotesquely around the grassy patch near their home like so much garbage. And yes, she did fear for herself. Tara was now utterly alone. Everyone she had come to know since awaking in The Realm had died: her friends, her suitor, her forever lover. She had no hope of escape, of understanding... of solace. She had no reason to care about those things anymore. All she had was hate and it burned within her like the flames in the inciner- ators tucked away in the basements of buildings where she had once lived. That gave her pause, the memory of some other life, some reincarnation of herself. What a pity she had never gotten it right.

Tara pushed the old memories away. There was no place for them where she sat crouched behind a bush bordering the house on the hill, the house where Mal dwelled. And just where was Mal? Surely, he knew everything that had gone on. He must, Tara reasoned. How could he not know that this right-hand man was dead at the hands of the newcomers. A wicked smile spread across Tara's face when she thought of the retribution Mal surely had in mind for them. They would suffer, she was sure of it. The pain would be enough to rival the suffering in Hell, or at least what she thought Hell must be like. Because it had to be worse than The Realm, right? The suffering - it had to be worse than simply being prey, didn't it, more than being afraid of the repercussions of every step? Tara willed herself to stop going off on tangents, to control her mind, to focus only on what was happening right in front of her, but this always happened. Whenever she got a moment to think, she always thought too deeply for her own good. All the 'what ifs' and 'whys' flooded in. And there were no answers for questions like hers, Tara knew. Many had tried to placate her, to give her rose-colored glasses to look through, both in The Realm and in the living world, but she still had more questions.

Why was she in The Realm and not Hell? Why was she allowed to be reincarnated, start life anew, only to link up with Mileeha again and again, doomed to repeat the same pattern as before? Why didn't she kill herself when she met Mileeha the last time in an attempt to stop the vicious cycle? She had toyed with the idea, so why didn't she go through with it? Would it have mattered?

Tara wondered sometimes if The Realm was just Hell spelled differently, all of it experienced within the confines of her mind.

Patrick and Doug swiveled their heads as they looked for something in the distance. Tara became more aware of the vulnerability of her position more keenly than ever as they did. Again, she wondered, where was Mal? Didn't they fear him? Were they really that bold? Tara couldn't believe they had waltzed into the house, killed Mal's second in command, and just took over the place without Mal saying a word? What did they know that Tara didn't?

Tara snickered. She had never trusted Patrick. There was something about him that rubbed her wrong from the day he entered The Realm, but she couldn't put her finger on it. No one would have been able to foresee what happened - them killing Mileeha. Strong Mileeha. How did they overpower him? Tara wanted to laugh at herself for thinking that there had to be witchcraft involved, but there it was. How else could an average joe and his less than impressive son take down a god?

Tara couldn't stop the tears from falling but she dared not draw in a shuddering breath for fear that the Hunters would hear.

Her head spun to look behind her before her mind even registered the sound. Uncontained movement pushing branches to and fro wantonly. The Hunters. They had found her after all.

Tara told herself to move, to run deeper into the woods and

escape to live another day, but her feet stayed still. She was tired. She was alone. She was done.

She was almost disappointed when they passed her by without a glance and loped into the dirt patch in front of the house to sit on their haunches before their new masters.

CHAPTER 37

Mal watched as Patrick and Doug instructed the Hunters, for the first time feeling the cold fingers of fear caressing the back of his neck. It wasn't that things weren't happening as they should, because they were. The pair had uncovered nuances to their skills faster than expected, actually. Doug was fulfilling his role as Mal envisioned he would – he was the embodiment of the sidekick extraordinaire with a dash of mistrust. It was the perfect combination to bring on the next phase. Patrick was honing his skills at an impressive rate as well. The role of leader suited him in more ways than one.

It was all the other things that had developed that gave him pause.

Mal hadn't expected Gabby to be a factor in how this whole thing played out, at least not in the way that she was. She would be important, yes. She was the impetus for Doug and Patrick's involvement. Saving her was first and foremost to them.

Reversing the family curse was only important after Gabby was safe and sound. But Gabby had thrown a wrench into the plans, hadn't she? Instead of just being there, just a girl waiting to be saved by her daddy, Gabby did something different. She went digging. True enough, Gabby didn't willingly dredge up the past. She hadn't deliberately opened doors that Mal expected would remain closed for eternity, but she had done it and that changed things.

Mal turned his attention from Patrick and Doug, who looked every bit as much of the pet store obedience trainer as the Hunters sat before them and cast a glance toward Tara tucked behind the bushes. She thought she was well hidden and that was all right. Any Hunter worth their salt would see her in seconds - she was so conspicuous that she nearly glowed against the landscape. But no one was looking for her now. The Hunters were being set to a task that would be different from anything they had ever done before. It would take all their attention to be able to pull it off, and pull it off they must if they wanted to please their new masters. And they did, the poor beasts. All they ever wanted to do was make their masters happy. He too had other things to do than worry about Tara at the moment. He had bigger fish to fry, as he had been wont to say in a previous life. The phrase came to him feely as things did most times - memories, melodies, snippets of times past. All unbidden. All unwanted. Remembering made him melancholy. Melancholy made him malleable.

Mal couldn't afford to feel right now, of all times.

He turned away from the scene unfolding outside, two separate scenarios building steps toward their inevitable end, one unaware of the other, unaware of the disadvantage this moment presents for them both. Somewhere in the recesses of Mal's mind he was concerned about Tara's presence and the aura that surrounded her. Revenge looks red when viewed through the right lens. Mal noticed the fiery tinges surrounding her place in the bushes almost absently at first, but now, as he walked into the recesses of the house, her presence and all that it might represent needled him again.

Tara, Mal spoke in his mind, sending Patrick an unspoken message, using the telepathic link he had formed with Patrick when he handed him the keys to the kingdom. It was nothing more than a whisper, but one that would not have been borne of Patrick's own subconscious. He would take notice of it, maybe not right away, but subconsciously he would hear the utterance repeating itself until he addressed it, the call having anchored itself to Patrick's thoughts. Mal did so swiftly, reaching into Patrick's mind and then retreating fast. That was a dangerous place for him to be. Even though he would have liked nothing more than to uncover what Patrick was thinking or to steer him in the direction he wanted like a puppet, Mal knew he couldn't risk reciprocation. And as strong as Patrick was, that was a real possibility. If Patrick gazed into Mal's mind, he might go mad. And that simply wouldn't do.

Mal looked down the hallway toward the corridor that led to Joanne's room. How long would it be before Patrick and Doug found her? He was surprised it hadn't already happened yet - the wife and mother they missed so much was under the same roof as them, right under their noses. But Mal supposed they had been preoccupied. And rightfully so. Gabby didn't have long. Mal thought that somewhere in Patrick's subconscious, he knew. The urgency he was feeling wasn't propelled purely because his lineage was in peril. Patrick must have known - must have *felt* - that a battle was to be lost sooner rather than later and they would have to start all over again with the children. Did Patrick worry that, at some point, they would run out of people to save?

Yes, Mal supposed he did.

But the girl kept reading, and reading, and reading.

Ah, Joanne. What have you done?

Mal heard Gabby's voice just then, a consistent sound that reverberated off the walls of the house, bouncing, turning, rising, falling. He caught only a few words here and there, but it didn't matter. He knew the story well.

Did you know what you were writing, dear one? Did you sing your words directly into your granddaughter's ear?

Mal thought of Patrick once more before taking his first steps toward Joanne's room. He felt an emotion that he couldn't readily define as he considered Patrick's form. He mused for the shortest of moments at how Patrick already seemed to stand taller. Even before the beasts that had hunted him down, snarling and salivating behind him as they snapped at his heels the moment his feet touched ground in The Realm, Patrick appeared poised. He was commanding them to do something that would change the existence of everything known to God, man, and beast, and his straight posture, upturned chin, and wide stance commanded obedience. Despite that, perhaps even because of that, Mal felt a sadness well within him. No, that wasn't quite it. As Mal stopped to consider the emotion that plagued him, it bloomed fully within him, encompassing his very being so totally, he thought he might be ill.

Pity. Mal felt a pity for his forced right hand man that was all-encompassing, debilitating, too real.

No.

Mal didn't have time to feel. Not now. Not after all the sacrifices he had made to get to this point.

As Mal resumed his steps, he pushed away thoughts of

letting Patrick know what was going to happen, of allowing him a few moments to ease his mind. He couldn't do that. Doing so would change the future as much as the success of Patrick's plan would. With emotions that Mal didn't think he would ever feel again, he squared his shoulders, refocused his purpose, and turned the corner.

CHAPTER 38

"I know! She called me yesterday to go with her to the bank."

"The bank? Who even goes to the bank anymore?"

"I know, right?"

"Did you go?"

"No! I mean, come on, Michelle. We can't just drop everything and cluster together to do every little thing," Carly, a thirty-something mom dressed in the stay-at-home parent uniform of the suburbs (a loose-fitting top with yoga pants and flip flops) took a break in her diatribe to look out at the kids who are playing together nicely in the backyard. A rueful smile formed at the corners of her mouth. She wondered how long it would be before elated giggles turned into shrill screams. "This isn't the '50s," she continued, "We don't have to huddle together, holding hands to go to the bathroom."

Carly took a sip of her coffee and looked out at the kids again.

Michelle, similar attire, similar posture, similar everything, took a sip of her coffee too.

Gabby watched them absently, fondling the handle of her own brew. She heard the kids, voices interspersed between the mom chatter and the Jhene Aiko playing in the background. Gabby caught the lyrics of "While We're Young" and mouthed them over her mug, curses and all. She hoped her friends didn't hear - she didn't feel like turning the music off even if it was in direct conflict with her current state of baby watching. Some-times, especially in moments filled with laughing children, moms with fly-aways and messy buns stacked on their heads, and the intoxicating smell of diaper rash cream and fresh coffee swirling in the air - during those times, when Gabby couldn't distinguish herself in the crowd - *then*, she needed a little some-thing cool, edgy, fun, something decidedly different from that moment in her life to call her back from the edge. Listening to music with curses in it - actually *saying* the curses in front of a mixed audience, albeit low low low, did the trick... sometimes.

Gabby sipped her coffee loudly, slurping, not caring, as she sang along and dreamed of the beach, sun on her neck, and running in the sand, a sarong flapping around her in the breeze.

The beach.

The sun.

Her neck.

Gabby felt a smile settle on her lips. She shot a quick glance over to the moms at the playdate (damn the person who came up with that term). They were engrossed in conversation about the killer and all the things people were doing to safeguard themselves. Gabby knew she should be listening. It wasn't like the situation didn't affect her. She still felt a chill run up her spine when she thought about her own supermarket incident, so

Gabby understood why the killer/stalker situation was being discussed in her kitchen over a cup of coffee... again. But right now, the beach called to her, the sound of the waves, the sun setting on the horizon, the warm breeze blowing through her hair. It would be time to go inside now, Gabby thought. Past time. To see the sunset was to linger too long to be safe anymore. Gabby felt her heart pick up its pace as she realized her mistake. Did she have a death wish? Was she trying to draw the monsters out and let them put an end to it all? Was there nothing le-

"- right, Gabby? I mean, she won't even try anymore. We tried to tell her - Gabby and me. Remember? Remember how out of it she looked?"

Gabby turned her head toward Carly in slow motion, as if coming out of a fog. They weren't talking about the killer anymore. Now they were just talking about people, picking, jeering, being catty. Fantastic.

Gabby nodded then looked away again. Carly kept talking. She probably didn't even realize how noncommittal Gabby had been, how distracted. Maybe she had noticed and it didn't matter, who knew? Gabby sighed and looked out at the kids making a bonafide mess of the backyard. The sand was smothering the grass instead of sitting inside the sandpit and sand toys were strewn all over the grass, discarded. The kids were dotting the lawn, playing separately but together in harmony, still. But that would change soon enough she knew as the other moms did, especially since the hour had changed and nap times grew nearer. That's what they were waiting for as they chatted within view of the backdoor, always at the ready to run outside and solve a problem, quell an argument, teach a lesson about sharing. That's why their words rushed out in a torrent, diarrhea of the mouth, her father-in-law would have called it. They needed to say it all and do it quick, before the kids ruined their fun.

Except Gabby didn't care about all of that. She never had, really, but on that day, she was more distracted than usual. She could feel the warm air of the tropical evening on her skin,: she imagined that the sun had set and removed its golden rays from view. The smell of rotted meat permeated the air, thickened it, made it hard to breathe. Gabby felt as if she might choke on it; the stench was so unimaginably bad. But breathe it she must, move she must if she wanted to make it off the beach alive. She had to get out of there before the vampires came. But Gabby knew she was already too late. They were there, watching her, standing in the shadows, just waiting for her to try to make an escape. Gabby's first step was tentative, as she turned away from the wa-

What was Robbie tearing?

Gabby stood slowly, eying Michelle's little boy. Sand stood on top in his hair as if he had dunked his head into it on purpose. Gabby had time to think that she didn't envy Michelle the chore of trying to get all that sand out of his curls before she moved toward him, panic prickling her skin like electricity. He was holding something white in his hands and ripping it into little pieces... pieces that were then being carried off in the wind. It was white, paper of some kind, big paper...

She never felt the knob of the screen door in her hands, never felt the grass beneath her feet (she had kicked off her flip flops at the table, imagining that there was warm sand caressing her toes). By the time she had the white paper he was playing with in her hands, her heartbeat had taken over all sound, thudding sound loudly in her chest, she couldn't hear Robbie exclaim in fear, nor Michelle asking her if she was ok.

It was just a stack of paper towels.

Paper towels - that's all.

Not the manuscript. Not her grandmother's work. *Not* the manuscript.

But where was the manuscript?

Gabby turned to go back into the house after a quick smile and chin flick to Robbie. Was that enough? Was that enough to calm the sweet little boy who had been damn near tackled on his back for some stupid paper towels? She didn't know. She didn't care right then either, though she might later. She didn't think she had yelled or cursed - the moms would have had a far different look on their faces if she had - but she probably snatched the paper towel stack from Robbie after getting to him with lightning speed. Inhuman speed? Gabby couldn't help but chuckle. Her grandmother's story was really getting into her head.

Gabby gave Michelle a smile and touched her shoulder as she walked back into the house. This seemed to allay Michelle's concerns and she came back inside too, taking up residence in her spot once again, and jumping right back into conversation where she had left off as soon as all the women were sitting down again. Gabby made a show of puttering around the kitchen first, masking the fact that she was looking for the manuscript behind straightening up the counter. It wasn't there. She hadn't really expected it to be left where it could get wet or greasy, but she had to look anyway. She'd like to think she would have taken care of it better than that.

Right?

"... freaking all the time!" Michelle and Carly erupted into laughter about something, leaning back precariously on their bar stools. Gabby smiled over to them, trying to look like she had been listening, but knew she failed miserably. Whatever.

She'd get back into the conversation later, after she found the manuscript.

"What's on your mind, Gab?" Carly asked, calling out to a fast-moving Gabby as she moved from the kitchen to the living room, in the zone.

Gabby heard her as an afterthought and said something back, but what that something was, she wasn't sure. Whatever she had said, it worked; Michelle and Carly started up a different conversation, this time about the newest streaming exercise program. As she passed in front of the TV, engulfing her in sound and coaxing her to sway along, a thought struck Gabby as funny but so very true: Jhene Aiko had never sounded so good.

She was starting to get nervous.

Not nervous, per se, but maybe antsy. The playdate was over and all the kids had left with their mothers in tow and a destroyed backyard in their wake. Gabby's kids were down for their nap. It was too early for her husband to be home from work. The house was empty. Gabby was ready to relax - naptime meant chill time for her, and God knows she needs the break in her cartoon-filled, mess-cleaning day. She wanted nothing more than to curl up on the sofa with a cup of coffee, some good music in the background, and a book in her hand.

But she still hadn't found the manuscript yet.

She had looked in the bedroom, on the coffee table, in the bathroom, on the front seat of the car, but she couldn't find it. Gabby felt an inordinate sadness washing over her every time she looked in one spot and didn't find the well-creased pages that her grandmother had left behind. A small part of her wondered why she was so affected. It was just a story - pretend. It wasn't an autobiography that could have taught Gabby about the woman she had never known. It wasn't even a finished product, though Gabby couldn't understand why considering how well the words flowed together. She was completely enthralled with the writing, and it wasn't just because the author was her grandmother. It was just plain good. The book could rival anything out in the stores now, Gabby was sure of it. But yet, it sat unfinished. Gabby had never heard that her grandmother had tried to find a publisher and received a bunch of rejections. She hadn't given it to a lot of readers, asked their opinions, and found that everyone hated it. To Gabby's knowledge, the only other person to have read the work was her grandfather. Something had stopped her grandmother from finishing the book, whether it was boredom, writer's block, or flightiness. Whatever it was, it clipped the wings of what could have been a decent writing career. The thought made Gabby sad.

She had to find the book. It was the only copy and another word would never be written toward the story ever again.

Gabby climbed the steps to sneak into the kids' rooms. Sometimes she read a page or two while she was in there, straining her eyes in the dim light, waiting for her babies to fall asleep. She silently cursed herself for not making a copy of the manuscript, just in case of something like this. She promised that would be the first thing she would do when the kids woke up... assuming she found it.

She had to find it.

Gabby checked Christopher's room first, then Autumn's and found nothing. She checked her own bedroom again, even her husband's side, on the floor under the bed, in the closet, in the bathroom. Nothing. She bit down hard on her nails, nipping down to the quick, like she used to when she was a child, and winced. Gabby hadn't realized she had brought her hand to her mouth, let alone have peeled away enough of the nail itself to make the skin beneath bleed. She sucked on her finger in frustration, trying to ease the pain, trying to think of where the manuscript could be.

Gabby remembered having it in the car with her when she went to get her nails done the day before. It was one of those rare days when the kids were able to stay home with daddy and she could get a few hours to herself. She had sat in the massage chair, her feet blissfully soaking some curiously blue liquid that was, by all rights, a little bit too hot to be considered comfortable, at least not right away, reading about Vernese and the hotel refugees making their way inland and up to the highest point on the island to escape the reach of the vampires. It wasn't that high as far as mountains go, even for the Caribbean, but at an elevation of over 1,300 ft, it was the best they could hope for. Vernese, Dr. LaFleur, and the remaining hotel guests were pushing past the resort area seated at the base of the mountain to brave the terrain. Surely, they would encounter all sorts of things on their way up - people driven crazy because of the madness going on in the world, those that lived off the grid before the event and didn't take kindly to the intrusion, mountain lions, cobras, all manner of beasts. Gabby didn't know if those animals were indigenous to the Caribbean or not, but it didn't matter. Maybe they had been on the island as part of a zoo, but then were set free by a good Samaritan when the outbreak happened and now they roamed free, every bit the predators that the vampires were. Maybe they came over in the ship with the vampires and were like pets, retrieving prey to offer as gifts to their masters. (Gabby wondered, not for the first time, if she should start writing too.) She couldn't wait to find out what was in store for her on every page. She just couldn't put the manuscript down.

But she had. And now she needed to figure out where.

She hadn't left it at the nail salon, that much she remembered. She could see herself picking it up after paying her bill and carrying it to the car gingerly so that she didn't smudge her nails. Then what?

Gabby remembered having it with her when she was at the supermarket that day - *the* day. She had read a page before going inside, hunkered down in the car with the cabin light on, trying to get through the words on the page before she started to feel the chill of the night air seeping in. She remembered smiling after finishing the section - Aaron had waxed poetic about wanting to meet Vernese on that page and Gabby couldn't wait to find out if his search of the civic center would allow him a glimpse of the woman he so pined for. Romance had never been her thing and it had been totally unexpected within the context of a novel about vampires, but she was really enjoying the change of pace. When she had finished the page, she closed the manuscript dutifully. She had promised herself that she would only stay in the car for a few minutes and she stuck to it. There was a killer running around, after all - there was no sense making it easy for him.

She hadn't brought the manuscript inside the supermarket, had she? Did she have it in her hand when she shopped, maybe putting it down on a shelf when she reached for a can of chickpeas or a box of pasta? Did it slip out of her cart when she made her escape, hellbent on leaving the phantom man behind? Had it been left on the Formica floor made sticky from a day's worth of dropped lollipops, fizzy soda, and grime, for the cleaning crew to sweep away? Her eyes widened in fear at the thought.

Had she really left the manuscript in the supermarket?

Before she knew it, Gabby was waking up the kids, disturbing them from their slumber (she would pay dearly for this later), and loading them into the car. Gabby never once thought about calling the supermarket to ask them about the manuscript. She knew better. All they would do was give her the run around, passing her from department to department, before some clueless manager got on the line and told her he was sorry that he couldn't help any further. No, she would force them to say that to her face.

Gabby was opening the trunk to grab blankets out, all the while wondering if someone had found the manuscript and taken it home with them. Worse, had someone found it, saw its yellowed pages, and decided it was trash? Her blood ran cold at the thought that her grandmother's words might forever be lost to the dump, thrown away by some pimple-faced teenager with food stuck in his braces. But, no, it wouldn't have been that kid's fault, would it? It would have been her fault. Hers alone.

The supermarket incident happened two days ago.

With tears in her eyes, she snatched the blankets out of the trunk, missing the thump that came after. Hand on the door, Gabby started to close the trunk when her eye caught on something white. Something big. Something magnificent.

The manuscript!

It was there on the flat board of the trunk, open to a page that was marked with big, block letters done in red ink that said 'FIRST PERSON OR THIRD? PICK ONE, JOANNE!!', waiting patiently for her to grab it and pick up where she left off. Gabby's heart leapt in her chest at the sight. Gabby instantly remembered where she was in the book and why her grandmother's note to herself had tickled her so much. The beginning of the tale had been in first person, from Aaron's point of view at least. In later chapters, she had slipped into third person, creating the distance she needed to tell the story from a different vantage point. Maybe she wasn't supposed to, but Gabby really liked the shift. Both approaches were important to the story, at least she thought so. There had been a lot of notes like that scrawled across the pages Gabby had read so far. Was that typical of an author to mark up their draft work before it was even completed? Probably so. She enjoyed reading her grandmother's notes. They were always direct and to the point. They often drew a laugh out of her too, though Gabby was sure Joanne hadn't found anything amusing. Sometimes she went in depth with her comments explaining new logic that she had come up with that, had she revisited the piece instead of abandoning it, would have taken the story in another direction. Sometimes she used shorthand. Sometimes she circled sentences and admonished herself with a simple, 'Come on!' Gabby could almost see her face, pieced together from photographs in her father's scrapbook, contorting in irritation as she marked up her work worse than any editor would have. The thought of her beating herself up over it bothered Gabby, but, more than that, Joanne's passion for her work shone through, no matter how raw. Gabby couldn't help but be floored by it. This woman, who loved her day job as a professor, teaching students how to write by day then toiled away writing her own novel at night, was speaking to her from the pages of her life's work, second-guesses and all. Gabby was able to interact in the most interesting of ways with the woman whose blood flowed in her veins but that she was never able to know in life. The concept was nothing short of amazing.

She'd *found* it.

Gabby wished she could say that such elation was an over-reaction to such a simple thing, but she knew differently. The manuscript had become everything to her. She *had* to read it, had to finish it, had to hear the words her grandmother wrote bouncing around in her head. It was as if reading it was more than just entertainment. It did more than satisfy her curiosity about a family member she never had the chance to know. Reading the story - Joanne's story - was like breathing, eating: being.

Her little ones had fallen back to sleep in their car seats while she was thanking her lucky stars that the manuscript was safe and sound. Gabby asked the stars for another gift as she executed the delicate act that the transfer between car seat and crib was, her eyes dancing at the thought: please let them sleep for another hour.

CHAPTER 39

He hadn't seen her yet, but knew she was there.

Instantly, the questions he had while still on the ship had faded away to nothingness. Now, as he stood under the palm trees swaying in the night breeze, as her breath caressed the nape of his neck as if she were sitting astride his back, he could hardly believe he had ever doubted she would be there in the first place.

Cecelia. Radiant. Elegant. And perhaps the descriptor she most enjoyed: provocative. Aaron's mind clouded as he felt her approach, nearing her steps slowly, making him wait until he could wait no longer. Cecelia was all of those things and more. She was captivating in the most amazing ways. Beautiful was not enough to describe her. Her entire aura was an elixir that, once sampled, was difficult to resist ever again. He couldn't deny the sway she held over him. Indeed, Aaron wasn't the only one to find her irresistible in the most literal of ways; her suitors numbered among mortals and immortals both. One look from her was capable of making the receiver beg for more. But Aaron knew all too well of other adjectives that described this ancient beauty. Words like vicious, ruthless, and indomitable to name a few. He quickly put such thoughts out of his mind. It wouldn't do to be thinking of such things with her in such close proximity, unless he wanted her to prove their merit.

Cecelia touched a wayward curl blowing in the wind and tucked it behind her ear.

Aaron shivered involuntarily.

"My love."

Cecelia had spoken first this time, unlike their last meeting when Aaron had spoken first and last, most and quickest. He wondered if this turn of events was to foreshadow what was to come. He didn't allow his mind to linger on the ramifications of that possibility.

"Cecelia." Aaron tried to keep his voice even, but it was hard to do when she looked like that. She was wearing a sundress, shoulders bared under spaghetti straps; calves golden in the waning light. The dress swayed prettily against her curves, clinging and billowing alternatively as the wind moved. Her hair was held back by a multicolored cloth headband, one of the hues a match to the amber of her dress. Her soft, dark brown curls danced around her head, animated by the wind, haloing around her head then swaying side to side. Cecelia wore no lipstick, no makeup at all. Aaron supposed she never needed it in life and her features had only intensified in immortality, settling into the masque of beauty that their kind assumed once the blood of the living coursed through them. She was older than he was even though they had died at a similar age; she was older than most of them by centuries. The life's blood had time to reanimate her skin with a vitality that fledglings pined for, her skin no longer the pale, graying monstrosity it must have been at her moment of awakening. Now she looked like a living woman, skin coppery and young, devoid of blemishes and wrinkles, and beautiful. So incredibly beautiful. Her brown eyes, more golden than they had been in life, were oval and ringed with the most lustrous eyelashes. They looked into his soul. Her full lips caressed the words she spoke. Aaron found himself staring at her lips, longing to run his tongue along her cupid's bow to elicit the intake of air she would surely make at the contact.

They had been here before.

"So formal, dear. How unexpected," Cecelia all but purred. The sound was anything but unpleasant, but Aaron understood her meaning as strongly as if she had slapped him with her bare hands. Cecelia was their coven leader, centuries old, and the most learned of their group. She spoke to only a few and, even then only when she deemed necessary, not the other way around. Aaron had been given certain allowances, liberties that others could never have dreamed of. This was so because she wanted it and there was no one in the world who would dare challenge her. But with those liberties came great constraints, sacrifices to his sense of self that made him uneasy. He had done the unthinkable. He had made Cecelia wait. Worse, he had made Cecelia *want*.

Aaron looked at her. She was appealing in every way. It wasn't just immortal beauty - had they been alive and well, breathing the air for necessity rather than out of habit, he would have courted her, slept with her, and claimed her as his. And here, in this afterlife on earth where she reigned by the batting of an eye, he could have it all if he did what came naturally to him. His body wanted her, craved her. Close proximity to her had always resulted in coupling and he had no doubt that she assumed this day would be no different, even after all the time between them. But Aaron wasn't so sure. He had left Cecelia for a reason. He had said goodbye to mortal life unwillingly, having been forced into the darkness by a fledgling on a rampage. He joined her coven unknowingly, having befriended other members by sheer luck upon awakening hungry, frightened, and alone. He became her lover because she named him as such, not that he was complaining on that score. Aaron wanted to become her partner in all things only if he so chose to and not by mandate. So, he bid Cecelia wait, and she had, until now.

"I should think you'd be happy to see me," Cecelia demurred. Aaron faltered. She was just so damned beautiful.

"And I am," Aaron said truthfully. It had been a while since he had seen her. So much had happened in between. Aaron was caught off guard to find that she cared enough to bait him, even now. "I wondered if this was all some elaborate hoax," he said, searching for his voice, "some game between you and Raymond. It was beginning to feel like we were all caught in the crosshairs of your lover's cycle, renewed passion and all that."

She closed the distance between them before he could even blink, her speed enchanting rather than jarring. Cecelia stared at Aaron, her head turned to the side as she looked into his very soul. She reached out a hand to stroke the skin of his cheek with a touch that was unnaturally soft for one of the undead. He found himself leaning into it. She felt like home.

"Never that, Aaron," she cooed. "Never with you."

Her lips were suddenly so close to his. Their bodies had moved together, seemingly of their own volition, and now their mouths were so close they shared the same breath. He wanted to kiss her. He always wanted to kiss her, and that was part of the problem. He couldn't think when she was around; Aaron's mind was always clouded when Cecelia was near him. All he could do was think of ways to get closer to her, to make her want him, when they were in each other's presence – to show her how much he wanted her. He had traveled land and sea to be with her in the past, had left a comfortable hunting ground to join her where she stood. When she needed him, he was always there. And even when she didn't Aaron had stayed close, the idea of putting down roots, finding a new coven, even having proximity to family that he could watch flourish from afar be damned. He didn't understand the effect she had on him and almost didn't want to.

Almost.

Aaron knew that Cecelia wanted him too - there was no question of it now and hadn't been for some time. He just wanted to be sure that he truly wanted her. Being mated with the coven leader would give him prestige and status, however it would also strip him of his freedom, and he wasn't sure that was what he wanted. Every time he set his mind to think about it, he would look up and see those beautiful eyes of hers or that sumptuous mouth and lose his train of thought. He would see the curve of her hips and lose focus, glimpse the round of her breasts and stop being able to form a coherent thought. It wasn't something she was doing to him deliberately, at least he hadn't thought so at the time. But now, in the dim light of the space in between night and day, as he felt his resolve slipping away once again, he wasn't so sure.

Aaron would be with Cecelia; he knew that to be true. Unless...

Cecelia pulled back abruptly, her lips that had been so invitingly close just seconds before, suddenly seeming a million miles away. They formed a thin, angry line before she was able to get herself under control and offer a placid expression that belied the truth. The question in her eyes confirmed what Aaron had suspected: she had read his thoughts and found the girl there.

"I haven't found h-"

She put her finger to his lips, stilling them, silencing him. With unblinking eyes, she turned to the water, watching its colors bleed from the teal of dusk to an inky black as the moon rose properly in the night sky.

Bleed. Someone would bleed tonight for Cecelia, if only so she could relish in their pain.

"A girl," Cecelia said, her tongue slithering over the words rancorously. "How common."

Aaron was suddenly enraged. Cecelia turned to face him curiously, sensing his anger and reveling in it.

"And Raymond? Nothing more than a toy?" Aaron spat the words out of his mouth, letting them cut the air like barbs.

It was Cecelia's turn to get mad. Her face flushed in anger. "You speak so disdainfully about your leader. So sure of your position, Aaron, that you can spit upon the ones who rule?"

"Raymond fell into position, Cecelia. It could have been any one of us. It could have been me."

"But it was not."

Aaron clenched his jaw. This was not a new conversation. Indeed, all conversations led to the fact that he was not a leader and she was. She was *the* leader of all things and he needed to learn his place. Between her thighs, unquestioningly, but decidedly beneath her in all ways.

Cecelia's eyes softened at the sight of Aaron's anger. She loved him, truly, if one had the capacity for such an emotion as one of the undead. She wanted him to end this separation, to finish his quest and come home to her. Standing there arguing on the beach wasn't getting her to that end.

"Raymond isn't you, my darling. No one is," she acquiesced because she had to, because it was the truth.

Cecelia stared at Aaron, watching as he melted under her gaze. He was a beautiful man. Tall with an athletic build. His black hair had taken on a wavy texture that it hadn't possessed in life. He had taken to wearing it long, at least for him. His thick mane curled just above the crest of his shoulders and Cecelia was mesmerized by the way it pushed off his forehead in the breeze. His nutmeg skin was smooth and clear, his cheekbones high. His smile, full and large, could light up an entire room. Aaron was never meant to be a bloodsucker, a killer, a vampire. He was too honest, too romantic, and selfless for this life. But he was a creature of the night, the same as she, and part of her was glad. Had he not been turned she would never have met him all those years ago. She would have lived and died not knowing the love of her life.

Aaron belonged to her.

She smiled into her stare, disarming him further. If she kept this up, she could have him on the beach in a matter of minutes, but that isn't what she wanted. Cecelia had nothing if not her pride. She wanted Aaron to come to her of his own free will.

"I kept my promise," Cecelia said after some time, releasing him from her spell.

"Which?"

Aaron had the urge to reach out and touch Cecelia's curly hair.

"The promise of food, of bounty here on this little island." Cecelia spread her arms to gesture at the tropical paradise that had been overrun by hungry vampires.

"That you did, and we are grateful."

"Are *you* grateful, Aaron? Do you know that I did this only for you?"

Aaron felt a lump in his throat. It would be so easy to kiss her, to pull her into his arms and tell her that he would love only her forever and ever. He moved to do it but stopped himself.

She is still out there somewhere.

And what if she wasn't? A voice in his head asked. What if she had already been bled by one of his shipmates? How far was he willing to go to learn her fate?

Cecelia's eyes had gone hard, like two black diamonds gleaming under the moon. Aaron didn't know if the voice in his head was his or hers.

"I love you, Cecelia." Aaron spoke the truth to her because, in the end, there was nothing else.

"Of that I am sure," she responded lovingly.

"But I must know if this is what I want to do or if it is what is willed for me to do."

Cecelia nodded curtly before turning away from Aaron. She started to leave him then, alone on the beach but returned to his side to place a chaste kiss on his cheek.

A smile crept over Aaron's lips as Cecelia pulled away, seemingly bashful. Whatever emotion she was feeling when she kissed Aaron's cheek disappeared as quickly as it had come. It was replaced with the bravado that only a person accustomed to getting their way can muster. Without casting another glance in his direction, Cecelia said,

"Do what you must, Aaron, but be quick about it. I won't be kept waiting for much longer."

Aaron wished he could have suppressed the gulp that his Adam's apple forced up his throat, but he couldn't. She could be so intimidating. It was incredibly appealing.

Cecelia had left the beach and made her way down the boardwalk, tracking the scent of her meal for the night, but when she spoke again, it was as if she were standing right next to Aaron.

"Be careful, my love... you might break her. But then again, toys are meant to be broken, aren't they?

Aaron opened his mouth to respond, but Cecelia was already gone.

CHAPTER 40

She could feel it. Burning slow in her stomach, roiling, festering with the threat of something more, something worse to come, Joanne could feel it. Sometimes it took a while for the sensation to show itself; sometimes she felt it before he ever entered the room. But it was always there, that recognition, and it terrified her.

She wondered if he knew.

Surely, if he knew he wouldn't let her live.

Could he kill her even though she was already dead?

Joanne didn't know what she meant, didn't understand her own thoughts anymore. Nothing had been clear to her since she showed up in the dark space he called The Realm. She hadn't seen much of it, just the four walls she had been imprisoned within. How big was the space outside of her small room? Were there others like her out there? Did they walk free or were they prisoners too? Joanne didn't know. She had never felt she could ask him anything. She didn't know why she was so afraid of him. He was mysterious, that much was true - he would never let her see him and stood far away so that she didn't touch him by mistake or otherwise. But he hadn't done anything to make her frightened. Somehow, though, she knew better than to ask much of him. Something told her that to ask many questions would not only yield nothing in the way of answers but might also bring forth his wrath.

His *wrath*, she snickered, voicing her thoughts aloud for the first time in what felt like weeks, if time could actually be measured in such ways anymore. But how bad could his 'wrath' actually be in a place like this, she wondered. The threat of death was nonexistent, at least from a physical standpoint, wasn't it? She was already dead, had already left her body to rot underground; she had already left her child motherless and her husband a widow. She was no longer there, gone, passed away as some might say. Wasn't that all there was to fear? Joanne wanted to believe that, wanted to hold that knowledge as truth so that she could stand up and walk out of that room, but something kept stopping her. Every time he came to her, just before he did whatever he did to make her insides shiver and her mind to turn away from thoughts of rebellion and towards thoughts of seduction, she thought about pushing past him and leaving the room. He couldn't do anything to her, not really. It was time she escaped the hell he was content with burning her in.

But something stopped her, begged her not to.

Because she knew more than she realized.

How could that be? Even she hadn't assumed any of it was connected. It didn't make sense and she hadn't tried to tie things together, so why would he? It just didn't make any sense that he would care about it. To her, there wasn't anything there to care about at all.

But that wasn't really the truth, and she knew it. There was something to it, something that sounded too real to be conjecture. Something that always rubbed her wrong. Joanne had never been able to put her finger on what made her feel uneasy, no matter how hard she tried to pin it down. Parts of it had floated into her brain unbidden. Some appeared to her in dreams. Joanne was nothing more than the conduit for those bits and pieces, the tool. And then it all stopped - the dreams, the whispers, the words. That's when *she* stopped. But by then she knew more than she ever wanted to know about it all. By then it was already too late.

He thought Joanne knew and he was right, she did. But just knowing wasn't enough. She didn't know what to do with the knowledge. But he didn't know that. He was afraid she would do something with it, she was convinced of it. That's why she had been locked away. That's why she was denied whatever life existed in this place.

But why visit her? Why make her feel like she would bed him if he was so inclined, without hesitation?

Because he knew who she was.

Joanne shivered involuntarily in her small, sequestered room, wondering what a second death, one by his hands in The Realm, might be like. She was terrified that she would soon find out.

CHAPTER 41

Up.

They went up. Vernese didn't know if that was a good or a bad idea, but there they were, their perch on Pic Paradis as much of a home as the hotel had been, albeit without the plush accommodations. She felt like they were kids at sleepaway camp. They bunked in a collection of lean-tos she had never known existed and ate dinner together around a campfire. Television shows from America always depicted the concept of sleepaway camp in that way - it was a place where relationships that would last a lifetime were formed in the creek and over a scary story in front of the campfire, all the while stuffing roasted marshmallows into yawning mouths. But there were no marshmallows to be blackened by the fire and there was no creek to play in. And the scary stories were all too real.

They weren't alone.

When they got to the first of the accommodating spaces on the mountain where the terrain flattened out a bit as it overlooked Pinel Island, they found people. A lot of people. Vernese thought she recognized some of them, part of details that had made up daily life on their little island. One of them was definitely her mother's old neighbor, dressed in rags and dirty. Another was a man she had seen every day as she walked to the bus stop for work. Maybe he worked in the store near her house, or maybe it was the gas station. Vernese didn't know, and none of that mattered now. He looked at her with vacant eyes. He didn't know her anymore.

Vernese tried to catch the eye of the old woman, the neighbor with whom her mother had shared pleasantries for over twenty years before her death, but it was if she couldn't see her, wouldn't see her even if she was standing right in front of her face. The woman kept turning her head, slowly at first and then almost convulsively, neck twisting, face grimacing. Vernese tried to will herself to look away but couldn't - the woman's thrashing seemed to draw her in, hypnotizing her. No one went to her aid. Vernese's hands fluttered to her mouth at the implications.

There were other people in the group that looked familiar, but Vernese didn't want to look too hard. She was afraid, now, of what eye contact could mean.

Spencer, the guard from the hotel who had been with her and the guests since the beginning, choosing to stay and help when he had the chance to leave and finding himself marooned in the high rise when there was no home to go to anymore, saw someone he knew too. He walked over to her, separating himself from the group without saying a word. It was as if he had been called away, hypnotized by some unseen force. The look on his face was that of confused bliss.

"Karen? *My* Karen?" Spencer had made his way to where the woman was sitting and situated himself right in front of her, but she had not turned to him. What Vernese could see from her vantage point was that the woman was young with long, muscular legs and a shapely waist. Her hair had been wavy but was knotted in a rat's nest now, locking and matting in ways that would require scissors to sort out if the time for proper grooming ever came again, which it wouldn't, Vernese knew, because she could see the back of her head where Spencer couldn't. Such trifles were over for that poor woman.

Vernese didn't watch as Spencer tried to rouse her - that privacy was a dignity she could afford him – but she couldn't help but hear him asking why she was there, why she wasn't in Curaçao like she said she was going to be when he left for work that fateful day. Vernese hoped he would stop talking to her soon, stop asking her questions she would never answer. It would be easier for him if he did.

She positioned herself behind him, several paces back, but there. She was there to receive him when he stumbled away from her lifeless body, head lolling on her neck after being shaken, eyes revealing themselves in their open, cloudy, unseeing horror. Spencer stumbled back under the weight of Karen's unfaltering gaze, her stare trained on him in death unrelentingly, as if she was seeking him out with laser focus. Vernese caught him on his way down to the ground, righting him steadily as she stroked his back, all the while keeping her eye on the people around Karen's body, and on the woman herself. Vernese harbored a sick type of fear of the woman in the pit of her stomach. She almost expected her to stand on those muscular legs and move toward them, muscle atrophy altering her step from a steady gait to a desperate lurch, but forward moving just the same.

Had she imagined the smile on Karen's stilled lips?

"Come, Spencer," Vernese said, keeping her voice low. People were starting to look at them. Vernese didn't think that was a good thing. Vernese and her little group didn't look as disheveled as the lot on the mountain. They had been living in the lap of luxury compared to what these people had experienced. When she thought about it, she realized how absurd it all was. They'd had beds to sleep in, fresh water to drink for most of the time, shelter from the elements. They must have looked like they just got off holiday only to find that their little island was under siege. Like tourists, relaxation still evident on their clean, unblemished skin. Vernese was afraid of what that meant among people who had been peeing in the grass beside where they laid their heads and slept with one eye open as a matter of course.

More than anything, Vernese wanted to go back to the hotel, back to the safety of the four walls, back to the sound of the surf at dawn. But she knew she couldn't. That place was gone forever, overrun, found out. Their future was up. It had to be.

Vernese could hear Spencer mumbling incoherently, calling out to Karen with the softest, most pitiful voice she had ever heard a man use. How long had he been whimpering in that way? Had others heard him too, noticed him, picked him out as an outsider? Vernese cast a glace around the camp, taking stock. Not many people were looking upon them, and that was good. Maybe they still had time to sneak away.

"Spencer," Vernese whispered harshly in his ear. "We must keep going. You can mourn her once we camp, but not here."

He kept mumbling as if he hadn't heard her.

"Do you want to die with her, man?" Vernese shook Spencer's shoulders roughly and he turned to her, snapping out of the trance into which he had fallen to look directly into

Vernese's eyes. "We have to go, Spencer. Now... before we can't."

Spencer looked around and caught the eye of a wiry man sitting cross-legged on the ratty edge of a woven rug that someone had lovingly made for a front room, maybe to go beneath the family dinner table. It was never intended to be used as protection from the roots and dirt and rocks upon which it now lay. The man was becoming more and more interested in Spencer and Vernese's conversation and this made Spencer's back tense. Vernese was right. They were in danger.

Spencer nodded imperceptibly and untangled himself from Vernese's grasp. He cast one last look at Karen, her eyes hooded and glaring now, seeming more accusatory than they had before, before walking away briskly but not alarmingly so. Reaching for Vernese's hand, he moved at a steady pace, getting in front of the group he had lived with since the nightmare had started - the group he would likely die with if what he had seen there was any indication of the way this thing would play out - and went up. They didn't need to talk about it - everyone had felt the disconcerting vibe of the camp. Going further up into the trees might prove to be fruitless, might spell their death, but that was better than offering themselves up to the desperate people they had just met. They climbed in silence, each of them wondering if maybe the next landing would have more resources or if they would meet another group of sick and dying people as unwelcoming as the first bunch had been. Vernese was the only one who wondered if Karen's dead eyes would be there to greet them.

CHAPTER 42

Up.

There it was again.

Up.

Gabby had read the word at the beginning of the chapter about the evacuees from the hotel trying to find higher ground. It didn't mean anything, was literally just a direction in that context, but it stuck with him, around the room inside his head. He looked over to Doug sharply, trying to determine if he was hearing it as well, but it didn't seem that he was. Doug was more focused on the Hunters they had deployed to protect Gabby.

The plan was simple: Send the Hunters to Earth to save Gabby.

Executing that plan was what was putting the fear of God into them. The Hunters couldn't go down to earth the way they were, but Patrick had it on good authority that they did indeed walk the Earth to pick up the dead when they had used up all their chances and were relegated to existence in The Realm.

They could be whatever the situation called for - a nurse clearing the body of all the paraphernalia left useless after the failed attempt at saving life or the dog sitting next to their owner as his shallow breathing stopped on a path in the park. Patrick wondered which person in his final moments was really a Hunter. Was it the nosy little kid peering out of the window over Doug's shoulder, trying to catch a peek at the old man dying in his son's arms, or was it the mailman who stopped in his tracks at the sight of Patrick on the ground? But that isn't how it happened, was it? Patrick strained, reached, trying to remember, but the memory was so far away from him now. It was as if his death existed in a land that lay just beyond the dense fog that separated them - so close, but yet so far. He continued to torture himself, clawing his way through the haze to figure it out. No, he felt sure that there was no child at the window, no mailman, his route broken by a son holding his dying father, no warm sunlight or submission in the strength of his son's strong arms. Just a cold, antiseptic hospital room smelling of blood, piss, and menthol and an unforgiving bed.

Patrick shuddered as if someone had just walked over his grave.

Doug was beside himself with worry about the plan. Patrick couldn't blame him. They had talked for a long time about what they proposed to do, understood how crazy it was to put their faith in those creatures, but had come to the conclusion time and time again that they simply had no choice. Time was not on any of their sides. The serial killer preying on Gabby's area seemed to be closing his circle as he orbited around her, bringing her closer and closer in his sights.

Something had to be done now.

Even as he sent the Hunters down to protect Gabby, Patrick couldn't help but wonder about the unanswered questions that bounced off each other in his head: What was the Hunter's role in those final moments? Was it there to fight off anyone who might try to intervene on the dying's behalf, be it angel, demon, or human? Had someone come to fight for him?

Patrick had not been there to fight for Doug. Had he missed the call? Had he been unable to answer it because he had already been condemned to The Realm? Patrick shook his head, frustrated with himself that he had gone down that rabbit hole. The past was the past and there was nothing he could do to affect it. Gabby was the only future that mattered.

While Patrick tested and retested the Hunters' ability to shapeshift, Patrick's head resounded with the singular word that set his hair on end: Up.

Up.

Up.

Up.

Said in intonations Gabby hadn't used, in voices she could never have recreated.

Up.

Echoing in his head so loud it seemed the sound would burst his ear drums.

Up.

The word so heavy it might crush his soul.

Up, damnit. Up.

Patrick stood and looked at the ceiling, the heat that caused his skin to burn in torment giving way to a chill that raised goosebumps, hard and fat, on his forearms.

"Up," he said aloud, understanding dawning in his mind and attacking his splintering reason.

Patrick left the room without uttering another word.

CHAPTER 43

Pic Paradis was full of scenic ledges, flowering trees, and natural beauty. As Vernese and the others moved up the mountain, they encountered rocky enclaves and cave openings that many on the island didn't know existed. They also came across a patch of relatively flat land near a thicket of bougainvillea trees in the most stunning shade of magenta. It seemed obscene to admire the blooms clustered together and flourishing amidst the mayhem that had befallen the world, but Vernese could no more deny herself the pleasure of looking at it, of being near it, than she could will herself to stop breathing. The bougainvillea meant something, signified some new aspect of their existence and though she didn't understand exactly what it represented, she could feel the power in the sentiment. They would stay there, near the bougainvillea. They would make this perch their home.

"This cave has been abandoned," called Liselle from inside

it, a disembodied voice carried along the wind. Vernese looked at the woman, contemplating her in a way she hadn't in all the time they had been cooped up together in the penthouse. Vernese thought she had been part of housekeeping at the hotel, or maybe she worked in the kitchen there. Her uniform, a slate blue snap-up housedress-looking affair, formless in its simplicity and tasteless in its functionality, didn't distinguish her as either. It didn't distinguish her as anything, really, and Vernese felt a sudden wave of shame that she had virtually looked past the woman, before and after the world fell apart.

Vernese walked over to Liselle, intent upon changing the way she had dealt with her in the past. It was a new day and she was going to be a new person. She stood next to Liselle, peeked into the cave and then, nodding, turned her back to it to look out at the sea. "It has a nice view as well." Vernese and Liselle kept looking out at the water as if it was just another day on the "friendly island" as Saint Martin had been so dubbed. "Is that Anguilla?"

"Likely," said Liselle, a smile forming on her lips. "That'll be nice to look at in the morning... for as long as we can."

For as long as we can. Vernese didn't want to acknowledge the truth in those words, but she had to. They couldn't afford to slip back into the complacency they had felt at the hotel before the knockers came. They would be fools if they did.

"It's big enough to fit us all too," Liselle continued, walking out of the mouth of the cave to join the rest of their ragtag group, leaving Vernese there to look out at the little island in the middle of the vast sea beyond. Vernese heard Liselle telling the others about the cave, about how safe they could be sleeping there, but she didn't join them. Instead, she kept her eyes trained on Anguilla. She wondered how many people were stuck on that island. They didn't have as many resources as Saint

Martin had. Food would have run out a lot faster there. Water too. People might have turned on each other early on, preying on the weak and taking to violence instead of working together to survive. She thought of the streets over there, most of them unpaved and littered with goats and chickens running wild. Were they still there, overtaking the island with their clumsy hooves and copious droppings, or had the vampires thinned the lot, deeming their blood as good as any?

They were flitting in and out of the cave, setting up camp. There was no discussion, no arguing about what they would do - it just was. And that was just as well. Vernese didn't feel like there was any place else to go anyway.

CHAPTER 44

She was so predictable.

Watching from outside, as had been her evening pastime for the past few weeks, she saw Gabby playing in the family room with her kids. She knew that Gabby would keep this up for another 20 minutes, then feed them while singing the alphabet song or some call and response thing she had learned from Sesame Street. Then it would be time for a little TV together, some cute show for little kids that taught about sharing and kindness or some such nonsense, and then it would be time for their joint bath. Thirty minutes of that and then they would be in bed, as they always were, by 8:00 p.m. Then the night was Gabby's. Her husband must work nights, she surmised. He hadn't been home at night during the week the whole time she had been watching. That was the only reason that Gabby was still alive. An altercation wasn't something she could allow to happen, not when she was so close. She didn't want to get caught before the deed was done.

She wanted to do it now, could feel the palms of her hands

itching for it, but she forced herself to wait just a little longer. What if Gabby's husband showed up? What if he had only been out of town and was coming back to resume their regular schedule? The thought irritated her - so much time had been wasted already watching this woman, her boring life and humdrum existence. Her hand twitched and she let it, watching it change from feminine to masculine, undulating under the pressure of the transformation; wavering under the indecisiveness. She clenched her fist, bringing it close to her heart where it would remain until it stilled, feminine and delicate, for now. She looked back at Gabby inside her happy home and smiled ruefully. Happy but bored. She thought, and not for the first time as she crouched in the bushes, that death might very well be welcomed. The thought made her chuckle out loud.

She pulled her eyes away from the window where she watched Gabby and cast her sights toward the neighborhood in which Gabby lived, darting them to and fro. The suburban street, with its tree-dense road verges and matching mailboxes, was pretty much devoid of foot traffic at that hour - the random dog walker or evening lawn waterer had been her only company, and those had been few and far between - and only the occasional car rumbled past. It was a quiet little street. Nobody looked in the direction of Gabby's house. No one had heard her laugh.

Nobody cared enough to pay attention.

Laughter from inside the house called her attention back. Anyone who might have happened by wouldn't have heard anything, so insulated were the houses in Gabby's neck of the woods. But she could hear it. She could hear all, even the thoughts that played in the woman's mind.

Gabby laughed at the upturned face of her little one in the highchair. Autumn - she thought that was the child's name. She had no use for that information now, but soon she would want to know. Soon she would be paying attention to her too.

The mess on the child's face would have turned her stomach - green peas and orange mash spit out and discarded to run down an already sticky chin - if she had the inclination to indulge in emotions she had long ago left behind. But she didn't. She didn't have much use for those anymore. If she had, she would never allow herself to sit where she was, to do what she had done over and over again to them. If she had, she would have abandoned this course, granting the unspoken wish that the soul before her whispered in the cosmos every night about keeping her and her family safe. But she didn't have those sensitivities anymore and would not have been satisfied walking away. She didn't know if she ever would be.

Gabby went upstairs with her innocents, right on schedule. Soon she would come back down with the papers she had been so desperately clinging to for weeks, the ones she fingered absently while singing along to some mindless nursery rhyme or while listening to her husband talk about projects at work. The pages were worn now, dingy, corners curled, but that didn't matter to Gabby. She would sit on the sofa, finding her place almost immediately, and begin reading with fervor the story that had led her right to this place and time like a beacon. She was amazed by the accuracy. It was as if the author had been recounting history instead of telling a fairytale concocted in her head. The likeness had been uncanny too, and that made her want to hear more. But soon she would have to silence Gabby as she had others before her. Soon she would have to send her home.

But not tonight. Tonight, she would settle into her hiding place and enjoy the tale of love and woe as if it were the first time all over again.

CHAPTER 45

SANGUINE PARADISE

They pilfered food and supplies from the resort at the base of the mountain, grabbing up everything left after other people had already cherry picked their way through the pantries.

They fortified their space, protecting the cave where they laid their heads by constructing lookout structures that reminded Vernese of closets pressed as flush to the face of the mountain as possible.

They trapped and slayed wildlife that ventured close, getting used to the taste of rat and snake, all the while hoping for the delicacy of the occasional goat.

The doctor created a makeshift laboratory using found materials and natural elements to create as good a test environment as he could hope for out in the open. He made concoctions to kill the vampires, ones to save the newly bitten but unturned, still hanging on to life by a thread and ones to protect the few unbitten that still lived on the island, a sort of immunization against a vampire attack - none of which worked.

They stared at the mouth of the cave, alternately and, sometimes, collectively, every night in terror of what might peek in to take a look.

They survived, though no one expected to.

The people on the ledge below, the ones who looked like they were knocking on death's door when Vernese and the hotel guests happened upon them, did not. Days later, when a few of them ventured off the ledge they had claimed as their own to see what else (and who else, if they were being honest) was around, they found the lot of them dead where they sat. Vernese was part of that reconnaissance crew, looking for food and potential adversaries. It had saddened her that she wasn't hoping to find fellow survivors, wasn't thinking of people in that way at all anymore. She had no interest in commiserating about the hellish experiences they had endured with anyone that hadn't lived it side by side with her. She didn't feel like she could trust outsiders, as they had come to be in her head now. They would all be like the people on the first ledge who had looked at them with suspicion, their eyes searching greedily for food and water, sizing them up to see if they could best them but knowing they couldn't, not in their degraded states. Vernese knew anyone they encountered now would be like the knockers.

When Vernese stood before the dead people on the landing, some looking as if they hadn't moved since, she felt a strange sensation that wasn't sadness but not joy either. The death of her soul lived in that in between and she mourned it more so than the people before her.

Vernese and crew had gone up the mountain first to see if there were other spots that could be inhabited before heading back down the mountain. The terrain turned rocky and less forgiving as the incline steepened and they quickly learned there wouldn't be anywhere else to run if the vampires came up the mountain after them. And why hadn't they come up yet? The question had taken up residence in her mind shortly after their first night in the lean-tos, exposed as they were to the elements. Surely the vampires knew they were there, Vernese thought. Surely they could... smell them. So, why hadn't they made a move yet? Why had they allowed Vernese and her group, the people on the ledge below them, and anyone else who might have tried inhabiting the mountain to live? It was as if they were marinating, stewing in their juices until properly seasoned and tenderized: ripened. With horror, Vernese realized how true that analogy might be.

Vernese looked out at the view from the end of a slim grassy patch above where their camp lay and watched the sun as it hung low in the sky, painting it with beautiful orange and pink hues. The pastel houses were beautiful against the tropical backdrop. Yellow, pink, and aqua blue facades; white balustrades and Bahama shutters pushed out to provide respite from the sun - all as beautiful in the waning light as they were in full sun. Some of the houses were nestled in the mountains, their porch lights having come on at the hint of sunset to illumi- nate the night as though someone would need safe passage to the front door ever again. It was those things that paralyzed Vernese, mundane and trivial everyday things that continued on even in the face of such change. Roosters still signaled morn- ing, though there were far few doing so now, so many of them having been taken as food. The tide still rolled in and out. Sunset and sunrise lights still flickered on and off as they were set by homeowners that had likely rotted in the rooms enclosed behind those beautiful lights. It reminded Vernese of a story she read while in school about a smart home going through the motions of cooking, cleaning, and preparing a fire for its masters who had been obliterated by a nuclear bomb just outside the house's protective walls. Time goes on, whether we like it or not.

Before Vernese knew it, she was walking again, going out alone, going up. She wanted time to process everything she had seen. She wanted to wipe away the memory of dead eyes and lifeless limbs.

Vernese found herself on the pothole-riddled road that led to the top of Pic Paradis, walking with her body angled toward the ground to keep her balance. She felt compelled to get all the way to the top, to see the beauty of the sea, the lights on Anguilla and St. Barts, the outline of Ile Tintamarre. Were people still alive over there? Questions kept coming back to her, niggling her like an itch she couldn't scratch. Were they looking over at St. Martin and wondering the same thing? Or had vampires landed on their shores and wiped them out the way they had on her little island?

Vernese fought her tears, sniffling loudly as she took in the citrusy smell of the red and yellow lantana growing wild among the bushes.

She reached the top with ease. It was a trip she had taken before, back when she had a job and an apartment - hobbies even - and a day off could be used as she saw fit. She often walked her little island, taking excursions on a whim and ending up at the beach when all was said and done. With over 30 beaches to choose from, she was never at a loss of where to go. The last time she had made the trek up to the top of Pic Paradis she rewarded herself with a dip in the clear water at Friar's Bay. There would be no such luxury that day, she knew, if ever again. Vernese didn't know if she could ever allow herself to indulge in the tranquility that floating in the crystalline waters used to offer her. How could it feel the same when life had changed so drastically? No, she thought. It would feel more like bathing in blood.

Venturing out so late was a mistake that Vernese became aware of when she found herself walking up that neglected road, but her subconscious had forced the issue and there she was. *Don't stay long,* she admonished herself silently, *unless this is the day you want to die.*

The view was as breathtaking as she remembered it.

Vernese was hypnotized by the lights in the French Quarter, where her mother was from. The people of that little village would have been awake at this hour, but not for long. Many would be taking a meal on the porch, talking kindly with their neighbors before settling down for the evening. Morning came fast in villages like this, where the people would set their boats out before the sun rose to fish for the day's bounty. It almost looked as if the scenario she was so familiar with, having experienced it in her grandmother's house when she was a young girl, was taking place right now beneath those lights. She could almost hear the easy banter spoken from house to house over the dirt road between them, a much more formal French than was found in Marigot or Grand Case to mirror the original settlers of the island who once laid their heads in the valley that seemed to be carved by the gods. Vernese wondered if there would be anyone left who remembered that after the vampires did their worst.

The air that blew Vernese's hair off her brow was cool.

Nightfall had come.

As Vernese turned to leave, she noticed a shadow at the far side of the ledge. It was impossibly close to the edge of the clearing, the base of it dangling precariously over the edge, taunting gravity. Vernese turned away but turned back at once, suddenly realizing what it was that she was looking at. A person lurking in the shadows. A man. How long had he been there? Did he slink into place while she looked off at islands whose shores, she imagined, she would never step foot on again or had he been there when she approached, challenging fate in the waning light of day? Vernese wasn't sure, but what she did know was that he had remained silent while she stood unaware and for that there must be a reason. She wasn't sure she wanted to know what that reason was.

"Pardon me, if I have frightened you," a silky tenor voiced, the words carried by the fragrant wind to Vernese's ears. "You were so lost in thought, I didn't want to disturb you."

"How long have you been there?" Vernese asked, forgoing pleasantries like 'Hello' and "Nice evening we're having, right?". The days of casual conversation seemed long gone as they stood on top of the mountain that was their salvation, their last hope. Now it was all about motivation and intention. Yet -

"Long enough to watch dusk turn to night," he said, clipping his words. He wondered if she noticed that he had more he wanted to say. He wondered if she could feel how much he wanted to approach her, caress her cheek, lean in and smell her hair.

Vernese watched as the man stepped from the shadows and into the light, which was fast disappearing. Even in the dimming light, she could see him, his dark hair swooped over his forehead messily, listing to the side in a curly bob that kissed his shoulders, the rest tucked behind his ear revealing a masculine neck that captivated her. His eyes were a warm hazel, seeming to light themselves from within. His skin, rich and brown, danced with amber that accented the curve of his nose and the strength of his brow. His cheeks were high, his jawline chiseled. His mouth, shapely lips over straight, white teeth, held an acquiescing smirk that made her insides quiver. "I got here a few minutes before you."

Vernese forced herself to look away, mentally poking herself in the ribs, begging herself to get a grip, but having marked trouble doing so. Gesturing toward the shadowed corner where he had stood moments before with her chin, she asked, "Why did you hide there?"

He took another step toward her and she was startled to find that she too was moving toward him.

"I'd hardly call it hiding," he said with a chuckle that set her more at ease than her rational mind was comfortable with. She could feel the smile spreading across her own face to match his. It wasn't a broad smile, neither of theirs was, and for that alone, she appreciated him. Their smiles were ones of shared struggle and acknowledgement of the momentary reprieve their time together at the top of Pic Paradis represented. She gave into it, let herself have that moment with this beautiful stranger, because times like those would likely be few and far between in the dismal future they faced.

Beautiful? She had referred to him as 'beautiful'. Vernese couldn't remember ever doing that before – calling a man such a thing. There had never been a context in the *bad bwoy* culture the men surrounding her tried to portray. But now, looking at this man who seemed to have been created by an artist's hand, each detail of his face perfectly designed, she knew that 'beautiful' didn't even come close.

Vernese had to get herself under control.

She almost shook her head to try and get her thoughts in order – was actually about to, but realized that he was closer to her now, close enough to touch.

Aaron noticed how close they were before Vernese had. They had taken steps toward each other together the way that people sometimes did when talking in open spaces. It felt normal, except that he could hear her heart beating out of her chest, could hear the blood rushing in her veins, could smell the sweet fragrance of it on her skin as though it prickled there, collecting on her skin like perspiration. No, there was nothing normal about that, Aaron reminded himself. He wanted to take a step back, to gain some distance between him and the beautiful woman before him, but he couldn't, not now. She was the one he had been looking for, the one he saw from the ship - *the* one. He knew it the moment she approached the landing where he stood watching the sunset, knew it as he made his way to the very spot upon which they stood. He could sense her, could pick her out from among the others to whom she clung, desperately trying to avoid the inevitability of their deaths. He knew she would come to the landing before she knew it herself, so he waited there, waited for the very moment when she would see him.

And... now what?

He almost leaned in, almost let his thirst take over and force him to sample her, but he stilled himself. Aaron would no sooner drink her blood that he would his own, no matter how much the thirst threatened to consume rational thought. She was his beacon. He had found her.

Aaron fought the urge to caress her arm. They were close. Close enough to touch.

"What would you call it then?" Vernese had found her tongue.

He didn't bother to suppress the sigh that forced its way out of his mouth before he spoke again, "I guess we both have things to think about."

Vernese looked down. He was right, of course. The past few weeks had been worse than any dystopian fiction she had ever read. Everyone had been affected in one way or another. That someone else had found solace looking out over the water shouldn't have been a surprise to her. She was disappointed in herself for thinking the worst, especially of someone with such kind eyes.

What?

"What's your name?"

CHAPTER 46

SANGUINE PARADISE

Vernese spit the question out, choosing the wrong emotion to express herself as she dealt with her inner turmoil. Why was she thinking the things that she was about this man? Why did she feel herself, the real Vernese who had hidden herself in a locked closet, tucked away in her mind to avoid the horrors her body encountered every day - why was *she* coming out to play right now? What was it about this man that made Vernese feel safe when she knew she shouldn't? He hadn't said anything to make her feel either way - there was just something about him that made her let her guard down. Was it his smile, as insecure and affected as her own? Was it the fact that he too found peace in nature, in feeling the wind flowing through his hair? Was it the curve of his lips or his broad shoulders? Vernese looked away from him and out over the water, turned inky black as nightfall. She heard more than felt the loud breath expelling from her mouth.

It was late.

Where was his accent from? The States? The UK?

"Aaron," he said, his face softening a bit, seeming to take pleasure in saying his name aloud.

"Aaron," Vernese repeated, though she thought she had only done so in her head. She was surprised to hear her own voice caressing the syllables and quickly quieted herself when she did. But still... *Aaron.*

"And yours?

"Hmm?" Vernese snapped her eyes toward him. She hadn't realized she had left the conversation, lost in thought. She couldn't put her finger on what she had been thinking. Just his name tumbling over itself in her head, curling, weaving, floating as if on water.

Aaron.

"I asked what your name was, but if you don't want to-"

"No, no, I'm sorry. I was," Vernese looked into Aaron's eyes, looking more emerald green the closer Vernese looked, and felt like she might fall into them.

He smiled at her.

She smiled back.

"Vernese," she said as she looked at him. His returned stare intimated something that she couldn't read. She regretted the blink that forced her eyes to look away. When she opened them again, the message was gone.

"My name is Vernese."

"Vernese... an old name for such a young woman." He wanted to ask her why she chose that name, her middle name, over her first name, Onika, but knew he shouldn't. To do so would be to reveal that he knew more than he should; that he could read her as easily as he would a book. He didn't want to admit that he was not like her in any way and could never be again. Aaron didn't want it to be over before it even began.

"It will be an old name for an old woman, God willing," Vernese replied, hoping to sound coy but thinking herself flippant instead.

Aaron's lips curled into a smile. For the first time in decades, he was at a loss for words.

"It was my grandmother's name," Vernese offered, her voice low and shy. "Everybody always said I have an old soul, so I just took to using my middle name instead of my first."

"And what is that," Aaron said, a little too eagerly. He wondered if she noticed. Had he been a living man, he feared his heart would have been beating loudly enough to hear from miles away. "Your first name, I mean?"

Vernese smiled at him, casting her eyes down toward her feet as she felt the heat rise in her cheeks. She didn't know why she was feeling so bashful all of a sudden. It wasn't as if they were talking about anything lewd or getting married or - Vernese jolted at the thought and then immediately looked away nervously. *Did he see that? Why is my mind bouncing all over the place all of a sudden? Why am I thinking about marriage?*

"He only asked about my first name," she breathed and clamped her mouth shut almost right away. She had said that aloud. Had he heard?

Vernese's face felt hotter than it ever had before.

Aaron heard and saw it all and fought to keep his face straight. Inside he was dancing, laughing, enjoying every second of it. Whatever this was, it was affecting her too. The prospect made him giddy.

"Onika," Vernese said, her voice hoarse. She cleared it quietly, trying to remember her mother's lessons about being a lady when what she really wanted to do was cough loudly into her hand. "My first name is Onika."

"Onika," Aaron said out loud, finally able to speak it without restriction. He repeated it again, letting the sound caress his ears. It was exotic, alluring, the accent in the second syllable commanding attention from all who would listen. *Onika.* He would hear this name repeated in his dreams.

"Beautiful," Aaron said, as he allowed his eyes to level onto hers. She returned the look for as long as she could before turning away, flushed. Maybe he shouldn't have done it, maybe he shouldn't have stared at her so intensely, but he couldn't help himself. She was infinitely more captivating up close than she had been from afar.

Vernese wanted to meet his eyes again but found it difficult to do. The way he spoke, so unabashed and free, was unlike anything she had ever heard before. It's not that the men she had been around hadn't said what they wanted - that was quite the opposite, in fact. Caribbean men weren't ones to mince words when they saw something they liked. Their antics put American catcalling to shame. But this was different. This man, this Aaron from a place wholly different from hers, wasn't using the simple words she was used to, ones that left no chance at confusion and left her cold in the process. Instead, he used inferences, perhaps even double entendres. She didn't know whether she should feel complimented or aroused and felt a strange combination of reactions because of it. Aaron kept her delightfully on edge, already.

"Where are you from, Aaron?" Vernese breathed, losing track of herself for a moment. The question seemed to float in the air between them, dancing on the breeze created by her breath. Aaron smiled - he couldn't help himself. He noticed her parted lips, the slight increase in her breathing, the look in her eyes, delectably faraway and at the same time enraptured in the present. She felt it too. He couldn't stop the smile from forming on his lips.

Vernese smiled too, hers self-conscious. She looked away from him and over to the vast black nothingness that was the sea at night. Something in Vernese scolded her; being there so late was dangerous, too dangerous, more dangerous than anything she had done since the outbreak. Being there then was like tempting lions with raw meat. If one of the vampires saw them up there, just the two of them, it would be over. She knew this just as well as she knew her own name. But there was something about Aaron that made her ignore what she knew to be true. Aaron made her feel safe. He hadn't done anything specific to bring that emotion from her, but there it was. His shoulders were broad, his arms strong; the muscles seemed to be chiseled naturally rather than cultivated in a gym. His legs looked powerful and his waist was slender. Vernese's logical mind tried to tell her that none of this was a match for a blood-sucking vampire, but she didn't listen. Listening would have meant she would have to leave the peak they stood upon and take shelter. She would have to leave Aaron. She wasn't ready for that.

"You have an accent..." she tried, hoping he would start talking again so she could listen to it once more, the gentle lilt nestled in his calming tenor feeling more and more like the elixir she had needed. Where had she heard his accent before? Her mind cycled through snippets of interviews on television and conversations she'd had with vacationers. Was that a Scottish accent? Irish? Scandinavian - what?

"America- New York," he said, pulling her back from her thoughts. She snapped her head toward him as if he had shocked her, eyes wide. Aaron couldn't help but feel like he was melting into them. "I'm from America."

"New York? You don't sound like - I mean, I've met people from there and you - I don't know, you just-"

Aaron laughed and then so did Vernese and oh, did he like the sound of her laughter. He tried to call up the thickest New York accent he could, but he could only find a cheap version of Pesci's Tommy DeVito from *Goodfellas*. This caused Vernese to laugh even harder.

"Are you sure you're from New York?" she teased between gasps.

"No, really, I am. I'm just not from the part you might have heard about most often. I didn't live in the city."

"No bass pumping out of boomboxes carried on people's shoulders?"

It was Aaron's turn to laugh, and he did so heartily. "You've definitely been watching too many movies."

"That's all we see out here about New York. Rap music, drugs, and - "

"Yeah, not my scene." Aaron didn't know why he stopped Vernese, cutting her off mid-sentence. He only knew that he had to interject, to change the course of the conversation somehow. He didn't want her to imbed those images in her mind to remember when she thought about this night. Aaron didn't want anything negative to be associated with him when she thought about their conversation later. *If* she thought about their conversation later.

"We used to call where I'm from 'upstate'. It's only about forty minutes away from Manhattan, but it's like another world." He saw her eyes shift and knew she wasn't listening to details like borough names and colloquialisms. Other things occupied her mind. That made him feel warm in ways he hadn't experienced in a long time.

"And you?" Aaron continued, realizing he had spent too long looking at her lips. "Are you from here?"

"Yes," Vernese replied, willing her voice to find itself. "Not far from Simpson Bay proper."

Aaron's stare was empty and full of emotion at the same time. Now he knew how it felt to be lost in a conversation. She smiled at him indulgently and pointed in the general direction of where she lived.

"Down that way, not too far from the beach."

Aaron nodded and smiled too. God, it was so easy to do that with her. *But not too wide, and not for too long*, he admonished himself. *Be careful, Aaron.*

He wanted to ask her if she went to the beach often, if she enjoyed swimming or if, after living on an island, the beach was just as mundane as anything else. He wanted to ask her about herself, what she liked to eat, what her hobbies were. He wanted to find out as much about her as he could, but instead, he stood smiling, his rapid-fire questions colliding in his mind and rendering him mute.

"How did you end up here?"

The question caught Aaron off guard. He was sure she saw it, how shaken he was. Aaron was suddenly sure she knew who he was, had seen him from the shore looking at her before, when he was just a vampire among many cruising to her island in search of food. Fear flashed in his mind, then anger at himself for thinking it would have been any different. He couldn't have hidden himself from her, not for long. And what was he expecting of her anyway? Did he think she would let him bite her throat before taking her into his arms? Did he think she would let him feed from her every day, blood for a kiss? In that instant, Aaron cursed his wretched sentimentality. He felt the primal urges he shared with his brethren well in his stomach, waiting to erupt and knew he couldn't have held back that need forever, if even for a night. How stupid could he have been.

Vernese looked at him expectantly, eyes innocent and interested.

Aaron could have fallen to his knees thanking whatever deity would listen to a condemned soul like his for not letting his bloodlust flash across his face for Vernese to see.

"Here? In St. Martin?" Aaron hedged. He wasn't ready for this - whatever it was - to be over, but he would make it quick if he had to, for her sake.

"On Pic Paradis on St. Martin after the outbreak or event or whatever people are calling it. Why didn't you leave, go back to New York to your family when you had the chance?" Vernese spoke openly. She was happy that he was there – happy that they had met, but still she wondered why it was so. If he had gotten himself to the island, surely he could have gotten himself off, even at the inflated prices that the ferryman proposed in those last days. Why hadn't he gotten out of there?

"Me, I'm stuck here - born, raised, and will likely die here, but you... maybe you could have gotten out," she finished, letting her voice trail off. Something about his face had changed while she spoke and she was instantly sorry. Maybe he wasn't a man of means at all. Maybe he worked on the freighters that came in every other day carrying supplies. Maybe he couldn't pay the inflated fare to get back home – maybe he couldn't have paid the regular price either. She had pressed him and now he was upset. The thought bothered Vernese to her core.

"Hey, I don't mean to pry, it's just..." she didn't know what to say to fix it, not really.

She hoped she was speaking under her breath when she said

she would rather be anywhere but there, but Vernese wasn't sure.

The guilt that tore at Aaron's heart was worse than anything he had experienced in his immortal life. He had lost friends over the time he had been a vampire, to overzealous hunters and suicide alike. He had murdered to live and murdered for sport. But nothing had felt like this. Nothing had touched him like the sadness in Vernese's eyes. He would take care of her, he knew then. Come what may.

"I - I didn't make it out in time," Aaron said, scrambling for words. He had started talking before he was ready, so eager to give Vernese the forgiveness her eyes begged for. "By the time I realized what –" Aaron paused for effect, letting his words break as he created a story that would placate her. "Everyone was gone... I got stuck."

"Unlucky," she said sadly, determined to let the issue drop. Vernese diverted her eyes yet again. She was finding it hard to look at him for long.

"Hmm," Aaron replied, needing to say something to fill the space.

And then they were silent. They were standing together on a mountaintop in the dark of night, saying nothing. And it felt right. They alternated between looking at each other and looking out at the sea where the moon shone bright. Both sights were equally captivating. Neither one of them wanted to stir, even as the wind grew cooler for Vernese. Were it not for a whisper carried on the wind to Vernese's ears, she thought she might have stayed there with Aaron forever.

Spencer was calling for her as inconspicuously as he could. His voice sounded as loud as an air horn in the amiable silence Vernese and Aaron had adopted.

"Shh, Spencer," Vernese hissed, turning toward the mouth

of the landing. He was close enough to hear but, but not close enough to see them. "I'm fine."

"Wat a gwaan?" Spencer replied, worried. "Dark come."

"Nothing. I'm jus-" Vernese smiled shyly at Aaron. Aaron hoped she couldn't see the hunger in his eyes as he smelled Spencer's blood.

"Coo yah. Yuh haffi come," Spencer said, adamantly telling Vernese to come inside as though he was speaking to a teenager lingering too long with her date at the front door. It didn't help that Vernese felt that very same way.

"Yuh mi dweet."

Vernese could still feel Spencer's presence. He was waiting by the road for her, swiveling his head to and fro anxiously. She could almost smell his fear. Under normal circumstances, this display of protectiveness would have made her smile – that her little group had come to care for one another was an unexpected result of the horror they called life, but now she just wanted him to go away so that she could be alone with Aaron again.

"Soon come, Spencer," Vernese said, looking over her shoulder at him and waving him off. Spencer took the hint and made his way back down the road, letting out the beginning of a sigh at first, then swallowing the sound earnestly, remembering where he was.

Vernese turned back to look at Aaron. There was something in his face that she couldn't read. It was only there for a moment, a quick flash of emotion that wasn't there before, and then it was gone. He had been looking in Spencer's direction while she was talking to him. Did he wonder who he was to Vernese? The thought made color spring onto her cheeks. Could he have been jealous that someone cared enough to brave the perils of the night to find her? Should she tell him he was just a guy that she worked with, that his girlfriend or wife (Vernese still didn't know which) had died on the first landing and that he had been extra vigilant about taking care of all the women in their group since then? Or should she let it lie, act like she didn't notice the emotion that crossed his face, and let him ask if he really wanted to know? These questions enthralled Vernese, making a smile that wasn't the least bit coy play on her lips.

She looked back at Aaron. He was smiling at her too.

"Are you out here alone?" Vernese said instead, chagrined enough to let the weird look on Aaron's face go unmentioned. "Do you have a place to stay? People to be with?"

She surprised herself with this question. She hadn't talked with her people to find out if inviting someone would be ok. They had never discussed the prospect. Of all the situations they expected to find themselves in, inviting someone to join their unit was never one of them. She remembered how they reacted when Dr. LaFleur had come floating up to them in those early days. They were less than hospitable. But surely they could see that there was nothing to be afraid of with Aaron, right? They would feel the same way about him that she did... right?

Aaron removed the conflict like it was never there.

"Yes, I do." Neither of them did much to try to mask their disappointment. "My friends are probably wondering where I am too."

Vernese nodded and cast her eyes around. It was late.

Very late.

There was nothing but the sound of their breathing for a few moments, hers deep and resigned, his mimicked, deliberate. He was hopeful that he was hitting the right cadence.

"Well, maybe I'll..." Vernese started, unsure how to say goodbye, not wanting to say goodbye.

"I live right..."

"Maybe I'll see you again... here?" Aaron filled in, shooting for casual but betting he sounded more desperate than he intended.

"Yes, sure. Maybe," Vernese finished, nodding vigorously, unable to stop herself.

"Maybe we will. Or you will, we-" They laughed again, full-bodied, unabashedly, in sync.

Vernese angled herself toward the road, deciding it would be best to go before Spencer came back and forcibly dragged her away.

"I'll see you again, Aaron," she said with a smile. She let her eyes linger a moment longer before turning away entirely and jogging down the hill.

Aaron watched her go reluctantly. He wanted to give her his number and get hers in return. He wanted to promise to call her later, do something that would assure her that he was interested - that he would be there - but those days were long gone. He would just have to wait. The thought drove him mad.

Aaron turned to look at the sea once more after she had moved out of his line of sight, trying to gather his resolve to leave the mountain. He needed that moment for two reasons: the most interesting creature he had laid eyes on in decades, was there - right there, within his grasp. The second reason, the one that might be his undoing, troubled him most. Vernese, his Vernese, was there on the mountain, surrounded by the untainted blood that ran through her compatriots' veins. Aaron could smell them all from where he stood, could hear the blood pumping through their veins. It made his mouth water. And god, was he hungry.

CHAPTER 47

Mal reached the door to the room that had been Joanne's cell faster than he intended. He knew the way like the back of his hand and had made the trip countless times over the past few years, but he found himself standing in front of it before he was ready all the same. This wasn't just a visit; it wasn't like any of the other times he had been there. This was the last time he would stand there, the imaginary barrier between them, adhering to illusion to the last. It was the end of a long story, even if only one of them knew it.

Mal didn't want to go inside.

He turned away from the door to pace the hallway again as he had done on many occasions. He used to plunge himself into thought of how to save her, how to make it so that she could actually come out of the room and stand by his side. But no matter how many ways he thought about the situation, regardless of the variables he plugged in or took out of the equation, he couldn't make it work. Joanne had woken up one day knowing things she shouldn't have known. She was doomed to die the true death from that moment on.

Did she know it? Mal often wondered about that. Just like she seemed to recognize him at times, at least some part of him, whether it be his voice or his essence, she seemed to know that she would never make it out of that room. How did that manifest for her? Did she know that to die in The Realm was to die the true, soulless death of the abyss? Mal hoped she didn't. He hoped she would go to her end without knowing that there was nothing - no existence at all - left.

He wanted her to live.

He wanted her to live because she didn't deserve to die.

He wanted her to live because he needed her.

Mal wanted Joanne to live because he needed her to be with him.

But none of that mattered anymore. Joanne had to die. She always had to, and, at long last, it was time.

Mal ignored the useless emotions his mind tried to throw at him, assaulting his eyes with the prickling of tears and his stilled heart with the heavy thumping of fear and dismay. It wasn't real, none of it was. He needed to understand that – to come back to the reality of the life he was living now- to do what must be done. He couldn't think of how her eyes squeezed shut when she smiled or how she worried her lip when she was puzzling through something. How her hair felt under his hand. How her lips tasted.

No.

Mal stepped away from the door, his chest heaving stupidly. "It must be done," he spat into the empty corridor. "It must be done and it is you who must do it."

Mal took one last deep breath to calm his heightened nerves and waited for the crisis to abate. His body was ready before his mind was. His legs carried him inside the room before he had finished saying his goodbyes.

Joanne sat in the far corner of the room, barely visible in the shadows. Mal was tempted to command the shadows to take leave, the walls to melt away, the façade to disappear, but he thought better of it. Why frighten her in the end? Why make her see that everything she had endured since dying - the seclusion, the cold - had been fake? There was no reason to be cruel. Not to her.

His eyes searched the darkness instead, trying to make out her silhouette. He could hear her breathing, almost panting, her body reverting to its remembered depictions of anxiety and fear as it always did. He could almost see her chest heaving from the effort.

"She knows," Joanne breathed in a small voice, one unlike any he had ever heard her use in all their lifetimes together. "You're too late."

CHAPTER 48

The door was open. Ajar.

Sort of.

Tara thought she could see a sliver of light at the seam where the door would meet the frame and close flush. She thought that if she could just get to it without being seen, she could sneak inside, find a hiding place, and then...

Then what?

Tara was appalled by her lack of planning.

What would she do if she got inside? Sneak around the house, looking in corners and crevices for... for what? The boogeyman? She knew him all too well already.

Tara's eyes darted to and fro wildly in their sockets as she watched the door flutter, almost undulate, moving under the command of a breeze she could not feel. She had to make a move before the door slammed itself shut, taking away her opportunity.

Tara stood, taking a step forward before realizing what she was doing. She hunched down, dropping as though shot. Then she crawled, advancing, but in smaller, camouflaged steps. Tara made it to the door uncontested, with only the bare bones of a plan constructed in her head, but it was better than nothing. That's what she told herself, anyway. *Flying by the seat of your pants yet again*, she thought, more than a little disappointed in herself.

1. Go inside.
2. Find a hiding place.
3. Find Patrick and Doug.
4. Kill them.
5. Find Mal.
6. Kill him.
7. Find others or end it.

That was the plan.

As she put her hand on the inordinately warm doorknob, grasping it from a low crouch on the splintered porch, Tara didn't think she would get more than four steps inside before a Hunter ripped out her throat.

CHAPTER 49

SANGUINE PARADISE

It was their spot, Anse Marcel.

Vernese and Aaron had made it their spot after their third meeting on the mountain in the waning light of the day. It was secluded; since hurricane Irene had leveled the hotels and restaurants in the little enclave, people had avoided it, choosing beaches that had recovered faster instead. After the vampire outbreak it had become a forgotten gem. Though the water was more shallow than Vernese liked to swim in, it was perfect to stroll through as she and Aaron had taken to doing at just around dusk. One could overlook the roofless structures and scattered debris if it meant uninterrupted time with someone special. Vernese and Aaron had talked about their lives before the outbreak, telling each other about the minutiae of their daily routines that they would never participate in again, not the way they had experienced it before. Aaron was careful not to say anything that would call time frame into question. It was difficult to speak in riddles the way he had to, but he didn't want Vernese to know that he wasn't of her time, wasn't like her in any way at all. He focused, instead, on being from different countries. He made much of the different types of food they had been exposed to, admitting freely that her description of Locri made his mouth water in ways that his mother's meatloaf never had.

As Aaron tried to make the comparison between the lolos that had littered the roads all over the island selling BBQ ribs and chicken to people on the side of the road to food carts selling hot dogs and gyros in city centers in the US, he fell deeper in love with the woman before him. She had dropped her guard, which released her brow, giving way to an animation he hadn't noticed in her face before. From the way she squinted to watch the sun set, surveying the brilliant pinks and oranges that painted the sky to the way her dimples showed when she let her unabashed smile shine bright, she was beautiful. Aaron saw the hope that had once dwelled within her, even the bit she had been unaware of before it had been smothered by the seeming apocalypse. It *was* an apocalypse, Aaron corrected himself, irritated that some part of him still tried to reach for a silver lining in the darkest of nights. He had brought on the apocalypse that had changed Vernese forever, he and his kind. There was nothing he could do to change that.

"Where'd you go?" Vernese asked, her eyes still smiling as the sun winked goodnight to her. "Seemed like you were a million miles away."

"I was," Aaron breathed as he wrapped his arms around her shoulders and drew her closer. They had started doing that the day before, the hugging, the holding hands. He had even touched his lips to her cheek, emboldened. She hadn't pulled away from his touch, hadn't started at how hard his skin felt or how cold, so Aaron did it. He kissed her. He wanted to do it again too.

Vernese let her hands rest on the small of Aaron's back, clasping together, locking him in.

She didn't find him uncomfortable to touch, odd to look at, unbearable to withstand. So, Aaron stayed, thanking the gods for that simple mercy. They started walking again, Vernese enjoying the wet sand beneath her toes. She was thinking about something; Aaron could tell by the way she nibbled her bottom lip. He gave her time to speak, all the while fearing what she might say.

Finally, Vernese asked, "Is there a woman waiting for you wherever you went just now?"

Aaron tightened his grip on her shoulders, being careful not to crush the life out of her. He thought of Cecelia, her beautiful eyes staring into his soul as he told her to wait for him, wait until he was sure, wait for him to decide.

He hadn't realized he had stopped walking until Vernese turned toward him. Something in the way he looked at her made her lower her eyes and look away.

"You don't have to answer- I mean, I'm sure there must be-"

"Vernese..." Aaron started but there was really nothing to say. He leaned into her, his eyes dropping to settle on her lips. He felt butterflies as she pressed a gentle kiss to the corner of his mouth before biting her bottom lip again, nerves getting the best of her. Aaron didn't know when he had last felt exhilaration like that. Stomach flutters and stuttering utterances were what he and Cecelia were about - they were all passion and heat. But this was different. Had he felt that way with Gillian, way back when he was a mortal man? Had someone before her made him feel as if he might happily fall over as long as it was into her arms? Aaron couldn't remember a time so sweet, so innocent. He felt positively nervous as he leaned into Vernese.

She let go of her bottom lip.

His lips quivered in response.

Her lips remained parted, waiting.

Aaron's tongue darted out to lick his own.

And then he kissed her.

It was tentative at first, Aaron afraid she would feel the chill of death on his mouth and recoil in disgust; Vernese in trepidation. It had been a long time since she had felt anything like what she was feeling right then. Aside from the moment with Andrew in the store, nothing had stirred within her for what felt like years. She had been too focused on her career, too focused on making something of herself to waste time on love. And besides, no one had turned her head. But, in the middle of mayhem, when the wolves were literally at their heels, Vernese found herself falling for someone. Hard. Aaron was different from her in so many ways, but alike in many too. It wasn't the frivolous stuff - life music or pop culture - that made them click. It was in the soul. Vernese could feel

... WHAT? COME BACK TO THIS... WHAT CONNECTION DOES VERNESE FEEL?

DOES AARON FEEL THE SAME WAY?

THINK!! TRY TO REMEMBER WHAT YOU SAW.

DOES THEIR SHARED CONNECTION MEAN ANYTHING?

CHAPTER 50

Gabby couldn't help but laugh as she was pulled out of the storyline by her grandmother's random notes. It was kind of cool, when she sat back and thought about it. Gabby was getting a glimpse of the creative process. Not many people did, so she considered herself lucky. Most people only saw the finished product, all polished and perfect, but Gabby was looking at misspellings, run-on sentences, shifting tense, continuity errors, plot holes, and raw notes that were sometimes scribbled hastily in the margins and sometimes penned in big, bold capital letters, like the last batch.

Peeking behind the curtain ain't always pretty.

Gabby got up from her spot on the sofa - she had worn a comfortable dip in one of the cushions because she sat there reading so much - and turned on the Keurig for a cup of coffee. As she listened to the water whirring in the machine, waking up and warming in preparation for her hazelnut coffee fix, she rinsed out the mug sitting on the counter and looked lazily out of the kitchen window. The fluorescent ceiling light highlighted her head and shoulders with an outline of pure, almost electric white, her frame almost backlit. She could see wisps of hair sticking out of the messy bun she had knotted hours ago, some of the strands standing up to halo her head. She could see the movement of her shoulders as her hands worked by rote, cleaning the mug in the sink to use again, swirling the sponge first inside then around the rim. Suddenly it wasn't her silhouette that she was looking at in the window. Her broad shoulders had been replaced by a thinner frame, bony clavicles reaching toward a slender neck... her grandmother's neck. She remembered how much smaller her grandmother's frame appeared in pictures; she was the only one in Gabby's family with such delicate features. It was Joanne's reflection, no question. Her arms moved in the same motion as Gabby's had, rinsing the mug, setting it in the strainer to dry, then rinsing the soap out of the sponge, but the movements were smaller. Gabby trailed her eyes over her form, the outline of the neck, then to the chin, then to face, peering as closely as she could at the reflection in the glass, but unable to make out any details. The hair was different. It hung loose, wavy, to her shoulders. It looked like one side had been tucked behind an ear and Gabby could see a dangly earring twinkling in that strange white light. Gabby cocked her head to the side and the visage did the same, revealing a sharper jawline than Gabby possessed.

Imagination or not, Gabby couldn't suppress a smile as she looked at her grandmother's reflection.

Her lips were moving.

Gabby's grandmother, Joanne - her lips were moving.

Gabby leaned closer to the window, trying to catch the light on her lips so that she could read them.

Remember... you...

Joanne wasn't looking at Gabby. She wasn't looking at the

sponge anymore either. Her head was turned a bit, casting her almost completely in the shadows, her hidden eyes looking off in the distance, as if she saw something across the street that interested her. Gabby tried to make out her face again. What was she looking at? Had she looked concerned? Nervous? Gabby didn't think so. She looked like she was thinking about something, her book maybe, like Gabby had snuck up on her, catching her mid-thought as she mumbled to herself under her breath. Gabby smiled at the idea. Oh, how she wished she could have done that in real life, snuck up on her grandmother as she had been thinking of vampires and sand.

Yes, that overactive imagination has made its way to me too, Gabby thought. *Definitely.*

Gabby looked in the same direction that Joanne's eyes seemed turned towards and saw nothing but darkened bushes and trees. She smiled coyly, like she had been let in on a side joke, as she surveyed the quiet evening outside. She imagined that Joanne had stood in her own kitchen looking out at the street in the same way, trying to gather her thoughts about the manuscript. Had nothing spoken to her on that last day when she looked out upon the bushes and trees? Had the characters in her head gone as silent as this night was?

Gabby would never know.

She could feel the smile on her face but saw something entirely different in her grandmother's reflected countenance. Joanne's mouth seemed to gape, the tips of her teeth showing between lips that quivered uncontrollably. The whites of her eyes, huge and almost comically round, were faintly visible above the blackened space in the middle of her face.

Gabby's smile faltered.

Beyond Joanne's terrified reflection, through it, outside of the glass and out into the night, Gabby saw something moving.

Black, it was all black, except for its white eyes. It possessed the body of a man but the grace of a woman. Lithe, strong, focused, balanced. At first the steps were tentative, creeping along the periphery then retreating to hide behind the bushes or a tree.

Black body, white eyes. Black body, white eyes. Black body, white eyes.

As Gabby watched, the thing outside (because that's what Gabby knew it was - a thing, not a person. There was something about the way it moved...) drew closer, taking more confident strides. It was coming closer, closer, right up to the window.

Joanne raised a skeletal hand to strike out at it.

Gabby shrieked, her hand raising to shield her eyes.

Then silence.

Then water running.

Gabby opened her eyes behind her hand and willed herself to move it out of the way so that she could see. Gabby's body obeyed reluctantly, pulling the hand down finger by finger. She looked. There was nothing outside except bushes and branches.

Gabby screamed when the window was suddenly flooded with light. She took a few steps away from the sink reflexively, her mind deciding that flight was the option at this moment, period - fighting was for another day. But as the sound of car doors slamming, an engine turning over, and finally, the lights moving closer to Gabby's house as the car exited the driveway across the street and made its way out of the community, Gabby felt more than a little silly. She snickered first then had a genuine, gut-clenching laugh at herself. She had spooked herself good.

Gabby looked over at the manuscript laying open on the sofa, her laughter dying down. She looked back at the window, a little afraid of what she might find, but resolved to do it anyway. Her own silhouette greeted her, wispy hair and all. She sniffed, more relieved that she wanted to admit.

Gabby turned the water off and put the sponge down to dry. She turned her back to the window, intending to walk back over the sofa, grab the manuscript, and go upstairs, thoughts of a cup of coffee abandoned, but she couldn't make her legs move. Suddenly she felt very aware of the fact that she was the only one downstairs, maybe even the only one awake in the house. And there was a black thing outside lurking in the bushes by the house. A black thing with white eyes, eyes that looked like they were glowing in the moonlight. No pupils, no irises, just white, white, white.

The hair on the back of Gabby's neck stood up.

Without looking at what she was doing, Gabby reached over to the coffeemaker and jerked the plug out of the wall, her hand knocking into it, water sloshing around inside. With eyes looking forward and unmoving as if she wore blinders, she made a beeline to the sofa, snatched up the manuscript, and nearly ran to the stairs leading up to her bedroom, taking them two at a time, calling her husband's name all the while.

CHAPTER 51

Aaron found himself on the floor clutching his chest, his mind muddied with surprise. He hadn't thought it would be that simple; he had expected to be leveled. Thomas had pulled his punch, and for that Aaron should have been happy, but he wasn't - not yet. He braced himself for another blow, one that he would struggle to recover from before dawn.

"What the hell are you thinking, Aaron?"

Here comes the monologue, Aaron thought. *Thomas won't be able to resist.*

"Jesus, do you know what would have happened if the others had been with me?"

Thomas had a point and Aaron knew it. He nodded sheepishly, not bothering to raise his eyes to meet his friend's. He didn't need to see them to know they were blazing red; Aaron could feel Thomas' anger - it was palpable, like humidity in the summer air.

He could still feel Vernese's soft lips on his, parting his, her tongue licking into his mouth. He -

"Are you fucking listening to me, Aaron, you piece of shit?"

A gruff snap right in front of his face, forced him back to the present. An angry Thomas looking at him from under a furrowed brow.

Aaron didn't know what was reflected on his face, but it wasn't what Thomas wanted to see. Thomas stumbled backwards, his entire body emoting incredulity, if that was even possible. He ran his hands over his face and hair so harshly he might have taken his skin off if he were a mortal man. "He doesn't get it," Thomas said to himself as he looked at the cars left waiting for owners who would never come back to the parking lot where he had unceremoniously dropped Aaron on his ass, talking just loud enough for Aaron to hear him.

Aaron said nothing. He said nothing because, while he understood why Thomas was angry, he really didn't care.

Thomas turned to Aaron, his face all raised eyebrows and surprise.

"You *don't* get it, do you?"

"I-"

"No, let me enlighten you, Aaron, since you seem to need a little help understanding," Thomas said as he approached where Aaron sat, still on his butt but no longer clutching his chest and gasping for air. Pointing in the general direction of where they had left Vernese, Thomas lost his grip on his frustration and yelled, "That girl is a human!" His voice boomed in the night air. "Flesh and blood. *Living* flesh."

Aaron closed his eyes and nodded. "I know, Thomas-"

"Bullshit, you know," Thomas cut in. "She's *food* for us, Aaron. She's the reason we're all on this godforsaken island - her and the rest of the humans hiding in their little holes."

Thomas took another step toward Aaron, now close enough to touch. "That's all she is - fucking food." Thomas let that sink in while he surveyed Aaron's face. He wasn't seeing the stubble that persisted on his chin, growing there like he was a living man, but never more than a dusting. He wasn't looking at the flat mole on his cheek or the tiny scar on his bottom lip, its origin story unknown to Thomas. All he saw was his misguided, overly emotional friend who was going to ruin everything if he kept going on the way he was.

"What do you even want with her, Aaron? If Cecelia finds out-"

Aaron turned to Thomas abruptly and locked eyes with his coven mate. He pushed him back, away from him, feeling suddenly that Thomas was standing way too close. His throat was dry; he wanted to stroke his neck to soothe it, indeed thought he had raised a hand to do so but saw them both sitting limply against his legs. He blinked. Thomas smiled.

"Did you think I didn't know?" There was a sneer in Thomas' voice. Aaron wondered if his friend had even tried to mask it. Thomas continued, snickering without a care, "Of course I knew - I've known from the very beginning. I know you thought you were keeping a secret, and you did, from some of the others, but not from me. I could see it in the way that you looked at each other. I always thought one day neither of you would be able to resist and would tear each other's clothes off right in front of me."

Thomas laughed at the thought as he began to pace.

"Tell me Aaron, why would you want this island girl, this

mortal woman who will grow old and die, when you could have such a beautiful woman as Cecelia? The power you would wield by her side," Thomas shook his head in disbelief that Aaron would jeopardize such a prospect. "How can you throw all that away for mere flesh and bone?"

Aaron had so much to say to that but nothing that would make sense to Thomas. Being called out about his relationship with Cecelia threw him for a loop; Thomas was right on that score. He thought he had been careful not to expose the relationship, even if Cecelia had not. She wanted to tell everyone so they would fear him even before they had become one, but Aaron didn't want that. He never wanted fear and adoration to be the motivators for people listening to him. Cecelia thrived on that kind of control where it only made him recoil. Aaron snickered, considering how much Thomas would ridicule him if he let that slip.

"I'm funny to you now?"

Aaron jerked his head up, seeing his error. "No, no. I wasn't laughing at you, Thomas. I wasn't laughing at all. I was just thinking-"

"That, my friend, is precisely what you have *not* been doing."

Aaron shook his head and Thomas looked away, both trapped in the details of their own headspaces. Aaron couldn't help but relive the kiss, the warmth of Vernese's lips on his; the way her kiss seemed to warm him to his very soul. He remembered everything about it, how she had been tentative at first, but that soon gave way to an almost kittenish teasing that he at once found endearing and alluring. He remembered leaning in, trying to catch her playful tongue as it moved around his mouth. He remembered tasting her smile on his lips when he caught her, ending the chase and engaging her in a new kind of game. He remembered feeling her melt as he kissed her slowly, luxuriating in the softness of her mouth, of her body pressed against his. Aaron felt Vernese respond. Just a little twitch that would have been imperceptible to him when he lived and breathed the same air she did, but that was like a ground tremor in its intensity now, to his immortal form. A moan escaped the back of Vernese's throat as she kissed him with abandon, their lips moving in sync, tongues colliding, dancing, circling each other in growing passion.

The only thing on Thomas's mind was what would happen to Aaron if someone found out he was harboring a human. They didn't have many rules but that was definitely one of them. Immortals stick with immortals and humans stick with humans. If you're caught with your face buried in a human's neck, it better not be to give them a hickey. How could he be so stupid?

Thomas couldn't believe how ridiculous Aaron was - had always been, what with the feeling and emotions he wore on his sleeve. Being a vampire had never suited Aaron - he was always one to lament the loss of life to the point of starving himself to weakness. It was during those times that Thomas wished Cecelia would force him into service. Just claim him as hers and command him to do what she wanted. Though she could have, she never did, citing freedom of choice, love, and some other such bullshit. They deserved each other.

Thomas looked over to his friend, his heartsick, idiot compadre, and sighed. Thomas got it. He really did, especially after he saw the movie that played a loop in Aaron's unconcealed mind. There was something to be said about someone else's touch, the kiss of desire. Thomas remembered well how it felt to have his lover's mouth on his own, strong hands controlling his hips as he tried to press forward again and again, begging for friction. Thomas remembered the way Dalyn would smirk when he would feel Thomas trying to press himself against his body; the way he would bite his bottom lip when Thomas' breath hitched in desperation. Thomas shut his eyes to the tropical paradise he found himself transported back to, went, instead, to the secluded deck he and Dalyn claimed as their own. It backed to the woods with centuries-old trees whose tops pointed accusatorily at the sky, and behind that stood the majestic Blue Ridge Mountains. Thomas envisioned Dalyn's face, lit golden by the setting sun; Dalyn's hair floating back from his forehead as he tipped back to take a drink from his ever-present can of orange soda; Dalyn's smile in the candle-light, warm and inviting; Dalyn's eyes as they sparkled when he searched for constellations in the sky; Dalyn's skin flushed beneath Thomas' hands. Thomas felt an unwelcome prickling at the corners of his eyes. He sniffed loudly, louder than he meant to, to push them away.

"Better lock that up, or there'll be hell to pay," Thomas said in warning, voice gruff with emotion as he tapped his own fore-head. The message was as much for Aaron as it was for himself.

Aaron looked at him, mortified.

Thomas couldn't help the smile that formed on his lips, but he wasn't entirely sure that it was for Aaron.

A rustling made them both look up and away, toward Phillipsburg, where the lights still shone from empty restaurants and bars. It was far away, enough distance between the sound and where they stood to run, to go back toward the French side of the island and regroup should the need arise, but it was moving steadily toward them. It could be an animal, Aaron guessed, but was saw no need in voicing it. He knew that was pure optimism at play; his sensitive side hoping against hope, so he kept it to himself. In the end, he was what he was.

In the end, Aaron knew better.

Thomas sniffed the air, filling his nose with the familiar scent, confirming what he already knew the moment he heard the sound, infinitely closer now, in the blink of an eye.

Thomas stood, squaring his shoulders at the unseen, "I think it's time to give the devil his due."

CHAPTER 52

Something was going on.

Gabby was at the park with her family. She was reading the manuscript, as she usually was when she had a few minutes to herself, and with her husband watching the kids as they played, Gabby could enjoy the warm weather with her favorite book in her hands.

The Hunters were doing their jobs. Some were children swinging on the swings, sliding down the slide, hanging upside down on the monkey bars. Some were parents helicoptering the play area and taking pictures on their cell phones. All of them had shapeshifted to Doug's specifications, blending into the landscape seamlessly, orbiting Gabby without her even knowing they were there. To the naked eye, they looked just like everybody else. It was only if you looked at them using your peripheral vision, a little off to the side and away from center, did you see that the Hunters were not what they seemed. Or maybe not. Maybe only Doug and Patrick could tell the difference. Doug couldn't help but wonder because over by the roundabout a little girl sat staring at a playmate in a strange sort of way, like she wouldn't or couldn't move her head from the chin up, head cocked, eyes downturned posture she had adopted. One second, two seconds, five before she snapped out of it. Doug was sure she would run away screaming, throwing herself at her mother and sobbing into her shirt. He could only hope that she merely sensed that something was off rather than saw the heinous countenance staring back at her from underneath the human costume it had donned. But she didn't. Instead she laughed and laughed, nearly toppling over with it as she reached for her new friend's arm. The Hunter-turned-playmate must have affected a similar facial expression because laughter erupted from the little girl again as she nodded her head and drew her hand to cover her open mouth. No screaming. No mayhem. The Hunters were working out after all.

No one looked at the Hunters closely. They were just parents out enjoying a pleasant day at the park with their kids - nothing more, nothing less.

Except for one.

Doug saw him near the fence. He didn't look out of place, not to anyone who might have been looking. He was just finishing up his coffee, reading the paper, and enjoying the weather. He wasn't watching the kids, at least not in any focused way. Nothing he was doing would raise any flags to anyone except Doug. Because Doug could see that the man with the coffee looked the same as his shapeshifted Hunters did: opaque, vaporous, superficial.

But he wasn't a Hunter, that one. Doug couldn't make out anything of the hunched form , the lizard-like skin, the shock of wiry hair beneath the veneer.

So, what was it?

"Do you see that, dad?"

No response.

Doug turned his head to look at Patrick but found himself alone in the room. When had his father left the room? Where could he be?

"Yay!" Doug heard the placating cheer carried from the living world to his dead ears and smiled. He remembered those days all too well. The 'look at me! Look at me!' years, when kids thought every single thing they did was a feat to behold, up to and including balancing themselves on one foot (or at least trying to). He had uttered his share of lukewarm praises to Gabby himself, topping it off with a smile that didn't quite reach his tired eyes. He remembered watching as his friends did it too, seeming to take turns with it as their kids bounced between them, squealing, "Watch this!" to anyone who would listen.

Parenthood... the most difficult job in the world.

Doug found Gabby's eyes and smiled. She had matured into such an amazing woman, one he was proud to call his daughter. He wished he could cup her face with his hands the way he used to when she was little and tell her how much he loved her. He wished he could let her know that she was not alone and that nobody gets everything right every single time. Doug wanted to share what he had learned from Patrick - how to apologize, how to admit his mistakes - and remind her that every day is a new day. He was so preoccupied with want for so many things in that moment that he almost didn't see the man position himself closer. He was getting a pretzel now, his back turned to the kids at the park, to Gabby on the bench, distracted by the manuscript. No one noticed him, but Doug did. He sent out a question, short and sweet, to the man, just to see what would happen.

Hey! What are you doing?

Nothing.

Not an eyebrow raised. Not a muscle twitched. Just calculated obliviousness to the scene behind him, so profound it was easy to miss.

But Doug saw.

And Doug watched.

CHAPTER 53

Aaron didn't have time to tell Thomas what he thought, how he appreciated him standing shoulder to shoulder with him against the dark; against who he thought were their brothers come to call. He didn't have time because he realized almost instantly that they were a diversion, a ruse to get Thomas out of the way. Cecelia had always been crafty that way.

That didn't mean his brothers weren't heading their way. They were. They were making the ruckus that both Thomas and Aaron heard - that part was true; theirs was the scent in the air that Thomas had smelled. They meant to pass by the parking lot where Aaron and Thomas stood, were indeed heading for the mountain in the middle of the island - the highest point on the island... the place where Vernese and her ragtag clan of survivors had hidden themselves, in search of food. And food they would get, without a doubt. Aaron knew all of those things were true and he wanted to run towards them, beseech them to turn away, to find somewhere else to hunt, knowing there was no place else to go. The vampires had depleted the food supply on the island, finding both the crude and the elaborate hiding places the morals had fashioned for themselves and annihilating the people that hid there. They had taken some of the people they found to use as endless founts to suckle upon when they had depleted the island's bounty. But they continued to hunt because they needed more. They continued to hunt because they could smell living blood in the air, still.

The end had come faster than Aaron had expected.

All that was left were the few who had ventured up the mountain. By now there were no worthy adversaries among them, if ever there had been. Aaron was sure that, after so much time had passed without adequate food and drink, the men's muscles would have deteriorated to a near atrophied state. Even the strongest of women among them would never have had a chance against he and his fellow vampires. The only one who Aaron had thought formidable in the group was the doctor because his mind, throughout it all, had remained sharp. But he never came up with a way to kill Aaron and his kind. The doctor had focused his research on the youngest of them, trying to reconcile what he knew about the test group of sanguinarians he had watched turn into vampires as he considered a way to kill them. Such limited understanding of the ancient evil upon them was his downfall. He'd tried to poison the blood, even going as far as injecting a sick boy holed up in a hovel deep within a parish close to the French/Dutch border with an arsenic cocktail and letting some blood from his wrist to entice the vampire's keen sense of smell. He only succeeded in killing the boy and nearly being killed himself when two vampires closed in on the dying child. He had attempted to capture sunlight - some business about optical cavities, mirrors, and resonating focal lengths that was beyond Aaron's scope of understanding past the fact that it couldn't be done, not with the limited materials the doctor had access to. He had even thought of injecting the vampires with liquid metal in an attempt to immobilize them as it solidified. If it could harden in their dead veins, it could keep them rooted in place long enough for the sun to destroy them, but the poor man couldn't get his hands on the mercury he needed to give his idea a go. The doctor's ideas were sound; Aaron was more than impressed with the logic the doctor had used to fight back, but none of them would have worked against the elders, those with the seasoned blood of age and war. The doctor - humanity itself - never had a chance.

He was gone now and for that Aaron felt a true sense of sadness. Knowing he couldn't stop the vampires, the doctor had walked aimlessly in the streets of Marigot, speaking French loudly, as though drunk, to get someone's - anyone's – attention on a balmy night. It didn't take long for one of Aaron's brothers to run the old man down and sink his teeth into his withered neck. Aaron heard the doctor's last words himself, attending the death to make sure it was swift, as a measure of respect. He would never forget the man's dying wish, whispered over the shoulder of the one who would take his life: "Si je ne peux en sauver qu'un... juste pour ce soir." *If I can only save one... just for tonight.*

How Vernese had cried when she found out.

Aaron knew the people on the mountain had no chance of escaping the vampires. The only reason they were allowed to live as long as they had was because of the abundance of food around the island. The people on the mountain were like dessert for a hungry man. There had been no rush to devour them - they weren't going anywhere. But now it was time. Soon the vampires would board the ship again and cast off in search of more food, but tonight they would be satiated by the lot on the mountain – however, they were tattered and torn. Their sallow skin wouldn't even register to the likes of his coven-mates, to Martin and Jericho and Jeremiah. They wouldn't notice how thin the lot was, how unwell. All they would see is the blood, its all-consuming beauty blinding them to anything else.

Vernese was there, on the mountain.

Aaron would have told Thomas to stop, to go to the mountain instead, to help him protect Vernese from the others, but he didn't have time. Thomas, loyal friend that he was, took off running out of the parking lot and toward the beach, because that is where the sounds he heard had led him. Driven by something inside him, something Aaron could only catch glimpses of before he was gone – a feeling of loyalty that sat in his stomach, the sound of laughter, blood at a hairline obscured by soft brown locks - Thomas took off. The word "protect" glowed brightly in Thomas' mind, but Aaron didn't know if it was meant for himself, Vernese, or the person to whom the blood belonged. Thomas was gone before Aaron had the chance to tell him that the sounds he was hearing had been misdirected and that Cecelia was moving him around like a pawn on a chessboard.

No, the vampires weren't congregating at the beach, having a bonfire and roasting marshmallows. They were going up the mountain to finish off the last of the humans on the island. Aaron didn't have time to wonder if they were the last humans left in the world, but some part of his mind settled there. The outbreak had been massive, spanning the globe with astonishing speed. They landed on St. Martin in desperation, looking for food where there had been sparse quantities elsewhere. How many of the other islands had been ravaged by other vampire clans? What would happen if there was no more food left anywhere?

He told Vernese he would protect her.

Aaron got up from the asphalt and ran toward the middle of the island, toward Pic Paradis. He could see its hulking form in the distance, its darker darkness noticeable against the inky blackness of the night. It stood there, a lone sentinel, watching the approach of death and being powerless to stop it. Aaron couldn't let her die that way. He couldn't let his brothers drink from her, kill her just to satiate themselves. He picked up speed, able to tax his body in ways he never dreamed of as a mortal man. Aaron didn't know what he planned to do when he got there short of standing in front of Vernese and claiming her for himself. There was the very real possibility that Aaron might be running toward his own death if one of his brothers was so blinded by hunger that he ignored the rules and fought him. Aaron steeled himself for that probability as he ran, seeing the base of the mountain up ahead.

He could feel their anticipation as they climbed Pic Paradis unhurriedly.

He could smell human blood too.

He was so hungry.

"Do you think she will let you have a taste?"

Aaron heard her before he saw her. She exited the shadows at the base of the mountain to walk toward him, her hips accenting every step.

"Your island girl, do you think she would have the courage to let you drink from her to survive?"

Aaron didn't know what to say. He stared at Cecelia, trying to read her expression, all the while keeping an ear trained on his brothers. They were close to Vernese's camp. Terribly close.

"Cecelia-"

"Tell me, Aaron. Do you think she loves you enough to let you take what you need over and over again, leaving her light-headed and vulnerable?"

Aaron could almost see his coven-mates licking their lips in anticipation.

He imagined their fangs biting into Vernese's neck.

CHAPTER 54

Mal stopped in his tracks. Joanne had said so many things with that one statement and he couldn't wrap his mind around it.

She knows.

Everything he had hoped for had been wiped away with those two small words.

She knows.

His eyes searched Joanne's as her face came into view. She had removed herself from the shadows, no longer afraid of who waited just inside the door. Resignation was etched on her face and it made Mal uneasy.

She knows.

He wanted to ask who knew what but there was no point in playing that game. Joanne knew too, that much was evident. She knew who she was, who Gabby was to her, who Mal was and how he fit into all of it. The knowledge was coming clearer by the second and Mal could do nothing to stop it. The ball that had been set in motion so long ago was barreling down the mountain to fall into the cerulean blue of the sea when it was done.

She knows.

"As handsome as I remember," Joanne said, suddenly upon him, so distracted he had been by her words that he hadn't noticed her approach, her hand touching his face. Her voice was her own, had been through time, but she didn't speak as Joanne then. Instead, she seemed to call upon Marcia or perhaps Danica, reincarnations from lifetimes ago, who could be talking with Paul or Jensen - he didn't know which. He had lost track of his reincarnations over the years, as tends to happen with each expression, each life. There were parts of his personality that had been irrevocably lost over time, unavailable to the newer manifestation as those that bore them were, alas, nothing but dust in his grave. But Joanne was much the same as she had been when he first laid eyes on her. The corporeal changes had been slight, but the soul seemed untouched, save for those made in search of shared understanding; of being a part of the world in which she lived. Mal knew he would have been able to find her no matter where she was - her soul was that strong, even after so many lifetimes, even after so much shedding.

Joanne laughed, the sound raspy and paper-thin, her voice hoarse from disuse. She croaked,

"You're too late," as she looked toward the floor. Mal looked in the same direction Joanne did, surprised to find that he could see Gabby reading in a park, his proximity to the woman he had come to love in her own right opening the world she called home in full view. How long had he lingered outside her door, milled in the hallway, delayed the inevitable, all the while giving her purview? Letting her see had never been part of the plan. He hadn't wanted to glimpse the despair that flashed across her face.

Children scattered everywhere amidst games of hopscotch, foursquare, and tag. The baby, Autumn, was playing with another little one in the grass in front of where Gabby sat, as immersed in their sandpit as the older kids were in their more structured games. Some part of Mal wanted to look for the boy, Christopher. Wanted to see his little head bobbing up and down as he played on the monkey bars or the swings, but he didn't allow himself that luxury. Seeing him now, as a beautiful young boy with the joy of childhood etched on his face, wouldn't help things. It would only make it harder to look upon him later, when death had cast its shadow upon it; would only make it harder to greet him at the gates of The Realm.

Joanne had looked down to see Gabby, the grandchild she never knew. The smile on Joanne's face as she watched her, the look of pride that etched itself there, filled Mal with love and pain in equal measure. It hurt Mal to know that what she had found such comfort in throughout life - being surrounded by family - plagued her in death, even as she stood in such a wretched place.

Mal wanted to ask Joanne what she meant, what she was talking about, how she could know anything at all after being locked away in that room, but he knew it was pointless to do so. Instead, he watched as the sunlight shone bright on Gabby's hair, watched as the breeze ruffled Autumn's curls.

He listened as Gabby's thoughts permeated the room and anticipated the moment when she would start reading again, telling the truths he so desperately wanted muted. He watched, wishing he could snatch the manuscript from her hands, indeed willing all the forces he could enlist into service to do so, until he felt Joanne's eyes on him once more and knew that wouldn't do. They were past the point where that would save them. No intervention Mal could make at this point would change the inexorable end.

***

G abby looked over at Autumn playing in the sandbox and smiled. She took a picture of her messy little girl playing with her friend and posted it right away, knowing she would forget to do it later if she waited. She cast her eyes around for Christopher, looking for the little boy who had been tearing through the equipment, getting on everything over and over again like someone was planning to uproot it in the night and cart it away forever. She found him, her smiling little boy, at the top of a slide waiting for another kid to get ready for a race on the one next to it. Her husband was there and he was smiling too, happy to enjoy the afternoon out with his family after so many back-to-back night shifts. Gabby was happy he was there too. Having another set of eyes watching over the two kids was a luxury she did not enjoy often. She usually found it difficult to relinquish control, hard to wrap her mind around the fact that she didn't have to bear the responsibility today - that the darting-eye syndrome, as she liked to call it, could take a breather for once - but this time, she had brought something along to help her mellow out. Gabby reached into her bag and pulled out her grandmother's manuscript. There were only a few pages left to the story and Gabby thought that if anything could help her relax into her afternoon of backup cat-herding parent, it was this. She couldn't wait to see how the story ended, or at least, how the story stopped. Gabby would have finished it the night before had it not been for her scratchy eyes and the first semblance of dawn peeking out over the horizon. The book had distracted her so completely, that she had lost track of time. What would she do with herself when all was said and done, when Vernese and Aaron took their relationship further, when the vampires bore down on Pic Paradis? How would she fill her days when the story was over?

Gabby didn't want to think about that.

All she wanted to do was read at that moment and, opening the manuscript to where she left off, she sank into the story so completely she thought she could smell the saltwater.

Cecelia touched Aaron's arm and blinked, transporting them to a darkened beach with waves lapping gently at the shore. The sound of water moving had become a favorite for Aaron and he couldn't help but acknowledge the way it diffused the tension between him and Cecelia instantly.

Pic Paradise was behind them, out of sight in the uniformity of night.

"Will she?" Cecelia prodded. "You will need to feed sooner or later. Will she let you? Will she put her life in your hands?" Cecelia's voice caressed the words, but they were formed with the most venomous of intentions. Aaron had wounded her, and she wanted him to know it.

"If she loves me the way she says she does-"

"You speak of love like it should mean something to me," Cecelia said, trying but failing to keep the distaste out of her voice.

"Doesn't it?" Aaron challenged, angrier than he should have been by her response. "Isn't that what you claim to feel for me?"

Cecelia stared at him, her eyes unwavering as she assessed the man before her. His face was different than it was before, softer in ways she wouldn't have imagined possible considering his immortal age. His chin was less defined, his eyes warmer. She wasn't sure if the look was endearing or immature.

She allowed a rueful smile to spread across her face before speaking again, ignoring his question for a line of thought all her own. "You play at something dangerous, making yourself pretty like that, Aaron." She moved toward him with uncanny swiftness: even Aaron was loath to see her approach. She touched his sharp jawline and parted her lips to gasp. "But your softness is only so to us. To them you are still as unnatural - as cold - as before."

Aaron didn't speak, didn't move. He wanted to. He could feel a response welling in his chest, but he couldn't voice it. Having Cecelia close was like a panacea to him and always had been. Every touch trailed fire upon his skin. He didn't want her to back away, no matter how much he needed to argue his case if he wanted to change things for Vernese. What he wanted to do was dip his tongue into the space created between Cecelia's collarbone and the column of her neck. He wanted to lave over it the way she liked, wanted to feel her respond against him. If he could do that, everything would be alright... except it wouldn't. If he did that Cecelia might leave Vernese alone, true, but then he would never know what could be.

"Vernese...?" Cecelia said languidly, letting the name roll over her tongue. Aaron sighed. He had let his guard down as his thoughts flitted confusingly around in his head. Doing so had allowed Cecelia to see into his mind, to pick out details he wanted to keep hidden. *That's what she wanted all along, isn't it?* Aaron realized. Control. That's what she *always* wanted. That's what she always got.

"Like a song sung upon a breeze," Cecelia mused, sarcasm lacing her words, deepening her tone. Cecelia stared into

Aaron's eyes, searching, appraising, for longer than he was comfortable with. She was reading him. Aaron stepped back even though his body protested mightily, in the hopes of breaking her gaze. Cecelia allowed it, but kept close attention to him, watching his every move.

"Beautiful girl," Cecelia said, finally, "A survivor."

Aaron didn't know what to say. He wanted to plead Vernese's case, wanted to ask for mercy for her, but he knew he shouldn't if he truly wanted her spared. Such requests uttered by his tongue, above anyone else, would incite her. Instead he looked away from Cecelia, shirking under her persistent gaze.

"I love you," Aaron muttered, knowing it would do no good but giving in to the truth once again.

"Speak you of love again?" Cecelia's voice raised with indignation and Aaron cringed away from the tone more so than the volume. The impetuousness of his words rang hollow in his own ears - he could only imagine what Cecelia must have felt. But he did love her. He loved her so very much. It's just that he had never been as intrigued by anyone as he had by Vernese. He wanted to understand how she had been able to draw him in so completely.

"You said the same when it was Raymond who stood by your side," Aaron attempted. "Such words didn't seem strange to you when you yourself uttered them."

Cecelia huffed, but looked away, letting go of the invisible choke hold she seemed to have applied to Aaron to keep him in place. His body relaxed from the tense position it had maintained in her grasp. Aaron spoke again after controlling the timbre of his voice,

"Isn't this, the self-exploration, the time apart - isn't this all to be sure that we know what we want? Sure, that there will be no problems between us when, finally, we rule?" Aaron spoke the words but was not entirely sure he meant them anymore.

"Sure of what *you* want, you mean, don't you?" Cecelia hissed, angrier than she was before. Cecelia moved away from him, turning herself toward the striated cliffs that show amber in the light of day, but will forever be a cold gray for those that rule the night. With her back to her love, she said, "I know what I want."

Aaron sank his head as he heard the words. As much as he didn't want to, he was hurting Cecelia. She was humbling herself standing there in the first place, a queen at the whim of a subject like him. But more so, he was dangling a carrot before her, promising happiness if she could wait a little while longer. And for what? Aaron looked toward the city, houses with lights that had never been turned off, empty and desolate, but illuminating the night just the same. Vernese was out there among those lights. She was prey running from inevitable death, but still clinging to the notion of survival. He knew she looked out at those lights at night, hope filling her heart at the potential for rescue, the possibility of fending off the bloodsuckers; the ability to survive his kind. Those thoughts had been futile. Their succumbing – their utter obliteration – had always been inevitable. There hadn't been enough of them growing food, planning for a time when there would be no meat to speak of and less fish by the day. They hadn't been planning for the day when there wouldn't be much of anything left to sustain them. They were pretty much just running and trying to survive the night. They had no idea they wouldn't last more than three months on the island after the outbreak. They hadn't known how little time was left.

But what about Vernese? He could help her survive. He could keep her safe. He could make her one of them...

"She won't do it," Cecelia said incredulously, turning to face him as the sound of the waves lapping the shore filled their ears. "And when she finds out what you are, she will run. God help you if she figures out that you only care for her survival to satisfy your curiosity. She'll try to kill you the same way her silly little doctor would have."

She was right, Aaron knew. Cecelia was always right.

"What is it about her that makes you turn your head away from me?" Cecelia asked with pure curiosity in her voice. "Is the lure of the throne not enough to keep you interested?"

Cecelia's eyes bore into him. Aaron melted into them as if he had been caressed.

"It is not that, my love," Aaron started, aware how insubstantial his argument sounded when spoken aloud. "The woman - Vernese - she is special. Different."

"Different? How?" Cecelia did nothing to mask the incredulity in her voice.

Aaron thought hard about that question. It wasn't something as simple as beauty or youth. Cecelia offered an abundance of those attributes such that no woman could ever compare. Aaron considered the innocence with which Vernese's eyes stared at him, even in the midst of a veritable apocalypse. Appealing, but a matter of circumstance. He wondered if Vernese would have found him so enthralling had they met when life was normal, when he was still among the living and sporting thick, unruly hair that was too long in the back to be considered fashionable. Would she have appreciated his skin in winter, when it wasn't quite as rich and sun kissed as she had grown accustomed to. He didn't allow his thoughts to linger there lest he find an answer he would not be happy with.

So, what was it? Her personality? Her sense of humor? Her body? Yes and no, to all of it. They hadn't explored each other enough to single anything out. As he considered how little he knew about Vernese, realization dawned on him. It wasn't so much that he was interested in any specific thing about Vernese over Cecelia. It was that he had *chosen* her of his own accord.

Words need not be said - Cecelia knew all.

"You trivialize this, Cecelia," Aaron said anyway, choosing not to answer the question. "It is not so simple."

Cecelia sized Aaron up, determination filling her obstinately. She was the queen, his leader as much as the others'. Cecelia would not tolerate this type of treatment - the utter insubordination - from anyone else. She had wanted Aaron to make his own decision without influence from her, but she had grown tired of waiting. All of this over a mortal woman? No, Cecelia would not wait any longer. She'd had enough.

"Oh, but it is," Cecelia crowed, "at least it is now."

Aaron looked at her, surprised by her commanding tone. He now saw the error of his ways. Aaron had danced too close to the fire and the wind had changed course to send flames flickering into his face.

"Decide," Cecelia said, her voice void of emotion. It was a sound that had raised the hair on the neck of her victims for centuries; one Aaron never expected to hear directed toward him. "Dominion over the coven and life with me by your side, or your mortal girl, who doesn't have long to walk the earth."

Aaron's mouth dropped open before he could stop it, questions, statements, pleas vying to be spoken aloud, but each dying on his lips.

Cecelia cocked her head, amusement playing around the edges of anger - a dangerous coupling to behold. "Oh, I won't kill her," she said, plucking one of the many thoughts out of Aaron's mind and giving it life. "I won't need to. Her life is already in peril. Any number of things will bring about her demise. And that is what makes your decision so important, Aaron." Aaron heard his own sharp inhale and exhale of breath, humanity coming back to him, washing over him in waves. He was perspiring and panting - he must have looked a sight.

Cecelia was not amused.

She walked over to the water's edge and let the waves splash her feet. She looked out at the water expectantly as her profile created waves of their own in the dim light. She was exquisite. Aaron couldn't help but admire the curve of her hip against the backdrop, as pure ebony as that of onyx. That he wanted to run his hand along the contour of her hip, that he couldn't control his base thoughts even at such a crucial moment disturbed him more than he could have ever fathomed.

And, in a flash of horrifying clarity, she knew.

Cecelia's head dropped, her chin grazing her chest for the most fleeting of intervals before rising above it defiantly.

Aaron's heart sank as he watched the posture of the woman he loved slump in on itself before righting even more rigid than before.

She turned to look at him.

Aaron shrank away from the stare, so cold and unfamiliar, he might have been regarding a stranger.

"I see," Cecelia whispered. Aaron started to speak, did utter a protest in an effort to quell Cecelia's anguish and buy himself more time, but she quieted him by simply blinking his words away.

Aaron had walked toward her unknowingly, wondering if he had been summoned there or if he moved of his own volition. He reached for her face. She let him cup her cheek, leaned into it, shutting her eyes at the contact. He wanted to hold her, wanted to caress her for as long as he could, but Aaron knew he would have to let go, would be forced to. There was a finality to the moment that left him cold.

"Cecelia-" he tried, but she continued as if she hadn't heard him speak.

"I'll spare her, you'll see," Cecelia said quietly. "You'll have the perfect vantage point to see everything that happens to her, every time."

A question formed on Aaron's lips, but he didn't voice it. Cecelia's eyes, coal black now, and alien, sclera gone as though it never existed at all, bore into him, rooting him in place. *Putting* him in his place.

He was afraid. For the first time in his immortal existence, Aaron felt the fear that had paralyzed him at the moment of his death. He couldn't speak, couldn't move.

Cecelia circled him, stalking him like prey, never taking her eyes off his face. She stilled her step behind him and ran her hands from his shoulders down to his hands. She laced their fingers together, her smaller hands on top of his larger ones, a gesture as sweet as love itself in the touch of another. But Aaron understood the truth of it all. In one soul-crushing instant, he knew that love was not what he was being shown here, and surely not mercy. He wondered if he would ever feel Cecelia's loving embrace again.

"Such a strong man," Cecelia cooed into Aaron's clothed shoulder blade. The material kept her lips from touching his skin, and Aaron was sorry for that. So very sorry. He could feel the dominance in her touch, could feel her hot breath at the nape of his neck. Would that he could feel her lips grazing his skin one last time. Because it was the last time, wasn't it? Aaron felt this was so, knew it with every fiber of his being. He had toyed with her for too long, had made a grievous misstep that would cost him the throne, though that he didn't care as much about. He had chosen by *not* choosing, had spoken without uttering a word. And she, the queen of the only world he could exist in henceforth, had heard him.

Aaron mourned Cecelia already.

Cecelia let go of Aaron's hands abruptly, as though wrenching herself out of a daydream. She pressed down on his shoulders lightly: Aaron knew what was expected of him - she need not exert much energy to make him obey. Aaron sank to his knees before Cecelia, waiting for her to move in front of him again. She regarded his back, broad and muscular beneath the summer shirt he sported. How easy it would be to punish him, bring welts across his skin and watch the wounds bleed then heel, bleed then heel, again and again until she grew tired. But would that be enough? Cecelia knew it would not. Aaron had demeaned her, made her look like a schoolgirl pinning after a cute boy, or so the reference went. He held her heart in his hand, knew it, and toyed with it without a care. Cecelia knew that was going too far, but that is how it felt. How dare he make her wait until he had decided - as if his feelings were the only ones that mattered? How long had they been at this push and pull, 40 years? Perhaps even longer. Cecelia could hardly remember a time when she didn't love Aaron. Even through Raymond, and Christoff, and all of the others, there had always been him.

Aaron had to pay for what he had done. She had to make sure he understood who he was dealing with.

Cecelia touched the curls at the back of Aaron's head lovingly. How she did adore him. He was beautiful, intelligent, strong, alluring. But fickle, this one. And because of that he would be made to suffer as she would in the midst of his pain.

Cecelia didn't bother concealing the sigh that escaped her lips. She walked in front of him, cementing a resigned countenance over the sadness that threatened to spill over.

Better to get it over with quickly.

"That strength will serve you well," Cecelia continued, her voice wavering ever so slightly. Aaron's punishment was only just now forming in her head and she was amazed by the degree to which she was willing to go to defrock him. But punish him she would. She had to. If they ever had a chance to be together, he had to know his place.

"... Serve me?" Aaron's voice roused her from her thoughts, even if they sounded small and uncertain.

He looked at Cecelia with wide, upturned eyes. She almost felt pity for him.

"My lord, yes," Cecelia said, her voice taking on the sugary-sweet intonation of an innocent. It made the hairs on Aaron's neck stand on end. "You will come to find that wielding power isn't all ornamental garb and debutant presentment, no. You, Aaron, will learn what it means to truly rule."

Aaron didn't know what Cecelia was talking about. He wanted to ask her but thought better of it. He was afraid of what he might hear. The truth was in her eyes, eyes that burned with a fire from within that he had never seen before. Aaron looked into those eyes knowing that he could not avoid her wrath no matter what he said or did.

"It will be a vast kingdom, yours," Cecelia continued, forcing herself to stand still and not give in to the nervous fidgeting her body clamored for. "Big enough to rival mine, in fact. And it will be yours. Yours to do whatever you want with, to share with whomever you want. Maybe your island girl or maybe one of the flower boys of the Far East you fancied for a time," Cecelia's lips curled lasciviously at the suggestion, "The choice - that is what you so deeply desire, is it not? Choice? Alas, my darling, it is all yours."

"What do you mean, Cecelia?" Aaron couldn't hold it any

longer. She was talking around it, dancing along the edge like a coin at the mouth of a spiral wishing well. Aaron didn't think he could take being teased, the way her beautiful mouth shot words out like poison-laced daggers, he-

"I'm talking about your kingdom, Aaron. Your future."

Aaron's eyes searched hers. He felt the tears prickle the backs of them, stinging the way he remembered they did when he was a child. He wouldn't have cared if they fell, indeed might have willed them to if only to relieve some of the pressure built up in his head, but they did not.

"My kingdom," he said, voice hoarse all of a sudden.

"Yes, all yours. You will rule over your people from the bowels of all creation, those wretches that come to you after seven lifetimes of failure to grovel at your feet, for life eternal. From all over the universe they will hail; the beaten and weary, the evil and damned, the broken, the downtrodden your very kith and kin. Not Heaven, not Hell, but The Realm will be ever-lasting for you and your kind, and of those there will be many."

Aaron shook his head slowly, the action purely a reaction to the words being said. He was unable to stop it, unable to close his ears from the deluge of judgment; unable to do anything at all.

Cecelia noticed his reaction and took a step toward him, the urge to touch him, to console him nearly stifling. She reached out to him but stopped herself, placing her hand back down to her side to grasp the hem of her dress. She regarded that dress, billowing softly in the breeze of the Caribbean summer night, carried by a wind that was ignorant to all it witnessed: the fall of a would-be king.

Cecelia looked at Aaron before continuing. His face showed the war that battled inside him, etched with both under-standing and disbelief at the same time.

Maybe they would never have the chance to be together after all.

Perhaps they never did.

Joanne wanted to call Mal a bastard, wanted to strike out at him for everything, but she couldn't. She couldn't because if she lashed out at him, she would have to confront her own selfishness as well. So instead she listened. She watched. She cried.

"Don't worry, my sweet, you won't be alone in The Realm, not even for a second," Cecelia cooed placatingly. "There are many past their seventh lives now and they will meet you at your door, shaken and afraid. It will be up to you to rule them, control them, keep them. They belong to you, incontrovertibly so, and it is up to you to make sure they obey your rule."

Cecelia had worked herself up and was meting out punishment with ease now. She knew what needed to be done and was eager to complete the task before she lost her nerve.

Don't look at him, she admonished herself. *Don't look.*

"Obey my rule? Cecelia, what are you talking about?" Aaron asked but he wasn't confused. He was searching for something to say to fix things, to change the course of the conversation; to save himself, but nothing came.

"That merciless in-between, that cold abyss shall be where you reign. Make of it what you want, you will have the power to do all things there when you take the throne. Carnival or

Gehenna - it is up to you. You can do anything you want there with those condemned to The Realm. Indeed, you can do anything at all except walk the earth again or step foot in Heaven or Hell. You will be left alone - all of you. Cast aside," Cecelia's voice hitched. "Forgotten."

Aaron drew in a shuddering breath. She had the power to do this thing she spoke of, he knew it. Had he hurt her so badly that she would put him through this? Was she so frustrated with him that she could not wait for his response?

"You're no witch," Aaron tried, unsure what he might gain from this new provocation. "How dare you try-"

Cecelia's laugh, mirthless and disdainful, ripped into his body to touch his very soul. "Fool," she spat. It was enough.

Aaron looked into her eyes for a long time before squeezing his own shut. *I could have been yours*, Cecelia cooed, her voice inside his head the balm he needed to surrender. *We could have had it all*. But as he envisioned Cecelia standing before him, her face beautiful in the light of the moon instead of contorted in anger, as he saw too a sumptuous figure silhouetted next to her, one with a crown of curly hair held away from her face in an elaborate hair wrap, stacking her curls up and up and up, he knew they - he and Cecelia - would never come to be.

Cecelia knew his heart had chosen Vernese. She knew he would always choose her.

Cecelia sucked her teeth, reading him like a book. She spoke low, her tone more ominous than Aaron had ever heard, "Even now, as you are on your knees..."

Cecelia wiped away a tear quickly with a ferocity that would have stilled the heart of a mortal passerby. She grabbed his neck, gritting her teeth as she did. She was so angry. She loved him. She hated him. She was so angry. She was -

"Kiss me, my love, once my intended, now my enemy,"

Cecelia said, cutting off her own thoughts to press her lips against his. The kiss was brutal, taut lips split open by teeth, tongues lashing at each other in a duel, stabbing, pressing, invading. Aaron reached for her, wanting to pull her back a little so that he could kiss her properly, show her the desire that still lived within him at the mere thought of their skin touching. Overpowering her was not a thought in his mind, his body giving way to arousal as instantly as always. But Cecelia would not allow it. She held both of his wrists securely in one of her hands while she finished the assault, giving Aaron time to think. He could never have overpowered such an old vampire. The battle had been won before it even began.

Cecelia broke the kiss without opening her eyes, without pulling away at all. Against his lips, she spat the words that made his insides quiver in fear, "As Lilith swore, I shall keep this promise. Your descendants will forevermore inhabit The Realm, spending life eternal locked within it like a doomed flame."

Aaron's face was wet with tears now. They flowed unabashedly down his cheeks. He was losing her. He was losing his life. He was losing everything he cherished. It was like dying all over again.

"Please," he whispered, detesting the desperation in his voice.

Cecelia's laugh, carried by the wind, hit his ear harshly. "Please?" she mimicked. "Please what? Forgive you? Save you? Save *her*?"

Aaron turned his head away from Cecelia's face, so rapt in emotion that her features appeared misshapen.

"I will do all of those, save one, my love. As I said, I will not kill her. You will know her, many times through many lives, for that you can be sure, but you will never be able to save her. Together you will fill The Realm with your children, made to sit side by side with those who could not repent, could not live according to God's law but were not suitable enough for the devil. You will watch as they pray for release; you will try to escape; you will wish for the true death because the guilt of knowing that it was you who condemned your descendants, the very fruit of your loins to The Realm for eternity. It was you, Aaron, who would not accept his position at my side. You, dear one, who spit in my face."

Aaron couldn't bear to look at Cecelia, not now. She was almost animalistic, crazy with her need for vengeance. Aaron cast his eyes around where they stood in desperation. His back was facing the mountain; the water was behind Cecelia. There was no one else on the beach, no one to hear his cries.

Cecelia, too, was crying. Oddly, Aaron took comfort in that.

He didn't see her finger, obscenely elongated and fashioned like a dagger, lining up with his chest.

The puncture felt like a pinch.

The gush of blood wet his shirt then his pants quickly. He was covered in it before he could will his legs to stand, to move away, to run. He pitched forward, digging his hands in the sand. He crawled once, twice, three times but she never faltered, wrapping her legs around his hips as he moved, straddling his back, weighing him down in a manner that would, at one time, have been welcomed. He swung at her blindly, reaching behind himself frantically as self-preservation kicked in, but she was unfazed, whether she absorbed the blow or not. He was no match for her. This, all of this, had been futile.

Cecelia hummed into his ear.

Aaron cursed the traitorous part of himself that enjoyed the sound.

Aaron sank down, his body lying prone as the blood of all those he had savored in the past few days ran down his legs, into his shoes, into the ground. It was only when Aaron's head lolled on his neck, eyes unfocused and incoherent, that Cecelia got off of him. She removed her finger from his heart and brought the digit to her lips. She licked at the blood, dark as pitch under the light of the moon, and moaned in appreciation.

"What a waste," she said. Aaron could only stare at her.

"You will die now, Aaron. Again,"

Gurgling sounds as the blood forced its way into Aaron's throat and lungs, a reflexive action that felt so very real.

"Once this body is dead, you will awaken in The Realm a king. Your vampire existence will be over and the residual that your soul left behind in your mortal body as well as in this immortal existence will be released into the ether to be reincarnated again and again. You will find your island girl time and time again. You will mate with her, have children with her for all time, both of you unaware of your connection but undeniably drawn to each other, whether you be lovers from warring countries, murderer and would-be victim, brother and sister. Oh, you will suffer to love her, dear one, so that you know the pain you caused the queen who offered you everything. Those children will be with you eternally in the nothingness that is The Realm, all of your descendants, always there, wanting to leave for Heaven or Hell even, as either would be better than The Realm, but they won't be able to. Because of you, Aaron. Because of the curse you have bestowed upon them."

Aaron could barely see Cecelia any longer, though his eyes were open.

Cecelia knelt down to guide Aaron's head into her lap.

She was so afraid.

She was so angry.

She was so afraid.

"I bind you to this creature, damned to come back again,

and again, reincarnating lifetime over lifetime," she said wetly, speaking to the soul that resided within the shell, as well as to that remnant of Aaron, that shedding that would stay behind in the hull even as it lay inanimate awaiting the sun. Aaron could hear the words Cecelia spoke, distant yet pure. The emotion in her voice let him know that she would mourn him forever, even if her words didn't. The thought made him smile as her fingers combed through his hair gently, gently, so gently, putting him to sleep.

The bleeding had stopped.

Aaron had stilled.

"And now," Cecelia said, sadness wracking her body in waves, "Goodbye."

<hr>

Gabby's mouth hung open.

"What happened?" she heard her husband ask, bringing her back to the world. She was in their car. They were parked in front of a restaurant; the same one they always went to on impromptu family dates like these. When had she gotten in the car? Had she helped pack up the kids at the park, helped get them into the car in the lot? She couldn't remember. In fact, Gabby couldn't remember anything except the imagined sound of Aaron's shallow breathing (even though he didn't need to draw breath, being a vampire and all, she still imagined him as a living, breathing being...who just happened to suck blood for sustenance), of how he must have looked bleeding out. She could only think of Cecelia, regal in her appearance, on her knees crying, her lover's blood staining her sundress. He's dead. Aaron was dead. He would reincarnate over and over, making more children that would end up condemned. And Vernese...

"Gabby?"

Her husband was staring at her.

"Yeah, I'm good. I just - wow, I'm really enjoying this book."

"I can tell," he said, glancing down at the creased pages of the manuscript.

Gabby was on the last page.

She blushed. She had virtually ingested the manuscript. The thought of it, what anyone on the outside looking in might think of her blind focus, made color rise in her cheeks.

"If it was that good, I wonder why your grandmother didn't finish it," he said as he climbed out of the car to unbuckle the little ones in the backseat. Gabby got out of the car too, placing the manuscript on the floor of the front seat, out of view. The story *was* good, but she didn't wonder why Joanne has stopped writing it, not anymore. There was something unsettling about the story now, something that made her skin itch just under the surface, right where she couldn't reach. It didn't feel made up anymore, didn't feel like someone spinning a yarn. It was authentic, real in an alternate plane kind of way and that made it scary – probably scarier than anything she had ever read. Gabby shook her head, her words jumbling together, not forming a cogent enough sentence to speak aloud.

Goosebumps had sprung up on her arms. She rubbed at them absently but couldn't shake the sudden chill. Words from the story, disjointed and disembodied, bounced off the walls of her mind, knocking into each other, pushing through each other. Something felt wrong. Really wrong.

Gabby vomited there on the sidewalk and they went home instead of eating out. She hugged her babies and went straight to bed, resisting the urge to bury her head under the covers to escape the boogeyman. Gabby had brought the manuscript upstairs with her, even though everything inside her begged that she leave it in the car, to maybe even burn it in the morning light. She found herself curled up with it in bed reading the last sentences her grandmother would ever write to the story over and over again, going numb with understanding.

S*he knows*, Mal thought sadly, *and now, so does he.*

CHAPTER 55

Patrick moved away from the door slowly, the fire that had burned so hot before dissipating a bit, as if redirected by the wind, as he entered the unfamiliar space of the hallway. Even so, his feet moved on, pressing forward without hesitation, as if of their own volition. It was his mind that was frightened, his thoughts that were tortured. His body knew what it needed to do. He had to go up.

Patrick left what seemed like a never-ending hallway and entered a non-descript common area. There was nothing there; bare walls with chipped paint, tarnished chandeliers, worn carpet. He snickered. He hadn't gotten around to imagining anything for that area yet. He'd have to ask Joanne to put some thought into what she would like later.

Was there a later for them?

Patrick wasn't so sure. What he did know was that looking for Joanne upstairs felt right. He hadn't felt anything so keenly since waking up in The Realm. He had to press on. He had to give it a shot.

Patrick walked through the common area briskly, eager to get to the center of the house. Once there, he turned around in a reluctant pirouette, peering into the dimness. It had to be there, didn't it? The stairwell should be right in front of him, but there was nothing. No gleaming marble steps, no rotted slates or broken handrails. Just nothing. Patrick looked down at the floor in the foyer, noting how the dust that coated it thickly did so evenly as well. It had never been disturbed. It wasn't that the stairwell leading upstairs had disappeared. It had never been there to begin with.

Patrick moved through the house with a purpose, going into every room except the one that Doug occupied. He didn't want to answer the inevitable question that Doug would have asked. He didn't want to voice what he was thinking and give it life. Patrick went to the far side of the kitchen, through the living room, into countless guest bedrooms, through the dining room.

Nothing.

Reluctantly, he came back to the foyer, standing next to the footprints he had left before. He had to be missing something.

"Joanne," he said under his breath, "where are you?"

Up.

Patrick let his head tilt back as he looked up at the ceiling. The word bounded through his mind again, deafening, smothering, colliding, crushing, until everything, all that he knew, all that he had ever felt, said, thought, whispered, screamed came together in a wild cacophony, the sound a psychotic crescendo from muted babble to raucous abrasion to blight the senses.

And then silence.

The suddenness of it drove Patrick to his knees.

He plugged his ears, the silence more deafening than the din had ever been. He squeezed his eyes shut, body swaying to an unknown beat, urged on by anguish and despair alone.

"Please!" he screamed, his voice echoing in the room harshly. "Please, let me go up."

Patrick didn't know if they materialized out of thin air or if they dropped down from the ceiling, but when he opened his eyes, they were there.

Stairs.

Stairs going *up*.

He remembered all of it now, words coming back to him in a deluge. The Realm was under *his* control. Patrick could do whatever he wanted - he could do more than just redecorating rooms to make them look the way he wanted them to. He could *reshape* the rooms, reshape the house, reshape The Realm itself. The Realm was his, his and Doug's to do with as they pleased. It was heady, this power. He couldn't wrap his mind around it, even still. As he took his first uncertain step on the mysterious stairs, then another, and the another, Patrick thought about how, if he had only realized what that power truly meant, he might have found Joanne sooner. Maybe he could have found her and she would have figured out how to save Doug? Maybe, if he hadn't been so simple-minded, so intolerably dense, Joanne would have figured out how to save them all.

There definitely wasn't any time for that kind of self-deprecation. He needed to find Joanne.

Patrick reached the top of the stairs faster than he expected to, only thinking once about how a stairwell materializing out of thin air was some horror movie bullshit. He turned his head from one side to the next. There stood a hallway with doors leading to rooms along it on his left. There was nothing on his right. Only it wasn't *nothing*... at least it didn't stay that way. It started out as a nebulous, hazy space that was just sort of there. There was no form, nothing that could be deciphered as anything whatsoever – no structure, no base - just an amorphousness that reminded him of fog in a meadow. There was nothing to pay attention to, nothing to be concerned about until it... changed. It went from nothingness to inchoate almost without notice, but then Patrick began to see more, as the wall took shape before his eyes, rising from a floor that hadn't existed a moment before. There was a surreal moment when Patrick could see beyond the forming wall into a smoky emptiness. It seemed to beckon him to look closer, to lean in and let the wall form around his neck.

Then the wall was solid, as though it had always been there.

Patrick turned in the only direction he could anymore with a huff and pushed on. There was no time to worry about the spontaneously generating wall and the murderous (suicidal?) thoughts that were filling his mind. He had left Doug alone in that room watching after his only child in fear for a reason. He was going to find his wife.

"Joanne?" he called into the corridor lined with doors, only half expecting a response.

Patrick was holding his breath.

He hadn't meant to.

He forced himself to exhale and walk down the corridor, even though he didn't want to. Patrick kept telling himself there was nothing to be afraid of, but something deep in his gut vehemently disagreed. There was something creepy about the hallway. It wasn't that there was something in the hallway, unseen, transparent waiting for him to make a move - Patrick had gotten over the feeling of being stalked when he watched the Hunters obey his command unflinchingly. The thing that frightened him about the hall was the ordinariness of it. The walls were painted yellow atop a chair rail and wainscoting done in white. The floor was carpeted with some cream-colored, tight looped variety. Normal. Something you might see in contemporary single-family homes. It terrified him, the normalcy. Where was the ghost? Where was the gaping maw of some unearthly animal dripping blood on the oh so perfect carpet? The lack of heart-stopping visages waiting to scare him threatened to push Patrick over the edge. He tried the first door he came to - the one on the left. It resisted, wood and metal rumbling petulantly as it refused to open. Patrick jiggled the doorknob once, twice, three times hoping it would give but knowing it wouldn't. He ran to the next one and then the next, pulling at them, tugging and pushing like a child might, trying to muscle the door to open, to move, wiggle, do something other than stay shut, keeping him away from whatever was inside. He grunted in frustration; virtually growled in anger.

"Fuck," he yelled in the empty corridor, turning on his heels to look at all the doors shut against him, eyes bulging with the effort. He was never going to get in. Never. Joanne was right there, just beyond his reach, and he would never ever see her again.

"She knows."

Patrick stopped in his tracks, arms still raised in front of him, fists still balled in frustration. But he heard something.

No.

He heard *Joanne.*

"Jo-" he started but then he heard her speaking again.

"You're too late."

"No!" Patrick yelled and sprang into action. He banged at the door in front of him, then at the next one, getting closer and closer to the end of the hallway with every step.

He heard something but couldn't figure out what it was. A laugh? A sigh? A shriek?

It was far away.

Or was it?

The sound echoed around him, came from inside him.

Patrick looked back the way he had come, the hallway seeming to stretch before him, an optical illusion that lengthened and shortened in wavering opposition. Patrick felt unsteady on his feet. He reached out to the walls to get his footing, not letting himself go down the rabbit hole, the one that reminded him that there shouldn't be any walls there anyway because there was no upstairs on this house, especially none that he had gotten to using some freaking magic stairs, and all of this was in his mind and he was probably asleep in his own bed having one hell of a nightmare and his son was still in fucking high school playing in a shitty-assed band and didn't have a daughter that they had to save or she would die, fucking die right in front of their eyes, the way Doug had died right in front of his eyes and his wife, his beautiful wife Joanne, was naked and she was sitting on his hips grinding on him slowly so slowly because she liked to feel him get hard beneath her and she had her hand on him and maybe if he laid real still she would put her mouth on him instead because she liked to wake him up like that sometimes and he could open his eyes and see her beautiful lips wrapped around him and he would fuck her in the early morning just the way she liked it and he would hope that the cat hadn't scratched at the door so badly during the night that Joanne had let him in because if the door was still closed, she would moan his name as she rode him, she would throw her head back and pant and moan and beg him to make her -

"There's nothing you can do to stop it now. He'll find-"

Patrick heard her. She really *was* there.

"Keep talking, baby," Patrick said, his voice low as he surveyed the door in front of him. "I'm coming."

Patrick braced his hands on the door and focused.

Open.

He squeezed his eyes shut, hearing Joanne talk, her voice getting louder, more excited.

Open.

Patrick's mouth was open now; he was panting from the effort.

Open up, you bitch. Open!

Joanne's shrill voice filled the air, deafening him, *"How could you? Did you do this to her? To all of them?"*

Patrick didn't recognize the whine that escaped his lips as his own. It was high and wild, desperate in its intensity, but it was most definitely his. Sweat beaded on his forehead, his imagination as active as it had been in life, as he braced his hands on the doorjamb and beseeched the door, the gods, anyone to listen.

"Obey me, you piece of shit. OPEN!"

It was as if he had said 'abracadabra' or 'presto change-o'. The doors opened like they had been blown by a gentle breeze, gliding inward in slow motion, languid like a summer afternoon. Patrick couldn't stop the smile from spreading across his face, even as he lurched forward to look inside the first door.

Nothing, just a few dining room chairs strewn around. Dining room chairs that belonged to the first set that he and Joanne bought for their first apartment together. He could see the silver duct tape wrapped around the legs of the one that lay on its side. It looked like it was in the same position it had settled into when it collapsed under him all those years ago. How old was he then... 25? Likely. He and Joanne hadn't gotten married just yet. They hadn't settled into careers yet either. The only things they ever ate while seated in those chairs were ramen noodles and peanut butter and jelly sandwiches.

"Stop! Stop, you bastard!"

How long had Patrick been standing there strolling down memory lane? He kicked himself and moved away from the door, looking into another room and yet another, checking for people and remaining ignorant to the rest, though somewhere in his mind, it registered that every room held something from his past in it. He would venture upstairs later to survey what was there. He would have the time, after all, more time than he would know what to do with.

"Did you know what you were doing when you wrote it? When you put pen to paper, did you know that it would be the cause of your demise?"

A male voice spoke that time, one that felt familiar, but in a very distant way. Patrick listened to the tone more so than the words, trying to place the voice, but failing. It bothered him. Something about not being able to pinpoint who that voice belonged to bothered Patrick to his core. Who else was in the house with them? Patrick had never even considered that there might be others. Who was it? And what was he doing with Joanne?

Patrick ducked into another room, one with posters of Janet Jackson and Vanity adorning the walls: Doug's old room. He wanted to stay there, wanted to walk into that room and sit on that bed and stay there, waiting for his son to come home from school and be pissed to find his dad sitting among his things. He'd give anything to live that moment again. But Joanne was yelling at someone, telling them to stop, begging them to.

He had to find her.

"Why do you think I stopped? My dream, it had been so real. It took me a while to realize that it wasn't a dream after all - that it was real, it was history. It was my history."

"But you went on for weeks, maybe months writing everything

down. How could you have remembered all of that to be able to get it down on paper with such accuracy?"

The man sounded genuinely confused. Patrick hoped Joanne was baiting him, trying to plan her escape. Good. He needed more time to get the doors open and find her. *Keep him talking, Joanne,* he thought. *Keep him occupied.*

"Weeks?"

Joanne's laughter filled the air but the sound left Patrick cold.

Patrick knew what was coming. He remembered the days when Joanne had sequestered herself in their home office, pouring over the computer as the words spilled out of her. She would take her meals in there when she would eat all, would sleep in there sometimes. When Patrick had tried to get her to come out of there for a little while, to come up for air and maybe take a shower, she would put him off. She said she needed more time, needed to focus on her work, needed to process what she was writing, needed to get it all out. So, he'd let her. He left her alone to do what she needed to do. And then one day she just stopped, leaving the manuscript unfinished. She just... stopped. When Patrick asked to read what she had written, she told him no, said she wasn't ready to share it. She never was. She started to - one day she answered yes to him asking to read it and handed him the manuscript, but after only a few minutes (barely into the vampire's monologue) she took it back from him saying it wasn't ready, that he shouldn't read it, that she needed it back. Patrick remembered how much Joanne had stuttered. She looked nervous, desperate to have the papers back in her hands. He gave the manuscript back to her willingly, more than a little concerned about what might happen if he didn't. He never asked to see it again. She never offered. The memory jarred him as much as the empty rooms he peered into in that impossible corridor on that impossible floor of a house just outside Hell did.

"I wrote it in one day."

Joanne's admission made Patrick stop in his tracks. One day? How could that be? To Patrick's memory, it had taken her a few months to write what she did. He remembered her going into their home office early and coming out late, hair wild, face taking on that sour-smelling sheen of sweat mixed with unwashed skin; looking like someone risen from the dead. If she had finished the manuscript in one day, what had she been doing in that room?

"You look at me like I should know this. I'm not Patrick, surely you've guessed that by now."

Patrick heard the man say his name. Something about that felt wrong.

"No, you're not. That much is clear. But don't you know all? Aren't you the orig-"

"You speak like you've seen things, child, but you are in the dark."

"Am I... Raone?"

Patrick felt like he had died a second time in the silence that came after Joanne had uttered that name. She had spoken it with a confidence that revealed a deeper understanding than Patrick was willing to acknowledge, to let permeate his thoughts, and it left him cold.

"You - the dream...?"

"The dream didn't tell me your name, but it wasn't hard to figure out," Patrick heard Joanne say. *"After all, I had time. I had the rest of my life, didn't I?"*

"That name is lost now, gone to the ground as surely as the one who carried it. It is meaningless."

"Perhaps, but the story of what happened to you is not."

Patrick opened another door - there were grass clippings

strewn around this one, enough to carpet the floor. He heard Joanne speak again, her voice full of emotion.

"How could *you-"*

"How could I what? You say you know; you say you saw. If you truly understood you would not ask that question, Joanne. I am condemned. Bound to this existence. I can no more stop what will happen to them than I can save myself."

The man's voice boomed when he spoke, growing stronger as he finished his sentence. Patrick was running out of time.

"But you relish it, don't you? The power - it fuels you. You love being in control, it was never about not *wanting to rule, was it? You wanted that, but only completely, unconditionally. That's what Cecelia didn't understand. You wanted to be the one in control, not her number two. When she sent you here to rule, she was giving you a gift."*

Open... nothing.

Open... nothing.

"That gift is paid for by our blood. Don't you get it? We are all dying because of you."

"And you, my darling Joanne."

Patrick started to run, kicking doors open and commanding them to obey at the same time. It was working, but the doors kept multiplying.

"Joanne... my sweet Severna, surely you realize your part in this?"

Patrick could almost hear Joanne's nervous breathing, could almost see her chest rising and falling in fear.

"But that's not fair, is it my love? The blame is all mine. You had no choice in the matter once I decided that we would be."

Patrick didn't like the pause, the insufferable silence, that descended upon the hallway. He was about to scream when the man finally spoke again.

"Remarkable, your ability to keep me from your thoughts. None of the others had been able to do so."

"None of them knew what was at stake."

The appreciative chuckle that issued from deep within the man's chest made Patrick's right hand ball into a fist.

"You are just as lovely as my Severna, Joanne. As resilient as the fabled Vernese you captured so well in your manuscript. The shedding process hasn't taken anything from your beauty."

"The what?"

There was a smile in his voice. It was a placating thing, soft and understanding. It made Patrick sick to his stomach.

"Reincarnation. When a soul leaves one body and is reborn in the next, it leaves something of the person behind. The portion left behind is an identifier that he has lived before, a remnant. Most times it joins the energy band and fuels the living, never making direct contact with another of its kind. But, condemned as we are, the sheddings of our past lives are here with me in The Realm."

Patrick was running, running, running, the silence as loud as a siren. Joanne had been quiet since the man said that Severna was Joanne's original and that she was a shedding of that ancient woman's soul. The idea of it was chilling – that she was nothing more than a copy of someone who had lived before, and not an exact one at that, missing intricacies that rounded out the original but left holes in the offspring – and Patrick had tried to blot out the thought by resuming his search, surveying the space around him, looking for her. He couldn't think about the fact that his Joanne was the discarded skin of a woman who had lived long ago, that he had been left with what had clung to consciousness after the other succumbed. Had traits he would have loved been lost to antiquity, forever gone into the soil? Had they been replaced by the bad, the evil, the ugly thoughts that lived inside, planning, plotting, waiting for the time when they could sun their slick onyx skin in the light of day?

No.

Not his Joanne.

Patrick needed Joanne to speak, to let him know she was still ok. He needed her to tell him everything was going to be ok and he didn't need to worry about what the man was talking about.

CHAPTER 56

"Patrick?" Joanne whispered, realization perking up all her senses at the same time. Patrick was there? In the house? She didn't let her mind linger on the fact that, in order to be there, her husband had to have died. She didn't let herself think about the pain he might have suffered through an illness or an accident. She couldn't. All Joanne could focus on was that her husband and the man that stood before her shared a soul. This man was the man she had lain with every night for most of her life, except not really. Her Patrick was a reincarnated version of this man, the one who caused all of this. He needed to know. Joanne was suddenly sure that this man had no intentions of telling him. Joanne's skin felt electric as she repeated her husband's name, this time screaming it at the top of her lungs.

Mal reached out, clipping Joanne's scream with a hand curled tightly around her throat, constricting her airway.

"Shh," he said. "Knowing won't change things. He rules The Realm now, not me, and he's taken to it like a fish to water."

He chuckled at her wide-eyed stare.

"Does that surprise you?" He carried her to the wall behind them, her body as light as a child's in his strong arms. Pinning her against it, he loosened his grip on her neck and inhaled sharply as if her lungs still needed air. He thumbed her neck, watching as the supple skin moved beneath his hands.

"So beautiful, Severna," he whispered.

"Don't call me that," Joanne hissed even as she felt her stomach twist in arousal.

Something in his eyes shifted and cleared. Joanne didn't like what she saw there.

"You're right," Mal growled. "You're not my Severna. You are Joanne. Patrick's Joanne."

"You should see him, dear. I was very impressed with how quickly he got the lay of the land," Mal continued. "He and Doug have taken to leadership quite well."

Joanne's lip trembled as she wrapped her mind around what she heard. Her mouth contorted to form her son's name, but she couldn't. Doug *couldn't* be dead, not her baby. He was too young. He was too innocent to be there. He wasn't supposed to be in such a hellish place. A flash of anger welled in her chest then subsided, replaced by an immense sadness that threatened to choke her. She wouldn't admit that the person she was angry with was Patrick, not even to herself.

Fat tears sprung from her eyes to wet her cheeks.

Mal looked away from Joanne as he reached into her body to take her soul. She writhed beneath his touch, trying to wrench away but was unable to budge.

"Sweet Joanne," Mal cooed, his voice echoing in Joanne's head, "I love you like I loved my Severna and the countless other reincarnations of her, but I cannot allow you to interfere.

Patrick... this one is special. If he learns the truth, if he succeeds in saving but one - well, I can't let that happen."

"Patrick," Joanne squeaked, her chest suddenly assaulted by an immense pressure. It felt like something was laying on it, compressing air and movement completely, paralyzing her. She tried to breathe and couldn't, tried to push at it, to claw at his hand, but couldn't raise a finger.

"To the sweetest among us," Mal said fondly, staring at Joanne as he separated her soul from her body to rub it between his hands like so much waste. Her eyes, now lifeless and fixed like a ventriloquist's dummy, stared at the floor that he lowered her to. He rubbed her hair. "By God, I would love you again. Every time."

CHAPTER 57

Mal felt him before he saw him, his soul reaching out to its shedding like raindrops gravitating to each other, desperate to puddle together. He turned around to look at Patrick as he stood in the doorway glowering at the scene before him: his wife on the floor lying dead for the second time and a man looking a lot like himself standing over her body. Mal marveled at how they wore the same facial expressions: open mouths gaping with exertion, eyebrows slightly raised in surprise, pain standing like stagnant water in their eyes. Not for the first time, Mal wished he could talk with him, help him understand. But he'd come too far now to let it all slip away. Cecelia was right: power was heady. Now that he had it, he wanted to keep it. Surely Patrick would understand that, right? He was the strongest of the reincarnated so far, Mal's equal in so many ways, including the physical (after so many sheddings he had given up on seeing his face reflected in one again, but there Patrick stood, his veritable twin). Of anyone, surely he would understand, right? Mal had gone over it many times in his mind and felt confident that Patrick would be the one to rule by his side, the reincarnated and the original sharing the throne. Patrick was strong enough, smart enough, malleable enough. But he needed time.

Mal put thoughts of communicating with Patrick out of his mind. Doing that, just like allowing Joanne's interference, was out of the question, at least for now. Resigned, Mal straightened his shoulders and squared his hips to his doppelganger.

Mal blinked.

So did Patrick.

Patrick saw Joanne's body crumpled on the floor like discarded paper in the empty room and sank to his knees.

CHAPTER 58

Tara sighed and looked back at the house. It sat still and unfettered, like nothing at all was happening inside. Certainly not the murder of her love. Certainly not the plotting and scheming that Patrick and Doug were doing with their new pets.

Tara wondered what happened to Mileeha's body, if it had dissolved quickly or if it had lingered for some time, fighting to remain present... alone. Her mind was consumed with he thought, suddenly. That and rage.

Tara had heard everything. She heard a woman, who sounded like she was speaking from the other end of a tube like the ones that kids pressed their ears to on the playground, deciphering tinny messages spoken from other ends of the park. The woman was telling the story of how The Realm came to be, of how some guy who loved someone he shouldn't have was to blame. She thought it must be Mal, and if so, she didn't really care. Mal had ruled The Realm forever, as far as she was concerned. When and how it came to pass was unimportant to her.

All of that talking was just background noise while she thought about what she was planning to do.

The time was right to go in. They were distracted by that woman's story - surely they could hear it inside if she could from outside, and much clearer, she thought. The house was only a one-story rambler, and not that big of one either. Tara could sneak up on Patrick and Doug and exact her revenge before they even knew she was inside.

No one would see her coming.

The palms of her hands itched. She was ready to do this. She had no knife, no spear, no weapon of any kind but that was all right. She'd killed men before with her bare hands, ones she hadn't held a single thing against. She had broken necks, ripped out throats, choked the life out of a few, and those men had been strangers to her. But she had a hard-on for Patrick and Doug — the biggest grudge she'd ever had in life or death. Now that she'd thought to do it, she couldn't wait to dig her fingers into the soft of their necks and strum their vocal cords, make them sing like songbirds. She couldn't wait to find out what their blood would be like when it spilled out of them, flowing like a faucet to soak into the insipid ground. Would it be warm like it was when they lived as men on Earth? She promised herself a taste, if it was.

CHAPTER 59

oug didn't know how to feel.

He was confused, more so than he ever had been.

The people in the story - who were they? Was Aaron supposed to be Mal? And who was the woman? Doug didn't know, but what was worse was that he cared at all. It had nothing to do with him. The origins of The Realm were inconsequential to him- all he wanted to do was get out and make sure his daughter never stepped foot in it. Why should he care about how it started?

Except he did care. Something in his soul turned over when he heard Gabby reading those words from his mother's book. His mother had *written* those words - it hadn't dawned on him that he was listening to his daughter read his mother's words until just then, not really. Doug hadn't thought about the implications of that, much less what the storyline could mean to his family. He thought it was pure fiction, some fluff his mother had started and abandoned. But he felt differently now. As soon as

Gabby had started reading, something about the words hit home in a way that nothing else had. That reality sent a shiver down his spine.

Oh yes, Doug cared quite a bit.

Doug watched as Gabby folded the laundry and he thought about what she had read. Again, he wondered if Aaron was supposed to be Mal. Who was Vernese? How did his father fit into all of this? As night turned into day in the real world, Doug's thoughts homed in on Patrick. There had to be a reason that he and Patrick had been hearing Gabby read the story so clearly. There were other descendants in danger of coming to The Realm alive, but Doug couldn't hear Autumn and Christopher's thoughts. So, why only Gabby? The story had to be connected to them all in some way.

Gabby took the kids to the movies.

Gabby had a girls' night out with her friends.

Gabby went on a date with her husband.

Gabby vacuumed the living room carpet, took a cooking class, drank a glass of wine by the fire after a long day.

Gabby did all sorts of mundane tasks, time flying by in a blur again, now that she wasn't reading.

Curious.

Doug almost hadn't noticed how quickly things had sped up for Gabby on Earth. He had grown so used to hearing her voice reciting the words of the manuscript that he had stopped noticing the details of what was going on in her world. It was then that he realized he hadn't heard her voice in quite some time.

Doug turned and peered into the haze, a veritable looking glass that never ceased to make him think of 1980s wizard movies, to see what was happening in Gabby's world. He was afraid to do it suddenly, cold reality knocking at the door of his senses. He might not like what he sees. He might not like it at all.

He almost didn't see her. In fact, it was Autumn that he saw first, young and vibrant. She was upside down on the monkey bars watching her mom read a book on a park bench. Her brother was on the other side of the park playing with his friends and Gabby was trying to split her eyes, trying to watch both of them at the same time. Autumn's pigtails hung down, reaching toward her cheeks as she swung listlessly in the summer breeze. There was a scab healing on her knee from when she'd fallen into a gravel pit just outside the mulch by the swings... the very swings that she had just catapulted herself off of. She had a scab on the pad of her right hand too, from that escapade. Her mom had said that one might leave a scar. And it would. Doug was sure he would see that scar, a scatter mark of lighter flesh where the rubble had engrained itself, with his own eyes when he met her... where? The Realm? *Oh god, please no.*

Autumn looked to be about 6 years old.

Doug's stomach dropped.

Time had passed so quickly, perhaps even faster than before. Autumn had been a toddler when Doug last saw her. He wondered absently if this had been what it was like for Patrick as he watched Doug's life go by. It must have felt like blinking.

Doug rubbed his face as he took in his daughter now, six years older. She didn't look so different, just subtle changes here and there. Her hairstyle had changed, her frame was more toned. Gabby was out of the stage where she was at a baby's beck and call and had stopped eating her dinner at midnight or showering for two minutes at a time. Gabby was getting back to herself and looked happy for it. A smile crept onto Doug's lips at seeing his daughter so content, but never made it to his eyes.

Six years had passed in the blink of an eye. Doug didn't let himself linger on the rest of the thought.

As he located the Hunters he had sent to guard Gabby, the need to get his bearings in her new world almost insurmountable, Doug's mind drifted to his father again.

His mother had written those words. She *wrote* them.

Doug thought back to that time. His mom had seemed obsessed with writing it, would lock herself away to do it, would leave for the library without saying anything, needing to do some research. This didn't go on for a long period of time – it was just a blip on the screen when compared to something the last month of school before summer break, but when it was happening, it felt like it would go on forever. She was engrossed in it, was all in, seeming to work night and day. Doug wondered how much of that was real and not just the imaginings of a kid. Had she really locked herself away in the extra bedroom turned office to write night and day or had she just told him she would have to watch his favorite cartoon with him later enough times that he remembered it? Perception's funny that way. And exaggeration's a bitch.

Doug really didn't know anymore.

Did it matter in the end?

He wasn't sure. Something kept bothering him about it, though - the time she spent working on the book that never saw the light of day... the fact that she wrote it at all. He thought his mother was writing a novel. It made sense to him that she would at least try, being an English professor and all. All that reading she assigned and critiqued and discussed with her classes had to trigger her creativity at some point, right? But to Doug, it never felt like her book was a work of fiction like she said it was. There was something about the way she researched ancient civilizations feverishly, comparing names and dates and things Doug didn't understand when he was a kid. He wished he could call the details up from his memory now but they just weren't there. Something about the way her eyes looked when she put two and two together in his presence. Doug remembered thinking she looked afraid. He remembered vowing to never read the book that had garnered such a reaction in his mom, even if she had been the one to write it.

There was something real in those pages that Doug was just starting to piece together.

He didn't want to listen to his subconscious self, the one that had figured it all out... the one whose quivering voice could barely be heard, muted by shock.

Doug looked at Gabby. She was asleep in her bed. The room was dark except for a sliver of light coming in from the far window near the full-length mirror she found in an antique shop, the same one she had nearly dropped as she hoisted it up the stairs, cursing all the way. The mound under the covers that was her husband moved up and down, up and down, breathing rhythmically in deep slumber. But then Gabby... Gabby was not sleeping anymore. Her eyes were open. She was sitting up in bed.

She was staring at him.

Gabby's nightgown had shifted in her sleep and was pulled uncomfortably across her neck and chest. It looked like it was choking her or maybe cutting off her circulation in the way the material corded around her, bound tightly as if she had been tossing and turning violently in her sleep. *She should fix it*, the little voice in Doug's head said, though he didn't care for the pleading quality it had assumed. *It has to hurt. Why won't she fix it? Gabby, baby, please* - Doug spoke his pleas aloud too, anything to stop himself from seeing her pointing at him, the makings of a smile playing at the corners of her mouth.

Doug squeezed his eyes shut.

Gabby knew too. She was telling him, wasn't she?

Doug was crying. Not for himself, as he had done so many times after waking in The Realm. He was crying for his father. His unsuspecting father who had been damned to relive some past life and pay for a transgression he didn't even remember, let alone one he was responsible for. Because it was true - all of it. Doug could see it in his daughter's upturned eyes.

The book was real, all of it was, and they were cursed. Because Patrick was Aaron in as much as Aaron was Mal. The book recounted tales of reincarnation and shedding and such, and that was where the truth hid - where it rotted and festered.

Patrick *was* Mal.

And he had no idea.

Doug's soul ached for his father. He must have heard Gabby's words as well, must have put it all together the same way Doug had and was out there somewhere, dealing with it alone. He turned to look at the door, wishing he could will his father back to the room so he could be by his side. He turned back to look at Gabby, contemplating leaving her to find Patrick. The day was bright in Gabby's world and she was walking toward her kickboxing class. The sight made him still, stop dead in his tracks. It was already a new day. Time was moving so quickly that Doug was afraid to leave. He might come back to find her standing in the room with him, time having run out for his daughter completely.

Gabby and Autumn were getting their nails done. Autumn was a little older than before, all glitter and ruffles. Her little legs barely made it into the soaking basin and she almost had to stand up to submerge them. The colors she had chosen for her toes were lined up next to the nail technician (pink, blue, and purple on alternating toes). The bubbles from the massaging jet tickled the bottom of her feet and she squealed. Gabby looked over at her from her own pedicure massage chair and smiled, faltering only slightly when she felt a nip at the cuticle of her right big toe.

Two years in 60 seconds. Doug could barely suppress a gasp.

A shadow blocked Doug's view of Gabby and Autumn for a moment, the person getting in his line of sight as they walked out of the nail salon. Doug wouldn't have seen it, wouldn't have noticed at all as enamored as he was with his family, except that she wanted him to. She lingered there, in front of his eyes, deliberately so. There was nothing remarkable about her – Doug couldn't decipher any real features except for the curve of her hips, and maybe the flip of her hair. It felt like the woman was looking at him over her shoulder. Doug could see the rest of the shop fluttering with activity behind her - nails being filed, colors being selected, heels being attacked with pumice stones. Doug would have looked away, would have tried to see how Autumn's nails came out, except that woman looked at him so provocatively, he couldn't turn away. He couldn't see her eyes, but he could tell they were boring into his soul, holding his stare. And he wanted to see, that was the kicker of it. He wanted to see what she looked like. Wanted whatever cloud that was covering the sun to cast her form in shadow to pass so that he could see her in full color. But he couldn't make her out - couldn't see anything save for her curvaceous hips, her rounded shoulders newly into view, that captivating flip of hair that he wanted to run his hands through, and her chin, clefted, he was sure, jutting out toward him alluringly for the tiniest of moments, then turning confidently to the door.

Then, suddenly, she was gone. Doug felt an immutable loss for which he couldn't find a source. When he turned his gaze back to Gabby and Autumn, the shop faded away, paling like a polaroid picture exposure in reverse.

CHAPTER 60

Joanne.

Patrick couldn't believe it, couldn't wrap his mind around it. Joanne was there. Right there. He could see her beautiful face, oddly serene as she lay on the floor. He could see her delicate hands outstretched toward the space where a window might be, reaching for something that only she could see. It was her. His Joanne. He'd found her at last.

Patrick raced to her side, his mind registering that she was lying in a heap on the floor, unmoving, a little too late. He called her name as he ran to her, repeated it over and over again, like a mantra, as he sank to his knees. He reached out his arms intending to wrap them around Joanne's shoulders. Patrick wanted to lift her into his lap and hold her close, press his forehead against her cheek and kiss her neck. She would rouse then, he knew. She would wake up. He could wake her up with a kiss the way he did when they were back in their studio apartment when the humidity was so thick, they had sweat through the sheets. He could wake her up that way because it worked that one afternoon when they fell asleep on the sofa after a particularly energetic romp and they had to clean themselves up before Doug came home from school. He could do it, he knew he could, because he had woken her up that way when -

Patrick felt as empty as he had when Joanne died the first time.

He reached for her shoulders but his hands went through them. He reached out a second time, trying to push her hair off her forehead and couldn't find purchase. His hand plummeted through Joanne's visage, hitting the floor with a sickening thump as it fell unrestrained. Patrick cried out, unable to control himself. He reached for Joanne again and again, missing every time, her image wavering with every disturbance, coming back more transparent each time it reconstituted itself.

She was fading away.

"No. No, Joanne," he rasped, his resolve faltering. He didn't think he could take losing her again. He also knew he didn't have a choice. "Please don't go."

She continued to fade, to evanesce, shimmering prettily as the cool air of night sometimes does when it meets the warm air of day as they trade places. A low whine permeated the room and Patrick was only distantly aware that it was coming from him, had been coming from him for some time.

Patrick sat there long after Joanne had disappeared, staring at the spot her body had occupied. Was she in Heaven now? Hell? Did she simply cease to exist? Patrick felt the same confusion, the same dismay that he had felt when Joanne died the first time; felt the same chill on his neck as though someone had walked over his grave.

Patrick's tortured mind wouldn't stop repeating the truth that would haunt him forever:

She never even knew I found her.

While Doug stumbled out of the house to find his daughter, hoping against hope she would be spared eternity in The Realm. Patrick said goodbye to his wife again, praying she had finally escaped, that she was finally at peace.

CHAPTER 61

They didn't see her coming.

Tara crept up on the house, her progress agonizingly slow as she crawled, slithered, crab-walked her way up to the side entrance. It was a door that she hadn't noticed before, but that was to be expected; she'd had a lot on her mind the last time she stood before that house. When she got to the foot of the stairs, she stopped dead in her tracks. Tara was out of the brush and out in the open, even if only her upper half was visible. She felt exposed. Tara was sure that any minute Patrick or Doug or Mal was going to come around the corner, see her, and snatch her up by her hair.

No, they wouldn't.

They wouldn't because they were all inside, preoccupied by that woman's voice. The Hunters were nowhere to be found. It was just Tara and them, and they weren't looking.

That's why this was the perfect time to do this. She had to go now.

Right now.

As Tara reached for the door, ironically screened in like a house in the south would be to ward off mosquitos in the summer heat, Tara focused on the question that had danced around the periphery of her consciousness since first hearing the woman speak of The Realm and its history. What did she really know about Mal? How were Patrick and Doug mixed up with him? She had always had a weird feeling about Patrick and the present circumstances did nothing to change that. Him getting away from the Hunters unscathed, evading them so well, even on his first night in The Realm, his rise to second in command after such a short time... Something stank, and it was good and rotten.

But did it matter?

Tara tilted her head involuntarily at the same moment as she grasped the paint-chipped doorknob. She needed to understand what was going on, needed to know who did what to who, especially considering that she was ready to gut the one responsible for Mileeha's death. Would it be Patrick, Doug, or Mal's blood that she'd spill to keep that promise? Would it be all of theirs for proper recompense?

Tara's mind looped around to the beginning, turned over on itself, and took another course. Did it matter how Patrick and Mal were connected in the end? They were all a jumble of arms and legs anyway, all tied up together in this house and waiting for her, guilty as could be - wouldn't be better if there was a big red bow on top. But was that really true? Couldn't Patrick and Doug be innocent? Couldn't they be stuck there, in The Realm, by some strange twist of fate and Mal was trying to corrupt them?

Shit.

No, she said to herself, the finality in her tone jarring to her senses. *No one in The Realm was innocent.*

With a curt nod that nobody saw, Tara opened the screen door, then the inner door and slipped into the house.

CHAPTER 62

One in four people.

That's what they said - one in four people die from Necrotizing Fasciitis, this bitch of thing that ate away at Gabby's skin, her tissue, her sinews, down to her fucking bones, burning into it like acid. One in four. 25% of the people who contracted this disease died. That means 75% live.

Gabby's luck had always been shit.

Her toe only hurt a little, she would swear to that even then, as she sat there post-op, her gangrenous leg conspicuously gone. It started there, at the cuticle, right where the nick from the clippers never healed. 'Flesh eating disease,' they told her over the beeps and buzzes of machines. 'Nothing we can do,' they lamented. As she breathed in the oxygen that flowed through the mask securely strapped to her head (she may have pulled the other mask off and broken the flimsy straps, hence the heavy-duty reinforcements), Gabby contemplated the stump under the blanket, the cut just above the knee - enough to make what was left of the leg look like it was separate from her body as it waggled incongruously. Gabby envisioned a black swathe of flesh covering bone, a new horror already eating away at the tortured flesh. She could feel it starting again, abrading the skin there, reaching up her thigh. 'Don't touch!' they said, 'It could spread.'

It's alive, Gabby thought ruefully.

She thought of herself grabbing the stump, squeezing it to let blood and pus and bacteria and death out to play. In her imagination, she grabbed at it with her hand and watched as the disease started there too, eating away at the skin on her hands and forearms, revealing the soft tissue beneath at once. Slowly but surely the flesh-eating disease devoured the tissue, then the muscles, then started working on the more resilient but equally doomed bones.

Gabby imagined reaching down again, grabbing a handful of the toxic concoction, and rubbing it on her face.

They said she might have 24 hours, but that was bullshit. If she had an hour left, she would be surprised.

One in four.

Oxygen for the sepsis. Dilaudid for the pain. The manuscript for her mind. Gabby knew that seemed like a strange request, but she had nothing left. The hospital wouldn't allow her husband and the kids to be in the room with her, even with surgical masks. The disease was highly contagious. The nurses and doctors even looked like they wanted to keep their distance, maybe stick her in a quarantine tent and leave her there to die so they could take her body and study it. She hadn't seen her family since she got to the hospital and wouldn't ever again. While that hurt her more than anything else, it was ok. Gabby would rather die than think they had contracted the disease that was eating away at her piece by piece. But she could read the manuscript. Even as her eyes dimmed and she conceded the fight, she could have it near. It would keep her company. It would set her free. It was the truth, wasn't it? Her grandmother had been writing about the truth the whole time. Gabby thought this was so, knew it the moment she read the last chapter. The enormity of it all made her laugh bitterly.

The oxygen wasn't working but the meds were. They were putting her to sleep. Good. That way she didn't have to think about the fact that some bacteria was eating away at her skin, lapping at the frayed edges, coaxing blood out of her flesh and into its hungry mouth. That way she could just float away...

No... not yet...

Gabby wanted to read the last page of her grandmother's manuscript again.

Her husband had looked at her strangely when she requested that he bring it along with a picture of himself and the kids for her bedside table. The question stood in his eyes, but he never voiced it. She had finished reading it a while ago, had mentioned at one point that she wanted to bury it in a closet somewhere and never see it again. Gabby had even tried to throw it out but couldn't bear the thought of her grandmother's words being lost forever, no matter how damning they may be. She wouldn't let him read it and he never pushed. This was her family's story to tell and he was determined not to pry. And even though her last request struck him as strange, he did it. He would do anything Gabby asked if it would give her a moment's peace. He and the kids had been poked, prodded, and tested in rotation for the better part of the afternoon to be sure they didn't already have the disease that would take Gabby's life. They didn't. Only her. He wouldn't be there when she left and they both knew it. Gabby knew that he felt helpless, that bringing the old, yellowed manuscript was the only thing he could actually do for his wife, so he did it without hesitation and she loved him for it.

Gabby reached for the manuscript on the nightstand, the pages creased and bent from use, and managed to drag it over into her lap. It fell heavily onto her stump and while she winced with pain, that was just a physical reaction. She didn't care about the stump anymore – none of the things that would plague the mind of a new amputee bothered her. She wouldn't have to wonder what life without her leg would look like. She wouldn't be around long enough for that.

Gabby sucked in a deep breath, the simple act becoming harder and harder to do. She wondered distantly how long she had to read before the nurses stormed her room, trying to save her from her inevitable end. A minute? Maybe two? Less? She'd better hurry up if she intended to read the page one last time.

Gabby's tongue felt thick and her eyes heavy. Color had drained from the world, everything taking on a strange sepia quality. Pretty. She wished she could tell someone that dying looked pretty to the one going even if everyone left behind might find it ugly, but there was no one to tell.

Gabby turned to the last page of the manuscript and let her eyes soak in the sight. This was the last time she would see the book; Gabby was aware that it was happening... she was dying. The thought didn't terrify her the way she thought it would. She was sad for her family - thinking about her kids growing up without her was enough to make her sick, but she knew that her husband would handle it and raise them right. She cried when she thought of their little smiling faces though, and almost didn't regain her composure. But as her head clouded and the haze thickening as she sobbed, Gabby realized that she'd better do just that. If she was going to read the manuscript again, she'd have to do it right then and there.

Gabby sighed and licked at the last wayward tear that ran down her face to pool in the corner of her mouth.

"Cecelia's tongue caressed th-the word," she read out loud, her voice croaking and ragged as though she hadn't spoken in years. Gabby wondered fleetingly if the flesh-eating disease had attacked her voice chords, pocking them with rotting open lesions, crusted white and bloody like a canker sore that has been bitten one too many times.

Gabby felt woozy. She fought to keep her eyes open.

She wasn't going to make it.

"… s-s-swirling it in her m-mouth before-" Gabby had to take a break.

A woman stood up from a seated position in the far corner of the room. Gabby saw her approach slowly, her black dress long, formless, and nondescript. Her eyes, full, dark, and empty like bottomless pits, matched her dress. There was a regalness about her form, her gait. Gabby was enthralled, even then, in the throes of death.

She didn't ask the woman where she came from or how she got into her room. She just was and that was all Gabby needed to know.

As the woman stared at her as if she could see into her very soul, Gabby's heartbeat slowed to a crawl. Her vision faded to a gray haze, engulfing the woman, who's beautiful face Gabby hadn't had time enough to appreciate, but that she recognized, nonetheless.

"Cecel-" Gabby tried, but her voice gave way to a rattle low in her throat. Her final breath hissed against her lips as she formed the full name of the woman before her.

Cecelia smiled down at Gabby, whose lifeless gaze was still trained on her as if she held all the answers of the universe. The manuscript lay in Gabby's lap. Cecelia picked it up, hefting its weight amusedly. Picking up where Gabby left off, Cecelia continued reading.

Cecelia's tongue caressed the word, swirling it in her mouth before uttering it aloud so low that only her intended could hear, even as he wailed her name in despair from the depths of his newfound home, but so loud as to span a distance unfathomable. In a smooth alto that could bring tears to the eyes of even the most seasoned of operatic connoisseurs, she said simply,

"Still?"

CHAPTER 63

Dark.

Darker than dark. Inky.

Nothingness.

Gabby opened her eyes to find herself in the middle of the blackest night she had ever seen. The grass beneath her feet had a weird grayish quality in the lightlessness, as did the trees, leafless branches reaching up into the black hole that was the sky. She looked around herself and saw nothing. She looked down at herself, but then clamped her eyes shut quickly, afraid. Gabby expected to see herself clad in a hospital gown, expected to see an empty space where her leg should be. She didn't want to see that ever again. But she had to look. She had to know. Holding her hands out to her sides for balance that she no longer needed, Gabby opened her eyes and took stock of herself in this new, blank world.

Jeans and a t-shirt: she was dressed in the clothes she had

worn to the hospital - not a hospital gown. Two legs held her up. Both feet looked normal, not the way they had... one inflamed as though it had been touched by the devil himself.

The devil...

Gabby spun her head around, looking in both directions. She turned from side to side, looking all around herself. No devil. No devil. Thank God.

But where was God?

Gabby brought her hands to her mouth quickly, covering her parted lips to smother the shriek that threatened to jump from her throat.

No God.

Gabby turned around again, facing the way she had when she awoke, and saw a house. The two-story tract house was missing its identical twins, standing alone in the blackness, but Gabby would recognize it anywhere. The windows, blinds closed against the night, watched over her like sentinels.

Gabby's smile was one of resignation as she took her first steps toward the apparition from her past, knowing that her future lay inside.

G abby never saw Mal as she made her way to the house. She passed by him, was nearly close enough to touch, but didn't notice. And that was all right. He didn't want to meet her just yet anyway.

The End

ABOUT THE AUTHOR

L. Marie Wood creates immersive worlds that defy genre as they intersect horror, romance, mystery, thriller, sci-fi, and fantasy elements to weave harrowing tapestries of speculative fiction. She is the recipient of the Golden Stake Award, a MICO Award-winning screenwriter, a two-time Bram Stoker Award® Finalist, a Rhysling nominated poet, and an accomplished essayist. Wood has won over 50 national and international screenplay and film awards. Wood has penned short fiction that has been published in groundbreaking works, including the anthologies *Sycorax's Daughters* and *Slay: Stories of the Vampire Noire*. She is also part of the 2022 Bookfest Book Award winning poetry anthology, *Under Her Skin*.

Her nonfiction has been published in Nightmare Magazine and academic textbooks such as the cross-curricular, *Conjuring Worlds: An Afrofuturist* Textbook. Her papers are archived as part of University of Pittsburgh's Horror Studies Collection. Wood is the founder of the Speculative Fiction Academy, an English and Creative Writing professor, a horror scholar with a Ph.D. in Creative Writing and an MFA in Speculative Fiction, and a frequent contributor to the conversation around the evolution of genre fiction. Learn more about L. Marie Wood at www.l-mariewood.com.

MORE FROM L. MARIE WOOD

About Horror: The Study and Craft

Telecommuting

L. MARIE WOOD

OPTIONED
FOR FILM
THE
REALM
THE REALM TRILOGY BOOK 1
BRAM STOKER AWARD® FINALIST AND GOLDEN STAKE
AWARD-WINNING AUTHOR
L. MARIE WOOD

www.ingramcontent.com/pod-product-compliance
Lightning Source LLC
Chambersburg PA
CBHW032011310726
48972CB00002B/364